CINDI MADSEN

SAILING at SUNSET

A feel-good romance
from Hallmark Publishing

Sailing at Sunset

Paperback: 978-1-952210-47-1
eBook: 978-1-947892-76-7

www.hallmarkpublishing.com

To my two pretty kitties, who spent most of the time I was writing this sleeping in my inbox, only to wake up, stand in front of my monitor, and demand attention.

Chapter One

A HAPPY *PING* ECHOED THROUGH THE cubicle, and Danae's heart beat faster. This was the moment of truth, and no matter the outcome, it meant doing one of her favorite things in the world: crossing off a to-do list item.

In glitter pen, of course.

People who thought organization was boring simply weren't doing it right. Tingles coursed through Danae as she flipped open her planner and found the goal digger sticker she'd placed next to the neatly written "Meeting with Mr. Barton."

Red was a power color, so she decided to go bold and use it to check the box.

Apprehension twisted her gut as she

smoothed a hand down her hair. Thanks to the humidity in Newport, Rhode Island, she'd given up straightening her dirty-blond locks long ago, embracing loose curls as her signature style. She bent and checked her teeth in her computer monitor, ensuring that none of the raspberry seeds from her smoothie had gotten stuck.

This wasn't just a meeting. It was *the* meeting. The one where she found out whether or not she'd be the new Chief Marketing Officer. If it went well, she'd be able to flip to the very front page of her planner and cross off one of the long-term goals she'd made six months ago—at the very beginning of the year.

That'd call for glittery orange ink, the color of success.

Let's not get ahead of ourselves. There was a difference between confidence and presumptuousness, and Danae knew better than to rely on anything that wasn't a certainty.

As she pushed to her feet, her hand automatically went to the golden Athena charm on her necklace. Although she wasn't superstitious—people were responsible for making their own luck—she rubbed the trinket. Mostly out of habit and because it reminded her of her mother.

Mom's obsession with Greek mythology was how Danae had ended up with her name. Dad had been unsure at first, but Mom mentioned the part of the tale in which Danae and her son, Perseus, were set adrift at sea, had help from Poseidon, and found refuge on a fishing island.

Everything came down to sailing and fishing with Dad. A bittersweet smile curved her lips, residual grief drifting up and squeezing at her chest. He'd passed away nearly two decades ago but missing him occasionally caught her off-guard.

Danae readjusted her chunky black frames, inching them up her nose, and then tugged at the red cardigan covering her black and white dress. In a sea of sensible, her red patent leather pumps were her one impractical indulgence.

The *clack, clack, clack* they made on the beautiful wooden floors of the Barton Boating Company office made her feel more confident, her chin automatically hitching higher. Each step was a punctuation, a reminder she could be firm and powerful, even if it'd taken her thirty-six years to get there.

Her pace faltered as she passed by Mark, who glanced up as she neared his desk. Like a deer in ex-boyfriend headlights she froze, and awkwardness crowded the air. Silly, considering they'd broken up before Christmas of last year.

Mark skimmed a hand over his trim, sandy brown hair, as if ensuring each strand was still in place. Naturally they all were, much like his suit, tie, and shirt, which appeared to be right out of a glossy magazine ad. "Best of luck to you on your meeting, Danae," he said, and while she searched for any hint of disingenuity, she came up blank.

Yeah, the other person up for the promotion was none other than her ex. Since Mark had dumped her out of the blue seven months ago, they'd done an odd sort of dance at the office, following the boundaries he'd made: no personal talk at work, always use a polite tone, and avoid being alone in a room if possible so they could remain amicable.

The guy loved his boundaries—namely ones that prevented people from getting too close. He had always been better at repressing his emotions, too, whereas she'd worn hers on her sleeve. Now she played things closer to the chest. "Thank you, Mark. To you as well."

"...been doing it this way for five years. Our target market doesn't care if their nail polish matches the boat." Paige's voice drifted over to them, and Danae peeked over the top of Mark's workstation to see Vanessa, Barton's social media manager, standing next to Paige, the head of PR.

The two women were opposites on every side of the spectrum. Paige was young and petite, with red hair and a fair complexion, and preferred the tried and true.

While pushing fifty, Vanessa was chic, savvy, and had a better nightlife than Danae ever would. Thanks to a background discovering and promoting beauty bloggers, her jet-black curls and bronze skin were always flawless, although her ideas were occasionally too hip and impractical for their boat-buying audience. "Well, if we don't change with the trends, we'll find ourselves behind them. And when it comes to my proposed yacht spa day, manis and pedis are only the tip of the luxurious iceberg."

"Hmm. When I think of icebergs and ships, I can't help but think of the *Titanic*. A good idea in theory, but I'm sure you'll remember how that turned out."

Usually their bickering made Danae's eye twitch—primarily because it drew out meetings for longer than scheduled. But at the present moment, it made it easier for her to disengage from Mark, call forth her confidence, and make the rest of the walk to Mr. Walter Barton's office.

Danae rapped on the open door and stepped inside. Too bad his floors were carpeted and muffled her formidable footsteps. Mahogany shelves with dozens of awards and framed news articles lined the back wall and matched the desk Mr. Barton sat behind.

He flashed her a smile, his round ruddy cheeks popping out above his wiry gray moustache. With his refined suits and penchant for fedoras, she could just picture him at home in a grand library, smoking a pipe and wearing a monocle. "Right on time, as always."

"And I always will be," she said.

As she turned to close the door, she caught sight of Franco, Barton Boats' web developer, through the open gap. He was just a couple of years older than her, and he was her closest friend at the office. His dark eyebrows arched encouragingly, and he gave her a big thumbs-up. The cardboard cup and the bag in his hand made it clear he'd chosen to go for a coffee run at their favorite shop instead of answering her email about how nervous she was, but since he'd managed to make her smile, she supposed she'd forgive him. She had a long history of heartfelt talks and happy dinners with Franco and his delightful husband, Justin, so she'd let him off this time.

As long as one of the pastries in that bag was for her.

The door closed with a *snick*, and a few more steps took Danae to the edge of Mr. Barton's desk. A golden frame caught her eye, one she'd never noticed before. "Is that new?"

Thanks to being a pinch nervous and a lot overzealous with her gesture, her trembling hand smacked the picture right off the desk.

"Shoot, I'm so sorry." Danae scooped it up, now grateful for the soft, forgiving carpeting. She returned the photo to the corner of the desk, plastered her arms to her sides, and prayed her face wasn't as flushed as it felt.

"Don't worry about it." Mr. Barton swiveled the picture his way and fondly studied the image of his younger self and three buddies in dark blue uniforms. "Back in my Navy days."

Thanks to extensive Googling before her interview, Danae knew Walter had been stationed at the naval base in Connecticut. Once he retired, he returned to Newport, where his family had founded and run Barton Boats since the 1930s.

"There's nothing like being out in the open water, on the confines of a boat, to get to know people very well in a short amount of time. Lieutenant Jeffers drove me crazy at first." Mr. Barton tapped the image of the guy to the right of him in the photo. "But having to work so closely with him led me to understand his viewpoint and how to best utilize our strengths and weaknesses. Now he's one of my oldest friends."

The way he talked about the lieutenant sent a warm fuzzy sensation through Danae. Surely this was the type of inspirational story that led up to giving her the promotion.

Right?

Deep down, she knew she was the perfect candidate for the Chief Marketing Officer position. While a tad biased on the subject, she worked longer hours, could multitask better than anyone else in the office, and was way more creative than Mark—who most certainly did *not* use color-coded glitter pens.

"I won't hold you in suspense any longer," Mr. Barton said, and Danae held her breath, alternating between visualizing her success and assuring herself she'd be okay either way, even if it would hurt her pride to lose one more thing to Mark. "As you know, I adored your pitch for our new campaign." Her boss made an invisible rainbow with his hands. "Barton Boats. Not just a boat, but a lifestyle."

This seemed rather like suspense, but Danae didn't say so.

"It's brilliant," he said. "As are you."

Is there a but *in there? Please don't let there be a* but. "Thank you, sir."

"That's why I'm appointing you Barton Boating Company's Chief Marketing Officer."

Time stopped.

Then sped up.

Since jumping up and down and squealing the way she had at a reunion boy band concert (not all that long ago) wasn't professional, she kept it to a contented expression and slight nod. "I won't let you down."

"I want you to oversee the changes that'll incorporate our new slogan, start to finish. This means you'll be heading up advertising, PR, social media, the website—all of it. You're going to be the team leader, and that comes with a lot of responsibility. Extra stress, too."

"I'm ready," Danae promised. She'd worked to put herself through college and had secured a job before graduation. Work gave her a sense of satisfaction she hadn't found anywhere else. Plus, the bump in salary would help her achieve her other long-term goals.

Nothing showed you how important it was to live well within your means like almost losing the roof over your head. Her parents had never bothered with a backup plan or savings, and after Dad died, the bank had come dangerously close to foreclosing on their home. *Never again.*

"Whenever you have time, I'd love to run a few ideas by you," she added. Over this past month, she'd felt a little crazy spending all her spare time on concepts that could very well go nowhere, but it'd been worth it. "I can't wait to implement them."

Mr. Barton held up a hand. "I appreciate your excitement, but for now, I'm considering this an interim position."

For now? Interim? The air whooshed out of her, taking her enthusiasm along with it. "I, um...What exactly does that mean?"

"It's important to build a strong connection with your team." The leather chair creaked as Mr. Barton leaned forward. "It'll be your biggest challenge, honestly. While I admire your drive, sometimes..." As he paused, her anxious imagination supplied a dozen caveats. "You need to learn to look at things from others' perspectives. To fully listen and process before you jump to do it your own way. I have faith in you, Danae, but I need to see what you're made of. I need to see that you're capable of being a team player."

Danae worked to hold her smile in place. Criticism—constructive or not—had always been hard for her to hear. Part of the reason she'd become so organized was to avoid making mistakes. "I'll work on that, Mr. Barton. I promise."

"Happy to hear it." He picked up the photo she'd accidentally knocked over and tapped the faces behind the glass. "As I mentioned earlier, there's a surefire way to do precisely that. And we just so happen to sell boats."

It felt like he'd given her half of an equation, and without the rest, how could she possibly solve for X? She didn't want to start off her trial period asking for clarification, yet confusion set in, leaving the wheels in her mind spinning.

Glee danced along the curve of Mr. Barton's smile and managed to catapult her apprehension to the next level. "I'm sending you and the team on an eight-day chartered cruise. Everyone's done so well this past quarter, so it'll be half reward, and half bonding exercise. It'll also be the perfect way for you to prove to me that I made the right call. Come back with a solid marketing plan that everyone's agreed upon, and I'll make the position official."

Danae's stomach dropped down in the vicinity of her pretty shoes. Mr. Barton added a wink. What did that mean?

That he was joking?

Please let him be joking.

Mr. Barton's gray eyebrows scrunched up, a couple of the wiry hairs catching the sunlight streaming through the giant window to his right. "I thought you'd be happy. After all, when you interviewed for your position, you mentioned how much you loved sailing when you were growing up."

Ah, yes. The reason he'd hired her on the spot—her sailing knowledge. Honestly, she *had* loved it. Those afternoons on the boat made up the best memories she had of her dad.

Once she'd helped Mom with the finances, though, Danae saw how much he had poured into the dilapidated boat. A vessel he'd had no idea how to fix, but sure spent a big chunk of change trying to.

There was an old saying, never repeated in the office: *The two best days of a boat owner's life are the day they buy a boat, and the day they sell it.* Boats were expensive to maintain. Add in a myriad of fishing gear, and the fact that Dad played hooky a little too frequently, and a stampede of creditors had nearly trampled their family.

Which was one of the main reasons that these days, Danae was all about *selling* boats instead of sailing them. "I do. I'm just not sure that right now, when we're launching a new campaign and website, is the best time to head out on the open sea."

"Nonsense," he said, swiping a hand through the air. "It's excellent timing. A change in environment will foster creativity, will push you to grow closer, and you'll be able to have meetings between ports. Vanessa has already planned an entire week of social media around it. She has so many ideas on how to improve our online presence, so I let her in on the secret, and then she was off and talking up a storm in that fast way she has."

As Vanessa was the newest member of their team, it seemed a bit strange that he'd confided in her first, but as Mr. Barton said, the woman was full of ideas. Not to mention, Danae had been preoccupied with landing the promotion.

Wait. That meant Vanessa and Paige would be on a boat together—no chance to retreat to their separate corners for some cool-down time between disagreements. That could get dicey.

Another realization barreled into Danae, one that made a tight band form around her chest. Eight whole days at sea with her ex-boyfriend. Despite their attempts to remain professional, there'd been enough guardedness following the breakup that the team had noticed. Even though it was better now, they worked in different departments for the most part.

She had already worried that with one of them getting the promotion, it would obliterate the barrier they'd erected to keep the peace. Take away a thousand square feet of office space, and things on the sailboat would get up close and too-personal, fast.

Vaguely, she heard the sound of a desk drawer opening and an accompanying flutter. "I've already chartered the trip and drafted the itinerary." Mr. Barton extended a sheet of paper, his expression making it clear she needed to get onboard—literally.

Danae tapped into her enthusiasm for her new title—one she planned on earning permanently—and let that shine through. "When's our push-off date? I'll get it in my planner and begin scheduling the entire trip so we can be as successful and productive as possible."

"You set sail this Monday."

Too many clashing thoughts shrieked through her brain at once, leading to a traffic jam that had her mouth stumbling over her words. "The...Monday that's after this weekend? As in four days from now?"

"That'd be the one."

While she adored her boss and his big ideas, he tended to dive headfirst before checking if the pool was eleven or three feet deep.

More protests crowded to the tip of her tongue about giving people—especially those with spouses and children—more of a warning and a chance to prepare, but Mr. Barton was up and out of his seat. "Let's go tell the rest of the team!"

Like a kid racing to see what Santa had left under the tree, he rushed out of the office, the hip he complained about on cold days not slowing him down one bit.

Guess I'd better get to planning.

Danae glanced at the list and worried her lower lip with her teeth.

I'm going to need more stickers.

Chapter Two

REGARDLESS OF THE FACT THAT Josh had been doing chartered tours for two years, every time he stood at the helm of his boat, salt water misting his skin, it hit him how amazing his job was.

No more cubicle, countless emails, or never-ending calls. No faster, harder, bigger, more, more, more.

Mr. and Mrs. Rivera, his current passengers, inhaled the fresh ocean air and basked in the glorious sunshine. Josh did the same as he gripped the weathered wooden handles of the antique steering wheel.

"It gives your boat a nice, rustic touch," Mr. Rivera said. Josh had found the wheel at a junkyard. To get his ship in shape, he had spent hours sanding and painting, but the discarded wheel he'd installed was still his favorite piece.

Sturdy and a bit cranky, the metal barrel and spindle always took a second or two of grinding before clicking into place. The muscles in Josh's arms burned as he turned, fighting the push of the water to aim the bow toward home.

"The entire boat is gorgeous. I still can't believe you did all the work yourself." Mrs. Rivera ran a hand over the wooden trim he'd added to the seats that no one would've wanted to sit on when he'd first bought the ship. Then she scooted closer to her husband and wrapped an arm around his waist. "This trip went by way too quickly. It's been so lovely; I almost don't want it to end."

The Riveras were on the last day of their week-long honeymoon cruise, a tour that had included stops at Martha's Vineyard, Nantucket, and Padanaram. While both of them had been married and divorced before, they'd found each other in their late fifties.

"You've been such a great guide, Josh," Mrs. Rivera said. "We'll absolutely be referring our family and friends—they were all so jealous of our trip."

Josh gave the couple a genuine smile. He'd had a lot of fussy clients in his day. The Riveras were a pleasure to have onboard. They kissed and hugged like teenagers, but that had given Josh plenty of time to stare out at the open water and be alone with his thoughts.

"This last week and a half has been perfect." Mr. Rivera lifted his wife's hand and kissed her knuckles. "From the moment the preacher declared this beautiful woman mine, to have and to hold, to frolic on the sandy shores with—that's right." Mr. Rivera's grin widened. "I said frolic."

Mrs. Rivera giggled, and a blush pinkened her cheeks. During the trip, they'd gone on and on about how this time around everything was so different, so much better. They knew who they were and what they wanted, and that was to spend every day with one another.

Nice to see, but Josh had been down the aisle before. After his divorce had been finalized almost three years ago, he'd vowed *never again*, and he planned on sticking to that.

The Atlantic Ocean was his beloved, and he had devoted himself to her for the rest of his life. Nothing hammered in that commitment like quitting his high-paying, stress-inducing job and selling his house and most of his belongings to buy a 1970s fixer-upper sailboat.

Now, at the ripe old age of forty, he got to set his own schedule and actually live his life, and that was worth every drop of blood, sweat, and tears. He pushed his tousled chestnut hair off his forehead and rubbed his stubbled cheeks. It was nice not having to shave every day, but he kept himself in good shape—a solitary life at the helm of a somewhat creaky boat made sure of that.

After sinking his savings into restoring this sailboat to full glory, he'd bestowed the name *Solitude* on her. He set the wheel, silently praising his mighty ship for how well she glided through the Atlantic. She looked dang good doing it, too.

Maybe that made *Solitude*—the boat and the term—his soulmate, and the ocean their blissful path. His life finally belonged to him. He never had to wear a suit and tie again, he set his own routine, and if the mood hit him, he could sail to Florida or Puerto Rico on a whim. His backyard could change every day.

His phone chimed, and he fished it out of his pocket. The Riveras were canoodling, and he wanted to give them as much privacy as possible. Although they'd seemed to forget anyone else existed, anyway.

Before Josh even opened his inbox, he suspected it would be Danae Danvers, Chief Marketing Officer at Barton Boats.

She'd been sending emails since last Thursday.

The first had led him to believe she had some personal vendetta against knots. She'd told him "The knot workshop is unnecessary and should be replaced with a brainstorming session."

Slightly bored one night as he'd been waiting for his clients to return from dinner, Josh had typed a reply: "Don't worry. It's knot as hard as it looks."

The joke had clearly flown over her head, as the next morning she'd replied with, "I assure you, I have all the knot knowledge I need."

Since Josh couldn't help himself, he'd asked, "What about your team? How aware are you of their knot-itude?"

"NOT enough to have a whole class on it. I'm more worried about keeping the trip positive and productive." Danae had then asked for his credentials and experience, even though the owner of the company had booked his services without requesting his life story.

So she'd sorta kinda replied to his joke, but then she'd immediately switched back to professional mode. Then again, her email signature was pink and included an inspirational quote that changed each day. A bit of a conundrum, to say the least.

Or maybe he'd had too much spare time to kill, studying her signature and searching for some insight.

After he responded with the information she'd asked for, Danae had sent him revised itinerary items Friday and yesterday evenings. A strange mixture of unease and curiosity coiled in his gut as he thought about meeting the woman in person. If Danae Danvers could nitpick this much over email, how much more would she attempt to call the shots once she got onboard?

The subject line of her latest email proclaimed it "The Final FINAL Itinerary."

Josh tapped on it and read the paragraph she'd written.

Josh,

Thank you for answering my questions and providing your credentials. I'm very much looking forward to meeting you tomorrow.

I've highlighted a few of the items I never received complete answers to in yellow and require your feedback. As I mentioned, it's more important to have sufficient strategy sessions as opposed to the more frivolous activities (i.e., the sailor knot workshop, mental scavenger hunt, and "Use What You Have" challenge.) Although fun, I hardly think those will help us finalize the marketing plan that needs to be established by the time we return to Newport at the end of the trip.

For instance, we can simply use what we have—our computers.

Please peruse the suggested changes and let me know your thoughts.

Best,
Danae Danvers
Chief Marketing Officer, Barton Boating Company

When it came down to it, a paycheck was a paycheck. However, one of the main reasons Josh had left his financial advisor position was so he could go with the flow and throw schedules and strict deadlines out the window. He'd do the job and do it well, sure, but life was so much easier once you let go of filling every single minute.

Since this was his chosen profession, as well as how he paid for his slot at the marina, he tapped the attached document. Then he glanced up at the Riveras to see how they were faring.

Mrs. Rivera lifted a bottle of wine they'd picked up at their last stop. "We're toasting to the end of our trip and the start of our new life together. Would you like a glass?"

"You two go on ahead," Josh said. "The Newport shoreline will be in view before we know it."

After a good minute or so of trying to open Danae's email attachment, the download timed out. WiFi was spotty at best out on the water, and if it hadn't loaded by now, it never would. He could glance at it later, once he returned to his dock sweet dock, where he had just enough modern comforts, like a strong internet connection. Which he primarily used for the occasional TV show.

I wonder if George and Nancy DVR'd our show, because I forgot to. They lived a couple of slips down and occasionally showed up in the morning bearing coffee, donuts, and hot gossip from around the marina.

In return, Josh brought them fresh fish and tales of his adventures on the high seas, since they didn't head out as often as they used to. They also watched crime dramas together and had a running contest going to see who could figure out the mystery first.

Thanks to a strong headwind that hinted at an oncoming cool front, he delivered the Riveras to the dock about forty-five minutes later than expected, which was why he didn't give out exact times, but ranges. Not that the newlyweds cared or thought twice about it. They thanked him profusely, took up their belongings, and skipped off into the sunset.

Josh visited the pump-out station, refueled, and gave his boat a thorough cleaning.

A quick glance at his watch revealed he only had twenty minutes to shower and rush into town. He'd scheduled a catch-up dinner with his little sister and her husband, neither of whom he'd seen in way too long.

From the sounds of the emails he'd received from the bossy CMO of Barton Boating Company, he'd better enjoy the break. The next eight days with the woman who couldn't stop changing the itinerary would surely try his patience and remind him why he'd left the corporate world in the first place.

Chapter Three

When Danae stepped inside her mom's house, her sister Selene was standing in the hallway, using the round mirror to take a selfie.

Selene glanced at her phone screen. "You're late."

"What? No, I'm not." Danae whipped her own phone out of her pocket, and sure enough, she was right on time.

Selene cackled. "Got you."

"Ha ha." Danae hung her purse on the set of hooks she'd installed in the hallway so that her family wouldn't dump their stuff in the main pathway. It hadn't kept her younger brother and sister from tossing their coats on the floor when they were growing up. They also liked to kick off their shoes the instant they stepped inside, so she used to trip her way in more often than not. "I don't plan out every single thing, you know."

"Are you kidding me?" Selene gave her a hug. "Your plans have plans."

"Oh, is that Danae?" Mom's voice drifted from the vicinity of the kitchen, so Danae headed that way. Selene followed her into the room and headed straight for the fridge.

Danae snagged a carrot from the veggie tray on the counter. "Did you apply for college yet?" Selene was twenty and had taken a couple years off after graduating from high school—something that had caused Danae's blood pressure to rise, while Mom had made a comment about everyone being on a different path—but had finally declared she was ready to continue her education. She intended to major in art history, and while Danae had wanted to ask if she had a backup, she'd managed to hold back. For now.

Her question was met with silence, which meant *no*. Her sister had been a baby when Dad died. She hadn't seen how hard Danae had worked to earn enough in scholarships to put herself through college, at the same time when Mom was also going back for a teaching degree.

Although she'd told her sister the story often. Enough times that it now earned her an epic sigh whenever she whipped it out.

The utensil drawer opened with a squeal, and Danae found the spare peeler and helped Mom with the potatoes. Sunday dinners were their time to catch up, and Danae had only missed a handful in her life—most of them back when she and Mark were splitting time between their families. "So, I wanted to let you know that I won't be able to make dinner next Sunday."

Mom lowered the half-peeled potato in her hands and blinked at her. Okay, so maybe Danae had become predictable. She rarely canceled and showed up when people expected her to. After having the rug yanked out from underneath her way too many times, she delighted in predictability. She had her cozy hundred-year-old cottage to return to at night, her set schedule, and—as of three days ago—the job title she'd been after.

Now she simply had to keep it. Danae's heartbeat accelerated as she explained how she'd gotten the promotion on what boiled down to a trial basis.

"Oh, I'm sure you'll get things all hammered out." Mom wiped her hand on the dish towel hanging from the stove and then sandwiched Danae's hand between both of hers. "You're so good at getting people to agree to your plans."

Nice, but not totally true. Danae's gaze drifted to the dry-erase board she'd hung on the wall of the kitchen. Organization had never been Mom's strong suit. Understandably, she'd been a wreck after Dad passed, so at seventeen years old, Danae had taken over a lot of the planning. Their lives had required intense management in order to get four people where they needed to be using only one semi-functional car.

Danae had organized their entire life on that board—well, technically it was their second, since at one point the countless lines of dry erase marker refused to fully erase. She'd helped them get through the rough patch, and the skills she'd learned had come in handy, even if she wished Mom and Selene had done a better job at picking them up.

With the potatoes on to boil, Danae circled to the other side of the counter, lifted her phone, and checked her email. Frustration bubbled up. They were taking off tomorrow morning for the eight-day chartered cruise, and Josh Wheeler still hadn't replied to her itinerary changes.

Sure, she'd been mildly amused at his jokes about knots, but it drove her a bit batty when people only answered a couple of the several questions she'd posed. She wasn't a fan of waiting for a response with a deadline looming, either.

She gnawed on her thumbnail, a habit she was trying to break. How could she get her team to agree on a marketing plan when she couldn't even coordinate with the sailor chartering the trip?

Vaguely, she noticed footsteps, but it

didn't hit her that they were heavier than Mom's or Selene's until strong arms circled her around the middle and she found herself a foot or so off the ground, her breath squished out of her.

"'Sup, big sister?" Leo asked, returning her feet to the floor.

She spun around to face him. Sometimes it was crazy to think that the tall guy in front of her was the little brother she used to cart to and from school. "Dude, I thought you were spending all your time working to pay off your student loans, not pumping iron."

Mostly she was kidding, but she also longed to hear he was taking care of things. Sometimes her family had told her to kindly mind her business, but they *were* her business.

"Legal files are heavy." Leo flopped onto the nearest stool and flashed Mom the winning grin that had gotten him out of way too much trouble growing up. "Hey, Mom." He nodded at their youngest sibling. "Selene."

Mom leaned across the counter to pat Leo's hand. "Yes, work is important, but are you taking time to go out and meet people? The offer to set you up with Principal Taylor's granddaughter still stands."

"I have a perfectly healthy social life, Mom. Why don't you give Danae the third degree?" Leo gave her shoulder a light shove. "She's older than me."

Danae shoved him right back. "'Older than *I.*' Anyway, I've had a relationship in this past year. You haven't."

"Oh sure, rub it in." His smirk made it clear he was far from hurt. Usually Mom took turns nudging them about setups and their dating lives. There had also been hints for grandkids.

When it came to priorities, solidifying her promotion currently held the number one spot. After the last company she'd worked for downsized—something that had definitely *not* been in her plans—she'd been out of a job for months. It had been right after she'd cosigned on Leo's student loan so he could get through law school, and she'd tossed and turned at night, worrying what would happen.

Once she sat across from Mr. Barton and saw the passion he had for his family's legacy and his employees, she was sure she'd found the optimal job for her skill set. Fortunately, he'd hired her on the spot.

Which was why she couldn't let him down, either. A weight pressed against her chest. Everything was riding on this upcoming trip.

When Mom turned to check on the potatoes, Leo leaned in. "You okay?"

"I've just got a lot going at work, but it'll be okay." It had to be. On a teacher's salary, it was hard enough for Mom to make it as it was, and once Selene started school, finances would get even tighter.

As soon as Selene was accepted at a college, Danae would help fill out financial aid and scholarship forms. Then the three of them would sit down and work out a budget—one she fully intended to contribute to. Her family counted on her, and she hadn't come this far only to lose the progress she'd made in her career.

Least of all because some sailor couldn't manage to return an email the night before they set sail.

Thanks to a combination of being overly tired, simply tapping the address his sister Jane had sent him, and the restaurant's recent name change, Josh hadn't realized they were eating at Midtown Fish and Oyster Bar until his GPS led him to it. His stomach sank, bad memories creeping in.

Since he kept his personal business to himself, of course Jane and Nathan would only think of the restaurant that had been renamed Jax's Fish and Oyster Bar as one of their past hangouts, one they hadn't visited in a while. Josh, on the other hand, thought of it as the place where things with his ex-wife had begun unravelling.

It had been their five-year anniversary, and Olivia had requested they celebrate with a romantic dinner at the same place Josh had taken her on their first date. She'd also been pushing hard for a five-year plan that included a housing upgrade and a baby.

To be fair, back then, Josh thought he'd wanted those things as well. A bigger house near the beach where they could raise a kid or two. Thinking he'd be able to surprise her with good news, he'd stayed at the office after hours to close a huge deal.

While he'd warned Olivia via text, he'd underestimated how late he would be. It seemed she'd sat there the entire forty-five minutes, seething and refusing to order food, just so she could reprimand him for his tardiness in front of a room full of people.

In hindsight, he should've sent another text or made a quick call. Or at the very least, done a better, more sincere job of apologizing, something he'd never been much good at.

After that, every tiny thing became an issue. Their future, their goals, their desires. How quickly they wanted those things. Money sat at the top of the list of items they argued about, so Josh would work harder, only to hear complaints that he was never home and didn't spend enough time with her.

It hadn't all been Olivia, though. The stress at work and constant pressure to earn more and advance through the ranks left him frazzled. Josh would come home short-tempered and snap at her.

That was the year he'd learned some things came at too great a cost.

They'd never made it to their six-year anniversary. Instead, he and Olivia had sat across from each other and divvied out their belongings like two rival teams determined to win, instead of two people who used to care deeply for each other.

Expelling a breath, Josh climbed out of his truck and fiddled with the collar of the button-down shirt he probably should've ironed.

The hostess greeted him with a wide, ultra-white smile. He mentioned meeting his sister and her husband, and she led him to where Jane and Nathan sat, a bottle of wine already uncorked. A loaf of crusty bread sat on a cutting board in the middle of the table. Josh's stomach growled.

"Nathan." He tipped his chin at his brother-in-law and then gave his sister a hug. "Hey, Janie. Good to see you."

She embraced him extra tightly, conveying that she'd missed him as much as he'd missed her. Despite the fact that she was a decade younger than he was, they'd been close growing up. From the moment she'd shown up, he'd considered her his responsibility. Overprotective would be an understatement.

While Josh had practically interrogated

Nathan at the onset of their relationship, the guy had been a good sport, not only winning him over but becoming a close friend. Best of all, Josh knew the guy would take care of his little sister, which eased his worries as he sailed off into the great wide open.

The charcuterie board in front of Jane held a couple of sweet pickles, and he popped one in his mouth as he settled in his chair. How nice of Jane to save them, knowing they were his favorite. He savored it and then opened the menu. "You guys already order your entrees?"

"Just the bread and the board," Jane said. "I was famished and figured you'd be extra hungry after a week at sea."

"Mmm," he mumbled, debating which cut of steak to order, and he might as well surf-and-turf it and add shrimp. Even though there were plenty of fine restaurants along his chartered tour stops, he often spent dinnertime alone in his cabin. Because he lived cheaply most of the time, he could indulge here and there. It was a good system.

Once the waiter arrived, they placed their orders, and then Josh turned his attention to Nathan and Jane. "So, what's new?"

"Funny you should ask." Jane's hand moved to her stomach. While her belly didn't appear any bigger, the protective move spoke volumes.

"Say it," Josh said.

"Sounds like you already know."

"I have a rule about not asking women if they're pregnant. I'm not going to risk offending you, of all people."

Jane giggled. "You realize you already implied it, though, right?" Her smile widened, and happiness wafted off her in waves. "But yes, I'm pregnant." She slipped her hand in the crook of Nathan's elbow and rested her head on his shoulder. "We're having a baby."

"Wow. That's..." A thrill fired through Josh as he imagined showing his niece or nephew the ropes on the sailboat. Teaching him or her how to sail and fish. It'd be healthy for Jane to leave her cares behind for a while and get out the water with him, too. "I'm so happy for you guys. Congrats."

Their food arrived, and as they ate, they discussed her early-winter due date and how Mom and Dad had taken the news. No surprise—they were ecstatic. It lifted a weight off Josh's shoulders he hadn't even registered had been there till now. Mom had been so disappointed it hadn't worked out with Olivia, especially since the chance of grandchildren had been dangled in front of her before being snatched away.

"What about you?" Jane asked. "It's not too late for you to settle down, you know. Nathan has a colleague who we think would be perfect for you. She's pretty and smart, and I really like her."

Josh stretched his arm across the table,

careful to avoid tipping glasses or dipping his sleeve in his food. "Jane, as I've told you, that ship has sailed. I'm already in love."

She stuck her lips out in a pout. "With sailing? Really?"

He bit back his smug grin so she wouldn't punch him—he'd taught her to throw her weight behind her swing, and she had a killer jab. "Yes. With sailing, freedom, the ocean, and *Solitude*. That's all I need."

While he appreciated her and Nate's attempts to keep him from becoming a hermit, he rather enjoyed being a bachelor. He only had to leave *Solitude* when he felt like it, which usually ended up being to see his family, hit the market, or walk around the marina and make small talk with his ragtag group of friends, most of whom were retirement age.

With a sigh, Jane let go of the matchmaking subject. They finished dinner, and he slipped the waiter his credit card before the couple across from him could.

As they walked outside, Josh congratulated them again on the baby. Then he headed home, his thoughts on his swaying house, comfy bed, and cool pillow.

Except when he arrived at the marina, there was a party going on. Come to think of it, he'd seen a flyer.

"Josh!" Tinsley ran up to him. She was in her mid-twenties, owned her own jewelry line, and had rented a slip near the marina entrance a couple of months ago. Her boat was decked out with "fairy lights," which meant tiny and blinky, and she could turn a one-syllable word into five. She also referred to boat living as "glamping."

Once the weather turned cold, he'd be shocked if Tinsley stayed, but for now, she'd taken to throwing community "mixers." Not parties. Those were for old people, apparently.

"You never RSVPd," Tinsley said, the beaded bracelets on her wrist rattling as she gesticulated. "So I didn't think you'd be coming. But don't worry. I always plan for extra guests."

"Ah, thanks, Tinsley, but I'm only passing through. Got a job early tomorrow I need to rest up for. I thought I'd just swing by George and Nancy's, and then—"

"Oh, didn't you hear?" Tinsley twisted a blond strand of hair round and round her finger.

Josh's lungs deflated as her question hung in the air. One of the downsides of his closest friends being in their early seventies was worrying about their health.

"They sailed down south for their granddaughter's sweet sixteenth birthday party." Tinsley's mouth formed an excited O and her hands went to swinging again, punctuating her words. "She's totally having a big party on the boat with all of her friends. Can you imagine how grumpy George is gonna be on a boat full of teenagers?"

Tinsley's laugh echoed through the cool night air, and Josh found himself chuckling along. George was a bit of a curmudgeon. It was one of Josh's favorite things about him.

A guy with dark hair walked up behind Tinsley and slid his arms around her middle. Before now, Josh had never seen the man bun in action. He supposed it fit the guy, if that was a thing that could be said about buns and dudes.

"Josh, meet my boyfriend, Sergio. Sergio, Josh."

Well, Nancy would be sad to hear that Tinsley was off the market. She'd been not-so-subtly hinting how cute Tinsley was, while Josh straightforwardly informed the woman that Tinsley was way too young for him, even if he had been searching for a girlfriend.

Josh shook Sergio's hand and muttered a "Nice to meet you." Sergio suggested hitting the dance floor, extending a pity invite his way, and Josh immediately felt like a senior citizen. His dancing days had been short-lived and coerced, to say the least. The idea of dating and dancing...it all exhausted him.

"That's okay," Josh said. "You two go on ahead."

"Sure you won't stay?" Tinsley asked as Sergio tugged her toward the steady beat of an unrecognizable song. "I made kale kombucha smoothies that'll power you up for your trip tomorrow."

Josh dodged the smoothie question and wished her goodbye. As quick as his feet could take his forty-year-old body, he headed away from the buzz of the party toward the blissfully quiet section of the marina. He paused at George and Nancy's empty slip, finding himself surprisingly sad at the idea of not sharing his usual trip recap. He reached into his pocket and fiddled with the barnacle-covered seashell he'd picked up for Nancy's collection.

Then he continued on, each thump of his soles against the wooden walkway loud in the quiet. The silence only intensified as he boarded *Solitude* and headed downstairs, into the cabin.

There were his bed and his pillow, and everything else he'd longed to get home to. Suddenly it didn't feel like the respite he'd been dreaming of.

He lowered himself onto the foot of the bed and kicked off his shoes. After shedding his jeans in favor of comfy shorts, he lifted his cell phone. The email that had refused to load earlier finally finished downloading, and Josh tapped the "Final FINAL Itinerary."

Most of the fun bonding activities had been replaced with strategy meetings and brainstorming sessions. What the difference was between those two, Josh had no idea. As he skimmed through the list, he envisioned an older woman with perpetually pursed lips and a buttoned-up cardigan.

What was the point of chartering a trip to sit in the ship and do exactly what they did in the office? During Josh's stint as a financial advisor, he'd been far too familiar with that type of work, work, work environment, with its suffocating cloud of tension and stress. If anything, he owed it to the people Danae worked with to resist at least a few of her changes.

Josh shook his head and tossed his phone aside. He could argue with Danae Danvers tomorrow. If he'd known he'd be dealing with her instead of the easygoing man who'd originally called and booked the trip, he might've refused.

Too late now.

As he sat in bed, contemplating TV versus sleep, a part of him missed the Riveras and their happy chatter. His nostalgia kicked into high gear as he recalled the years when he and Jane had bonded over wizard books. Those days when she used to show up at his house during her college years to ask for advice on classes, her major, and boys.

Now she was living her own, grownup life.

His sister was having a baby, Nancy and George had their family, and he had...well, he had his solitude.

The thing he swore he wanted. He didn't want to be one of those people who finally achieved their dreams, only to find themselves unsatisfied. But as he climbed into bed, loneliness wrapped around him, heavier than his blanket.

If only coupledom didn't come with so many complications...

Even as his logical side balked at the notion, Josh couldn't help thinking that once in a while, it wouldn't be the worst thing in the world to have someone to come home to.

Chapter Four

"SERIOUSLY? WE'RE HALF AN HOUR away from pushing off for eight whole days, and still no response," Danae muttered, and her Uber driver glanced at her in the rearview mirror.

"What was that?"

"Nothing. It's just..." She gripped the headrest on the passenger seat and scooted forward as far as her belt would let her. "If someone texted or emailed you, you would take the time to answer, right?"

"Um, usually."

"Exactly." With a harrumph, Danae sat back and refreshed her email. No reply from Josh magically appeared, and her nerves stretched to the fraying point. She was already going to have her hands full with her team, and she didn't need another person to manage.

Since he hadn't bothered responding yet, she might as well make a few last tweaks. While she hated to mark up the papers she'd printed for everyone last night, she had a handy roll of correction tape in her purse. Thanks to all her practice in writing in tiny print in her planner, she doubted anyone would even notice they had been altered.

We can definitely squeeze in a think tank session as we cruise around the harbor. That sounded better than brainstorm, especially since the word "storm" wasn't always welcome at sea.

Danae rolled correction tape over the hour reserved for learning the parts of the boat. If anyone hadn't memorized the sailboat diagrams while working at the company, she could cover the basics in ten minutes. Then they could use the rest of the time to get a jumpstart on the campaign.

To cut down on complaints and make sure there was some fun time, she scheduled a twenty-minute break.

"Here, right?" the driver asked, and Danae glanced up, surprised to find herself at the marina already.

She thanked the driver, climbed out of the car, and immediately added a tip and a positive rating so she wouldn't forget. She pushed her glasses up her nose and headed toward the beautiful Barton Boat in front of her. A Fortune 703 model, which was their biggest, most luxurious sailboat.

Perhaps she should've worn her contacts instead, since out on the water her lenses would likely be speckled in no time. But she disliked her contacts, and the wind might dry them out. Constantly wiping her glasses on her pink cardigan seemed like a better option than applying an entire bottle of eye drops a day. Besides, she'd seen the harbor before, so she'd stick to the middle of the boat and work while everyone else took their break.

Naturally, she was the first of her team to arrive. Possibly before their captain, as she didn't see anyone else. *Ooh, if Mr. Wheeler doesn't show, does that mean we can go back to the office to do our work?*

Since Danae had put so much effort into planning and re-planning the trip, she couldn't decide if she'd be more frustrated or relieved.

As she climbed aboard the sailboat, nostalgia slammed into her, transporting her back in time a couple of decades. There was the familiar sway under her feet, the sound of flapping canvas and lapping waves, and the scent of saltwater and wood. She ran her hand along the railing, which wasn't nicked or rusted in places, like it'd been on Dad's boat.

Be careful near the edges, NaeNae,

Dad used to warn, since she'd lean over the railing as far as she could to peer into the water. That was back when she was young and trusted things to catch her, before she'd had enough life experience to realize there weren't a whole lot of guarantees in this world.

Franco's husband dropped him off at the dock, and when Justin unrolled the window to call out a greeting to Danae, their bulldog, Jack, and cairn terrier, Rose, blocked her view, yipping and barking.

Franco pushed his sunglasses on top of his dark hair and continued to wave goodbye to his family. It had cracked her up when she'd discovered the dogs the men had owned before getting together shared the name of the couple from *Titanic*. She had declared it was totally meant to be in the early days of their relationship, and while Mr. Web Developer had rolled his eyes, he hadn't refuted it, either.

One by one, everyone else began showing up: Vanessa and her two chic matching suitcases, Mark and his leather duffel bag, and then Paige, who said a fifteen-minute goodbye to her fiancé before climbing aboard as well.

Finally, there he was, the one person she didn't recognize. Danae gripped the handle of her compact roller suitcase and strolled over. "Josh Wheeler, I presume."

Slowly, he spun around, and it shook

the Etch A Sketch in Danae's mind, erasing everything she'd planned to say. The early morning sun danced across strands of his disheveled hair, highlighting the copper streaks hidden in the brown.

A groove formed between his eyebrows as he studied her, and her throat went dry as she superimposed this guy's image over the one she'd expected—an older, grizzled seafaring type who grumbled about "new-fangled technology."

So what if Josh Wheeler was mildly attractive—hold the mild? Or had eyes the same azure color as the water in the harbor behind him?

"Go ahead and get settled, and we'll be pushing off shortly," he said.

His voice jerked her back to herself, the words she'd intended to say slowly reforming in her brain. "Actually, I wanted to talk to you about the final schedule, and a couple of the last-minute changes I've made."

His mouth flattened into an ambiguous line. "You must be Danae. Sender of all the emails."

A prickling sensation swept across her skin, leaving her unsure how exactly to respond for a couple of seconds. Deciding professional was never the wrong way to go, she held that part of her façade firmly in place.

"I am." She hugged her planner and stack of itineraries to her chest and extended a hand. "Danae Danvers, Chief Marketing Officer. And you must be the guy who doesn't reply to emails."

Okay, so she'd failed at remaining strictly businesslike there at the end.

Josh didn't make a move to shake her hand. Simply skimmed his hand over the boom and fiddled with the backstay. "I replied to most of them."

The frown couldn't be helped, nor could the thread of exasperation. "Did you at least look over the final itinerary? I've made a few more tweaks—"

"To the final *final* itinerary?" One corner of his mouth kicked up, emphasizing the unkempt scruff on his face and the dimple in the middle of his chin. "Do you know what *final* means?"

"About as well as you know how to reply to emails," she quipped. She plucked the top paper off her pile of copies and extended it to him. "Fortunately for you, I have extra copies. You'll see that I've shortened the activity for learning the parts of the boat. Fifteen minutes is all we have time for."

The extra humidity made her glasses slip, and she readjusted them. "Oh, and when we pass by Ocean Cliff and the Jamestown house on the rock, can you get as close as possible to the coast? We're selling luxury, and our social media manager wants to take several video shots. Once we finish up there, I'd like to arrive at the next port in plenty of time because we have a strategy session planned for this evening."

The paper crinkled as Josh took it from her. Instead of studying it, he folded it in half and half again, jammed it in his pocket, and said, "We'll see."

Then he headed to the helm of the boat.

Danae stared after him, mouth agape. She spun around and narrowly avoided colliding with her ex-boyfriend. "Oh. Hey, Mark. Sorry. Um..." She gestured him ahead of her. "If you'll gather the troops, I'll give everyone their cabin assignments so they can put away their stuff."

"I realize you got the promotion, but that doesn't mean I report to you. Mr. Barton is still my boss."

Danae gritted her teeth in an approximation of a smile and focused on keeping her tone polite so she wouldn't break any of his at-work rules. "Yes, I'm aware. What I meant to say was that I could use help gathering everyone so we can settle in and be ready to leave on time. Would you be willing to help me with that?"

"Of course. I just want to be clear. Keeping our boundaries in place is going to be more important than ever on this trip."

"They're already crystal clear. No need for a recap."

Great. Now she was going to have to spend eight days in a confined area with *two* men who didn't want to listen to her.

Josh welcomed everyone onboard, introduced himself, and covered the safety features, as well as what to do in an emergency.

Toward the end of his spiel, his gaze snagged on Danae. While he'd been right about the cardigan, it was about the only feature he'd imagined correctly when it came to the Chief Marketing Officer. She had pale skin that suggested she didn't get outside much, which was a shame when you lived near the beach. She was also younger than expected—he'd guess her to be in her mid-thirties. Prettier, too. Her dirty blond hair was pulled half up, and the breeze toyed with the long curls that hung around her shoulders.

A smile tipped her lips as her attention drifted toward the horizon, her features calm for the first time since she'd climbed aboard. Was that a spark of adventure in her eyes? The same one he felt before sailing into the deep blue?

Slowly, she looked back at him, and Josh lost track of whatever he'd been saying.

"Is that it for the safety talk, then?" she asked, already lifting the planner in her hands—to check the item off her schedule, no doubt.

Part of him wanted to find something to tease her about. Maybe point out that if she'd read the safety guide he'd sent upon booking, heels weren't recommended. At least the brown ankle boots on her feet had a smaller, chunky heel, unlike some of the stilettoes other women had worn so they could endanger their lives every time they clacked around too close to the edge.

But even in email form, the humor had been touch and go. Not to mention they had an audience, and what was he thinking? He had a job to do, and it didn't include making jokes with one of the clients.

"Not quite. One thing everyone should be aware of," Josh said, drawling his words, "is that the ocean and the wind don't care about schedules. No two trips are ever alike, regardless of how many times you've sailed the same course. Each time is different—that's one of the beauties of sailing, and it's better if you know beforehand that sometimes plans have to be rearranged."

Danae's eyebrows drew together, the scrunch of them suggesting she didn't like the idea, which was why he figured he'd better warn her sooner rather than later. Managing expectations at sea was important.

After briefly pointing out the parts of the ship, he nodded in Danae's direction. "Now, I believe your fearless leader has a whole list of items for you to get started on."

The preppy guy with the neat sandy

hair and the button-down shirt lifted a finger in the air, not as if he were testing the direction of the breeze. More like he couldn't be bothered to raise his whole hand. "While Danae is leading this particular project, she's not our boss. Or leader, or whatever."

Josh wasn't sure what to say to that.

Franco and Danae shared a glance that spoke volumes without saying a word. Then Danae said, "Thank you, Mark. Now, let's leave our captain to the sailing while we start our first meeting of the day, which I do happen to be in charge of."

Within twenty minutes they were clear of the more crowded part of the harbor. Josh studied the fluffy clouds overhead, noting the darkening undersides. Yesterday had been inordinately hot, and a cold front was predicted to roll in later this afternoon, although with the breeze, maybe they'd manage to miss any of its effects.

The engine growled as Josh sped up, the sound softer and smoother than the grumbly motor on *Solitude*. He had to hand it to the Barton Boating Company—they made one beautiful sailboat. The Fortune 703 model cut through the water like a dream. It was bigger and shinier than what Josh was used to, with a wheel that moved easily, no grinding required.

While Josh got the allure, this ship was a little too smart for its own good. Auto features were fine and well until they broke, and you didn't have enough experience to get yourself out of trouble. Then again, it'd be a long while before any of the bells and whistles on this hunk of—

Hmm. I suppose calling it a hunk of junk doesn't fit. Occasionally he lovingly referred to *Solitude* as a hunk of junk. Particularly pre-remodel, when the term was painfully accurate.

With the course set and the boat steady, Josh locked the wheel, and dug out the so-called final itinerary that Danae had given him. Oops, he'd already missed her second requested change, but with a few alterations, he could switch up which part of the harbor tour they would end on.

With that done, he headed to check on the passengers. While the boat was twice the length of *Solitude*, he could still hear snippets of conversations as he moved around the first cabin. The Barton employees had split themselves between the two bench seats, and while Danae was facing the center of the boat, the others were straddling the bench or turning around to enjoy the view.

Danae struggled to keep her team focused as they peered over the side of the boat and pointed at birds and the large suspension bridge that connected Newport to Jamestown. In the distance, several sailboats bobbed along, looking more like seagulls than boats, especially when compared to the giant cement-and-wire structure they were sailing underneath.

"...two hundred and fifteen feet of vertical clearance to accommodate the Navy's largest ships," Mark was telling Franco, who was the company's tech geek. It was a factoid Josh shared himself when people wanted to know more. Perhaps with a crew of locals, today he could coast. Not that he was unwilling to play tour guide, but some clients preferred to take in the sights without his chatter, and he wanted to give people their best possible sailing experience. Bigger groups made that a bit trickier because of the varying personalities, likes, and dislikes.

That was why a lot of his first day was spent sussing out his passengers.

"Paige and Vanessa, do you have a list of social media contacts who can announce the launch of our new campaign as soon as it's finalized?" Danae asked. "Really spread the word and drum up some good publicity?"

The fair-skinned redhead kept her eyes fixed on the Rose Island Lighthouse. They'd see several lighthouses during the trip and had a tour of the one on Block Island scheduled for tomorrow, but the squat white one with its pale green shingles stood out. "I started to compile a list last night and will get it to you soon."

"I already have a spreadsheet ready to go," said the woman with thick dark curls—Vanessa, that was it.

While Paige hadn't turned to address Danae, she gave Vanessa her full attention. "As head of publicity, I'll need to see it first for approval."

"As social media manager, I'm always happy to add more contacts to my ever-growing list, so I'd love to combine our efforts and reach more places. Once you get your list ready, of course."They shared a tight smile that made Josh want to back away, which was pretty much how he always felt nowadays when he encountered any kind of drama.

Danae raised her voice and spoke in a placating tone. "It's going to be more important than ever for us to *all* work together, so if you could both send those lists to each other and come up with a finalized version to send me, I'd appreciate it."

The light tapping of keys filled the air. "Done," Vanessa said, and Paige lifted her open laptop and began furiously typing away.

Ah, the bad ol' days, when he'd had to play nice in conference rooms, even when it felt like he and his colleagues were competing rather than collaborating. What a waste of time. Although remembering how hard it could be to keep coworkers on task and happy made him think he should cut Danae, with her emails and constant itinerary alterations, some slack.

A subject change might do everyone

some good, so he switched into tour guide mode. "Coming up, you'll see Fort Adams State Park." He swept his hand toward the approaching peninsula and the gray brick fort that looked more like a castle without turrets. "Anyone been to the Newport Jazz Festival?"

Paige, Franco, and Vanessa chimed in that they had, and Josh asked how they'd enjoyed it. The four of them began chatting and comparing who they'd seen, and Danae's toe started tapping, her posture growing more anxious the longer the stories went on. Couldn't she see that Vanessa and Paige were now talking about something they had in common, the earlier tension gone? Possibly not. But Josh had done several of these corporate retreats, using the skills he'd had to learn when he worked in the office world.

"Okay, well, let's talk about what prompted you to go to the festival," Danae said. "Flyers? Social media posts? How can we tie that into our marketing strategy?"

As they began discussing that, Josh returned to the helm, where he stayed until lunch.

After they ate, he readied the boat so he could loop them around and get close to the famous mansions, as Danae had requested. Call it a peace offering. Although with the wind kicking up and more dark clouds rolling in, he wasn't sure how long the sailing would be smooth.

About thirty minutes later, the mansions were in view, although the sun no longer was. Josh walked across the deck, to where everyone lined the portside. The boat rocked more than it had earlier today, before the temperature began to drop, and a spray of water came over the side and made the passengers jump back.

Strike that. Everyone but Danae—heedless of her doused shoes—scooted back.

A green lawn led to a beige brick house with several chimneys and even more windows. The property owners kept the trees trimmed to allow those windows a view of the bay, which gave people who sailed by a peek at the luxurious life. Around the bend was an enormous neoclassical house with floor-to-ceiling windows, columns, and an atrium with a fountain. From their current position, it wasn't easy to see, and the thick gray fog that had come rolling in certainly wasn't helping matters.

"This is as close as I can get," Josh said, and Danae glanced at Vanessa.

"Will this work for you?" she asked, automatically gripping the railing and shifting her weight to the back foot as the boat swayed again. Either she'd recalibrated in record time or she'd been on a boat a few times before.

Vanessa lifted her phone and frowned at the screen. "It's too hard to get a good shot through the fog. With my eyes, I can sorta see the pale brick, but once I lift the screen..." She made a disgruntled noise low in her throat. "The phone isn't picking up any details through the fog, and if I zoom in, it's just more convoluted."

"What about the three-story mansion with the red roof and all the cool archways? Ooh, and check out that beautiful balcony." The glimmer of excitement Josh had seen in Danae's eyes before they set sail reignited. "Suddenly I want to stand up there and shout, 'Romeo, Romeo, wherefore art though, Romeo?'"

"I tried that trick at a club once," Vanessa said. "I don't recommend it." She and Danae laughed, while Josh did his best to remember his high school literature class.

The sigh that came from Vanessa as she zoomed on the massive Vanderbilt mansion led him to believe that she still wasn't getting what she wanted.

Danae glanced at him, as if she expected him to help.

Josh held up his hands. "Hey, I'm not in charge of the fog."

"Isn't there anything we can do?" Danae asked. "Will it burn off?"

While he'd cursed the weatherman's inaccurate predictions before, Josh also knew better than to put himself in the guy's shoes. "The one constant at sea is that nothing's ever constant. But if you want my honest opinion, the sun will set before the fog clears in this area of the bay."

"Shoot. I guess I should've made the mansions the first stop, but it didn't make sense to zigzag across the bay, only to have to sail back." Danae moved closer to Vanessa and squinted at her phone screen. "Can you use any of the footage you've taken? Even if it's just a teaser?"

The woman played a few seconds of a video, swiped through the pictures she'd taken, and shook her head. "Not without it coming across as completely amateur, and I would never upload anything less than the best." She tapped her lip and then her eyebrows shot up. "You know what we should do?"

All eyes focused on Vanessa, but she didn't immediately rattle off the answer, leading him to believe she enjoyed people hanging on her every word.

Eventually, Franco asked, "What?"

"Did you guys see those mini videos on Trendster?"

"Trendster?" Danae asked, saving Josh the effort, although he reminded himself he was the silent partner on this ride, so to speak.

"Oh my gosh, it's the coolest app. Franco, you've heard of it, haven't you? I figured you'd be up on all the happening events."

The guy blinked at her. "Maybe in my early twenties, but these days I'm an old married man who stays home with his husband, playing endless games of fetch with our babies."

"They have two dogs," Danae surprised Josh by whispering. "In case you thought..." Her nose crinkled. "I mean, you probably figured it out, but sometimes it makes me picture babies crawling after a stick, and that'd be super cute, but possibly not recommended, and..." She placed a hand over her face, which was slowly turning an adorable shade of pink. "I'm gonna stop now."

"Don't stop on my account," Josh said with a smile. "Especially since that was right where my mind went. Diapered babies with sticks in their mouth."

Her head tilted, as if she wasn't sure whether or not he was joking. Either he'd been at the marina too long and had forgotten how to tell a joke, or Danae worked so hard she'd forgotten how to laugh at one.

"It's the hottest of the hottest, and it's always changing," Vanessa said. "People check in, and post these super short, hyper-aesthetic videos that show off the location. If you're going to check out the place because of someone's video, you tap the go button, and that user gets trend points."

Their brazen social media manager tapped her phone screen and then swiveled it toward her audience. "I've been trying to build up Barton Boating Company's points, as well as my own. Everyone take out your phones and download it right now so you can follow me at Vibe With Vanessa. Trust me, it's going to be huge in no time."

One by one, the passengers pulled out their phones and added the Trendster app, although a bit begrudgingly.

"Click the link for the Castle Wines Vineyard. Isn't it gorgeous?"

Franco leaned in and watched the video with the rows of green leafy vines and clusters of people wandering around enjoying the scenery. At the end, the camera zoomed in on a group seated around a wooden table, laughing and chatting as they shared a bottle of wine. "I recognize that logo," Franco said. "Justin loves that brand. I'll have to pick some up for him."

People remarked on how beautiful the place was and how lovely the wine-tasting looked. "I bet they'll agree to give us a tour in exchange for a boost on Trendster," Vanessa said to Danae. "I can take lots of beautiful shots in the vineyard that will fit the lifestyle angle we're going with for the campaign. That far inland, we won't have to deal with the fog like out here."

"But I already made a reservation at a restaurant close to where we're docking tonight, and I made sure they had a private area so we can have our big strategy session during dinner."

Vanessa slung her arm around Danae's shoulders. "Hello. Strategy sessions are always better with wine. Seeing where it grows somehow makes it taste better, too. I'm not sure about the science behind it. Only that it's true."

Paige now sat on the deck in the middle of the boat, her gaze focused on her lap. Given that her skin appeared paler than usual, she must be seasick. "I agree," she said. "Plus with the water getting choppy, I'm ready to take a break from the boat." Her comment set off a chain reaction until everyone except Danae had spoken in favor of heading to the vineyard.

"If that's the plan," Josh said, "I suggest we sail over to the Jade Pond Marina. I can make a quick reservation online, and for a small fee, we can dock and order a couple cars to take us to the vineyard."

Danae glanced from him to her team, back to him. Clearly she was outnumbered, and he worried he shouldn't have put her on the spot. He was simply trying to ensure that the Barton Boating Company had a great trip. Not only because he prided himself on getting even the most hesitant to enjoy themselves, but also because they were a big Newport company and it'd be good for his charter business as well.

At long last, Danae gave him a tiny nod, although she couldn't bring herself to say the words that would mean straying from the itinerary and the reservations she'd made.

Josh returned to the helm to change course.

Like it or not, by the end of this week, Danae was either going to blow a blood vessel or learn to go with the flow.

Chapter Five

DANAE AND THE GROUP WALKED past a rocking chair that'd been fashioned out of weathered logs and twine, and followed their tour guide into one of the leafy green rows.

The entire place had the rustic atmosphere of a simpler life—one she was struggling to feel, considering the upcoming strategy session.

"The land at Castle Wines Vineyard is protected farmland," their tour guide said. "You'll notice we plant from north to south, so that the sun will hit both sides of the rows and produce the best, healthiest grapes possible. Our estate also includes two lakes, one that we use for irrigation..."

Danae hung back from the rest of her team as they continued on with their tour.

The tour that wasn't on the itinerary. Which was fine. She could improvise.

After she formed a solid strategy.

Her pulse thrummed faster, and she sucked in a lungful of air before gradually letting it out. Part of the reason she'd taken the trouble of reserving a spot for dinner where they'd be guaranteed privacy was because she'd never led a meeting on her own. Since a big part of this trip included proving herself as someone who could take charge, she needed the strategy session to go well. They were a diverse group who rarely agreed, and somehow she was supposed to get them to do just that.

No pressure or anything.

Danae lifted her planner and skimmed the notes she'd jotted down. The top three items were underlined.

Listen better

Consider others' perspectives

BE A TEAM PLAYER

"You okay?" a deep voice asked from behind her.

"Gah!" exploded out of Danae's mouth as she jumped, dropping her planner in the process.

She reached for it at the same time

Josh did. Their fingers brushed, and a shock tingled up her arm. Josh's eyes met hers, and she wondered if he'd felt it—did shoes get staticky on grass? She'd thought it was only carpet.

Her beloved planner lay on the ground, its pages exposed. Danae hastily scooped it up. In a lot of ways, having someone see what she'd written in the compact squares and along the margins felt like allowing them to read her diary.

"Sorry," Josh said as he straightened. "I thought you realized I was here."

Danae swiped at the dirt and blades of grass stuck to the back cover. "At the vineyard, sure. In my own private row, not so much."

"Ah, so this is *your* row." He flashed her a smile, his tone teasing.

Danae slipped her planner in her laptop bag, thinking of how far they'd strayed from what she'd scribbled in today's square. "I just hate things I can't plan for, you know?"

Josh nodded. "I got that vibe, yes."

She arched an eyebrow, warning him to be careful.

"Don't know why you're giving me that look. Take it up with Mother Nature."

"Maybe I will." Danae stuck her thumb under the strap of her laptop bag so it would stop cutting into her shoulder. Thanks to the extra notebooks she'd packed, assuming her team would forget theirs on the boat, it was heavier than usual.

The wattage on Josh's grin kicked up a notch. "I'd like to watch that."

A laugh slipped free, and she imagined herself shaking her fist at the sky and asking why it couldn't cooperate. Mother Nature would likely respond with one of those cartoon storm clouds that followed characters around and rained only on them.

"Come on." Josh gestured her ahead of him. "We're gonna miss all the good stuff. Like hearing about the kind of grapes they use in the wine we'll drink later."

They continued down the row, the dappled sunlight turning their path into dancing circles of light as the leaves fluttered in the breeze. The earthen scent drifted up with each footstep, a rich mixture of dirt, sunshine, and greenery, and she realized that she *had* been missing the good stuff.

This time when she inhaled, she took the time to enjoy how crisp the air was as it filled her lungs. The rows made perfect lines that covered acres of land as far as the eye could see, but the individual trunks were twisted and gnarled, each one different from the next.

Danae slowed to study the clumps of green grapes next to her. "I wonder how many grapes it takes to make a bottle. If it's anything like fresh-squeezed orange juice, it's a whole lot of effort for not that much juice."

"Let's guess, and then we can ask." Josh's shadow stretched across the leaves in front of her, turning them a darker shade of green. "Whoever's closest gets to set tomorrow's schedule."

The speed at which Danae whipped around to face him nearly gave her whiplash. The corners of his eyes crinkled, his smirk bringing out the dimple in his chin, and her exasperation faded in an instant. "You're teasing me."

"Guilty. You make it too easy. Then again, maybe it's all part of my master plan."

"You? Have a plan?"

"Hey," he said with a chuckle. "And yes. A dastardly plan, one that requires you to answer my next question honestly." He took a step closer to her, and her heart quickened. "Are you as stressed out as you were before I crossed your path in the vineyard?"

"You mean before you scared me half to death?" Danae asked. Then she took a second or two to truly check in with herself so she could answer his question.

The pressure that had been building in her chest when they'd first begun the tour had eased, any remaining nerves having more to do with how close Josh was. She wasn't sure why she was having such a nervous reaction to him, besides his aversion to following an itinerary.

An inkling tickled the back of her brain, whispering that the reason might have *something* to do with his being a relatively charming, ridiculously handsome male, but she promptly shut those thoughts down. She was on this trip to earn her promotion, not to flirt with the sailboat's captain.

"Admittedly, I do feel less stressed. As long as I don't go thinking too much. See, I'm new to my position." She'd blurted out that last part before thinking better of it—hazards of an overactive, noisy mind. She suspected it also had to do with Josh's directness, and how long it had been since anyone seemed to notice or give weight to her stress level.

Since the admission was already out there—and she needed to talk to *someone* about the concerns her family had brushed off as silly—she pressed on. "I'm good at my job, but I need to prove to my boss I can handle more responsibility in order to keep my Chief Marketing Officer title." The pressure that had temporarily eased began building once again, and she had to dig down deep to find her confidence. Sometimes it was about faking it till you could make it. "But don't you worry, I'll figure it out."

"I wasn't worried for a second."

She laughed, surprised at how easy it had come—twice in a matter of minutes, too. "That'd be more comforting if you actually knew me."

"Sometimes you can just tell. You strike me as a person who achieves whatever she sets her mind to."

Warmth flooded her, making it that much easier to keep hold of her assuredness. "I don't even care if you're buttering me up. I'm going to run with it." She started down the path again. "And my guess is nine-hundred and fifty grapes per bottle."

"I think you're underestimating the grapes. I bet four hundred would do." A mischievous gleam hit his blue, blue eyes, one that left her a tad wary and a lot intrigued.

Within a few more minutes, they caught up to the rest of the group. As the tour guide answered questions, Danae noted how relaxed everyone seemed. The clouds that had dotted the sky were dispersing, leaving behind clear skies that looked straight out of an oil painting.

Okay, maybe touring a vineyard in place of a foggy sail hadn't been the worst idea.

Vanessa moved to Danae's side and showed her the video she'd recorded. The endless blue sky she'd been admiring glowed bright, the perfect backdrop to the leafy green vines and the restaurant down the way. "Doesn't it look amazing? Like you just want to step inside and stay for a while. I'll end it with a shot of wine glasses and a bottle. Maybe a cheese plate. It's going to be perfect. 'Not just a boat, but a lifestyle.'"

She smiled as she quoted Danae's campaign slogan.

"It's gorgeous," Danae said. "I'm here, and I still want to step inside the video."

Their tour guide led them into a room lined with large wooden barrels, and Danae blinked as her eyes adjusted to the dimmer light. Then the woman began explaining the varieties of wine.

"If you hold the glass up to a white napkin, you can see if the wine's more opaque or translucent, which helps us ascertain the quality." She unfurled a white linen napkin and held it up to the glass. "See?"

Danae inclined her head to Vanessa and whispered, "What's the difference between opaque and translucent? It just looks red to me."

"I was about to ask the same thing," Josh said, turning their duo into a trio.

Vanessa lifted the glass the woman had set in front of her and gave it a swirl. Then she borrowed the napkin and held it up. "Think of it like your relationships..."

"Nonexistent," Danae joked, and Josh snorted. She ducked her head, working to cover her embarrassment over blurting that out, although she suspected the wine wasn't the only thing red right now. At least he'd laughed.

Did that mean he was single?

You're not going there, remember?

"What I mean is," Vanessa continued,

"we want transparency in both our wines and our relationships, not murky or hazy."

That clicked on the lightbulb over Danae's head. "Hmm. Things I never knew before."

"Me neither," Josh said, and then he took the glass the tour guide handed him and clinked it with Vanessa's and then Danae's.

Danae and Josh sipped as everyone else paused to sniff their wine—apparently they'd missed the memo. Since no one seemed to notice their gaffe, she and Josh shared a smile over the rims of their glasses. The red was dry, earthy, and a little bitter. Not nearly as sweet as she preferred, but she suspected it was right up Mark's alley. His entire family was into wine, and she'd always felt out of her depth whenever the subject came up.

Sure enough, Mark made an *mmm* noise after he swished and swallowed. "Can't beat a nice pinot noir. They say it's a notoriously difficult grape to grow, but a glass like this is well worth the effort." He chuckled. "Easy for me to say, I'm sure." The tour guide giggled, complimented him on his knowledge, and talked about the extra steps they took to ensure they had the best grapes for their pinots.

Danae lowered her glass to the table without drinking the rest, and Franco nudged her. "Aren't you gonna ask for a fruity white?"

"I always feel like wine people roll their eyes over how sweet I like mine. As if wanting to avoid puckering up after every sip is a bad thing."

"It's perfectly fine to like what you like," Josh said, and Franco pointed at him.

"What he said. Wine is supposed to be enjoyed, not endured."

"If I had my way, they'd roll the rim in sugar, too. Like, why can they do that for a cocktail, but not a glass of wine?"

The tour guide moved to another section of barrels. "Would your group like to try another red, or does anyone prefer white?"

Franco, Josh, Vanessa, and Mark all pointed at Danae, and muttered variations of "She does."

"We have a lovely dry sauvignon blanc, or a dessert Moscato that pairs well with berries and pastries," the tour guide said. "Which would you prefer?"

Danae ran her fingers along the edge of the table. "The Moscato, please."

"You want me to ask if she'll roll it in sugar?" Franco asked.

"Um, no," she whispered. "I'm doing my best to appear as if I know what I'm doing. Pretty sure that'd give me away."

Their tour guide handed Danae the first glass, and this time she remembered to swirl and sniff. The citrus and honeysuckle notes made her taste buds do a jig in anticipation. She sipped, relishing the sweet flavors as they coated her tongue. "Wow. This is really good."

They tried a couple more options, and everyone shared one last toast with their favorite before they readied to move on to the restaurant.

"Yes?" Their tour guide asked, pointing at Josh, who had his hand up.

"Before we go, I was wondering if you could tell me how many grapes it takes to make each bottle of wine?"

Instead of looking at the tour guide as she answered, Josh's gaze moved to Danae.

She perked up her ears, wanting to be right even though she'd merely taken a wild stab in the dark.

"A typical vine will produce about ten bottles. So forty grape clusters per vine, which produces approximately ten bottles, makes it four hundred. Give or take."

Josh couldn't help the smug expression on his face, and it took everything in him not to laugh and give himself away when Danae turned wide eyes on him.

"How did you know?"

Ever so casually, he rubbed his fingertips along his jaw. "Would you believe it was a lucky guess?"

"Didn't you see the plaque up front? I took a picture." Vanessa swiped a couple of times and then pivoted the screen toward Danae. "It says it right there in bronze, almost word for word."

Danae's mouth fell open. "You read the plaque?"

Josh hooked his thumbs in the front pockets of his jeans and shrugged. "Let this be a lesson to you. It's remarkable how many things you miss if you fail to live in the moment."

A smile spread across Danae's face, a charming little groove forming in her cheek, even as she shook her head at him. "Oh, I missed something all right. It's called you cheating."

Amusement radiated through her features, casting her in a whole new light. While he'd only caught hints of this version of her on the ship, her cheery side had come out more and more as they'd wandered through the vineyard.

Once she noticed everyone else was watching, a few of them with crinkled foreheads, it faded faster than he would've liked.

Mark, on the other hand, frowned as if he'd stepped in mud, or something worse than mud.

Danae rubbed the side of her neck, and the more serious businesswoman he'd met first thing this morning returned. "Time for dinner. Just remember, it's a working meal, and we're gonna need all hands on deck."

The tour guide escorted their group to the farm-to-table restaurant, where she handed them over to the hostess and, with a wink, told her colleague to take good care of them.

Rustic light fixtures hung from the ceiling, which boasted wooden beams. Large windows overlooked the vineyard, giving it an open feel. More than the usual amount of wine glasses covered the tables, as jovial groups and couples sat around enjoying the food and drinks.

The hostess gestured to a table, but Danae pointed at one in the back corner of the room. “Actually, could we sit over there? We need to have a strategy session, and it’d be easier if we had some privacy.”

The hostess accommodated her request, and they settled at one of the few tables without a view. A waiter arrived and described the extensive list of wines, a handful of which they’d already tried, and they each ordered a glass to go with their meal.

After the waiter left to put in their order, Danae withdrew a notebook. “I jotted down the best ideas we had during this morning’s think tank session, and now I want to plot out how to implement them.”

“Oh, I forgot my notebook on the ship,” Paige said, and Mark and Vanessa echoed that they’d done the same.

“Fortunately for you, I’m prepared.” Danae passed out notebooks. The covers were paper-bag brown, with motivational sayings stamped across them. Things like *Everyday I’m Hustlin’*; *Work, Play, Slay*;, and *Like a*

Boss. She also handed out colorful gel pens, adding that she would like them back at the end of the meeting.

Josh sat back in his chair, attempting to put as much space between himself and the meeting as possible. "I can go eat alone if you need me to."

"No need," Danae said. "That'd make me feel bad. Besides, you already signed the non-disclosure agreement." She inhaled, and when she picked up her pen, he noticed a slight tremor in her hand. "As you all know, we need to have a cohesive marketing plan in place by the end of our trip. Vanessa, why don't you start by telling us how you're going to tie in today's photos and videos so we can all provide feedback and support?"

Vanessa began a rundown of her ideas for the social media launch, and since the cheese plate had arrived, Josh tuned out and nibbled on that.

"...have the statistics. Men are our main target market." Mark raised his voice, vehement enough about making his point that Josh was pulled back into the conversation. He'd obviously missed something.

"That doesn't mean we should ignore our female subset," Danae said.

"I never said we should. But our efforts—and our budget—should still be geared toward men over fifty with disposable income. So far, you and Vanessa are listing images and concepts for women."

Vanessa huffed, clearly offended, and threw out a "Seriously? Are you saying that beautiful scenery is just for women now?"

"Of course not," Mark said, holding up his hands. "I'm simply pointing out what I view as a minor oversight."

Danae crossed one leg over the other, the table rattling as she bumped her knee into it. The purse of her lips suggested she had to work at remaining calm. "There are plenty of men who care about wine. If I recall correctly, you happen to be one of them."

"Yes, but you're still missing my point." Mark glanced at Josh, and a sense of foreboding pricked Josh's skin. "Would an image of wine or a vineyard make you think about buying a boat?"

"Uh, excuse me," Franco said. "I'm a guy."

"Yes, but you and your husband don't feel the need to buy flashy yachts and sailboats to compete against other men for female attention. To buy one not only for sailing, but as a status symbol you can bring up on the golf course or over bourbon at the end of a long day."

"That's because I have more interesting things to discuss and brag about," Franco said in a teasing tone, but Mark's expression remained unchanged.

"Before you were hired as the web developer for Barton, how much did you know about yachts and sailboats?"

Dead silence.

"My point exactly. I bet if we asked Mr. Wheeler—"

"Josh is fine," he said out of habit, unwittingly jumping into the debate with both feet when he'd resolved to stay out of it. All because he'd gotten sick of phone calls and meetings where it was Mr. Wheeler this, and Mr. Wheeler that. Out at sea, most people were stripped down to the simplest version of themselves.

Except maybe the woman seated to his right. Judging from the rapid tapping of her pen, the conversation wasn't going the way she'd hoped, either.

"Anyway," Mark continued, "if we asked you about the people you usually charter for, I'd wager that most of them are older gentlemen. Some who are going out with their fishing buddies—in search of a trophy catch, no less—and some with their wives or girlfriends."

Josh paused, and everyone awaited his answer. "Most of them are, yeah."

"At the caveman level, that's what drives men to believe they need to buy a faster, shinier, bigger boat. Even if they don't realize that's why." Mark peered across the table at Danae, and there was something about the way he looked at her that Josh couldn't quite put his finger on. "Just because you want men to be more evolved and use things like use Google calendar to run their lives, doesn't mean they are. Do you really want to risk putting too much emphasis on the wrong target market to prove a point?"

His challenge hung in the air.

While Josh might've been more tactful about it, Mark wasn't wrong. In addition to the charter trips, most boat owners at the marina were male, and while there were a handful in their late thirties to mid-forties like Josh, most of them were over fifty. People like Tinsley were the exception, and her boat was a rental—and hardly a yacht. Although he wasn't sure what Google calendar had to do with anything.

In this instance, he hadn't been asked a direct question and was going to keep silent. He and Danae had just formed a sort of truce among the vines and tasting barrels, and he didn't want to undo it, because it would make sailing easier.

Yeah. That was the sole reason. Not because he'd enjoyed those few minutes when it had been just the two of them, or how her laugh had made his pulse quicken.

A muscle ticked in Danae's cheek. "I see your point. We'll come up with more images that'll appeal to primitive men who think the only things that matter are money and impressing the ladies."

Josh bit the inside of his cheek to keep himself from laughing at the jab. Most everyone else in the group studied the spot in front of them like they'd never seen a table before.

"Mark, I'd appreciate it if you could write up a list of at least ten images or video ideas to incorporate and share with Vanessa."

"Gladly."

"I guess that's the end of my presentation, then." Vanessa slumped lower in her chair and crossed her arms. She fired a tight smile across the table at Mark. "I do hope you won't be offended when I point out minor oversights on your end as well."

"I expect you to," Mark said. "Pushing each other is how we'll make the entire team better."

Danae scribbled notes, and then their food arrived.

After they'd eaten and their waiter had cleared their plates, Danae turned to Franco. "Let's talk website. We want to portray elegance and the luxurious lifestyle while keeping it simple. You said you have a beta version for us to look at?"

"Yep, which is why I brought my laptop, as requested." Franco smiled at Danae, who returned his smile and thanked him. Then he opened his computer, clicked a few buttons, and swiveled the screen toward everyone.

The excitement in Danae's features faded a touch, and a contemplative crinkle creased her forehead. She tilted her head one way and then the other.

Franco raised his eyebrows and scanned

the faces of everyone seated around the table. "Well?"

A couple of beats of silence ticked through the air, each one adding a layer of tension, and then Danae tapped the end of her pen to her lips. "Why is there an anchor in the middle of the menu bar?"

"That's actually the main menu button." Franco maneuvered the cursor over it and clicked. "I thought the anchor would be a fun change from the norm."

"Super cool idea," Danae said. "But I don't think I'd realize that I could click on it if you didn't tell me. You know?"

Franco tightened his lips until they nearly disappeared and nodded. "Okay, I guess I can understand how that might be confusing."

"Are those graphics moving around like that all the time?" Vanessa asked, indicating the swipe of blue that came from the right and then the left, like two ships crossing in the night. "It's a bit...dizzying. My eye's working so hard to follow them that it's all I can focus on."

"If you hover over one"—Franco moved the cursor to one of the sailboat graphics—"it stops so you can click it. Then you get the information on the different types of boats we sell."

Vanessa wrinkled her nose, which made it pretty clear she wasn't a fan, and Josh eyed one of the empty tables, wondering if it was too late to make a break for it.

"There's hardly any copy." Mark pointed at the screen. "And what is there is far too tiny for our older demographic to read."

"I think that's partially because of the simplicity and color of the font." Chair legs scraped the floor as Paige scooted closer and squinted at the screen. "What are the other options?"

"Do you really want me to start rattling off every possible font and color combination?" Franco asked.

Now Paige was stung, her face crumpling, and Josh recalled enough from his time in a conference room to raise his shoulders in preparation for the moment this went south. "All I'm saying is that the font and background need to be more distinct from each other so people can read what little information is on the homepage."

"I can tell you've done a ton of work, and I like where you're going with it," Danae said. "But as Mark pointed out, our audience does skew older. Think sleek yet simple. Classic and straightforward. Along with a pinch more copy to help guide people who visit the website."

The laptop snapped shut with a *click* and Franco jammed his computer back in his bag, although it snagged on the fabric at first, leaving him to fight with it for a couple of extra seconds. The line of his jaw tightened.

Danae said, "We should take a break." A wise move, Josh thought, under the circumstances. "Paige can make her presentation tomorrow morning."

Paige nodded, and Vanessa sent a conciliatory smile Franco's way. "Let's go wine-shopping," she suggested to him. "You said you wanted to bring some back for Justin."

He looped his bag over his shoulder and stood. "Sounds good."

His exit set off a chain reaction, everyone else muttering that they were going to go take a few last pictures or head to the gift shop.

Then Josh and Danae were alone, and he didn't know what to say or do. Perhaps he should've gone with the rest of them, but he couldn't bring himself to leave Danae at the table alone after that tense exchange.

Danae pushed her fingers to her temples. "This is why strategy meetings shouldn't be done over wine."

"I'm not sure that was the problem," Josh muttered before he thought better of it.

Danae frowned, and the stress that had been weighing her down when he'd stumbled across her in the vineyard crept back in, tightening the line of her shoulders. "Let me guess, if we'd tied knots for an hour after lunch this would've gone better." He opened his mouth, even though he wasn't sure what to say, and she held up a hand. "I'm sorry. That was out of line. I just..." Her breaths came out shallow. "I needed for that to go well, so I've got a long night of brainstorming on how to fix it ahead of me." She pushed out her chair and followed after her team, and then Josh was the one alone and sighing.

Not only was the fifteen-minute ride to the ship going to be awkward, everyone was sure to be bumping into each other as they prepared for bed, and tomorrow they all got to wake up and do it again.

While the lighter moments with Danae in the vineyard had been nice, this was a much-needed reminder that relationships were complicated and involved a lot of hassle, whether between coworkers, friends, or couples.

The version of him that had wished for company last night had clearly been delusional.

Chapter Six

TODAY NEEDED TO GO BETTER.

No, today *would* go better.

Danae strolled up to the very tip of the ship's bow, inhaled the brisk saltwater-scented air, and held it in. *Live in the moment.* What an easy phrase—one she couldn't afford. People who lived in the moment were the same ones who later foreclosed on houses or left their loved ones without a safety net.

She was the leader, and that left the responsibility for last night's tumultuous meeting on her shoulders. While she'd been known to overthink and overstress about every possible scenario that *might* happen, she wished she'd been better prepared for how everything went down when Franco showed them the beta version of the website. Maybe if she'd written more notes, or studied tips for leading meetings, or...something.

A tight band formed around her rib cage as she rehashed the last ten minutes of dinner, as she'd been doing for the last twelve hours. Franco was very talented, and a total whiz at technology, but he could be a little sensitive about his work. Then again, most people were, it came to their department and their specialty.

While she was trying to remain optimistic, she was seriously doubting her boss's theory that shoving them all on a boat would miraculously erase their differing opinions. If anything, it seemed to highlight them.

Considering that they were about to sail away from the mainland, leaving her without any escape from the ship for an entire week, she contemplated walking the plank and making a swim for home.

But she wasn't a quitter.

Besides, that wasn't on the agenda.

Heavy footsteps cut through the whirl of thoughts messing with her mind, and Josh walked up beside her and gripped the forestay. "Morning."

"Morning. Sorry about yesterday's—"

"Look, I—"

Their words crashed in the middle, and Josh gestured to her. "You go ahead."

Danae fiddled with the charm on her necklace. "I feel bad about how everything went last night, including the fact that it put you in an awkward position. And I'm sorry I snapped at you. I was upset because it felt like I'd already failed, day one."

"Don't worry about it," Josh said. "I know it's not easy getting people to see eye to eye, and I'm plenty capable of getting myself into awkward situations. I usually prefer to put my foot in my mouth." His crooked smile left her slightly off balance.

"Is that so?"

He nodded, and relief flickered for the first time since the meeting. For hours she'd lain in bed, trying to come up with a strategy for making today go more successfully. Up here at the front of the sailboat, chatting with a scruffy sailor wearing an army green jacket that suited his rugged style, her inner turmoil calmed, as smooth as the azure water that stretched on for miles and miles.

The early-morning sunshine sparkled across the face of the silver watch on his wrist, turning it into a beacon. While a lot of people had given them up in favor of telling the time on their phones, there was something about a guy with a sleek watch. Or maybe that was her penchant for being on time talking.

And I'm staring. In order to avoid being caught, she turned to the two platitudes written across the notes section in her planner. Since she apparently didn't understand men or the "caveman drive," she figured she'd ask a dude who had plenty of brute force skills.

"Which quote do you find more inspiring and motivating?" Danae lifted her book and read, "'Great things in business are never done by one person. They're done by a team of people.' Or 'Talent wins games, but teamwork and intelligence win championships.' It's Michael Jordan, so—"

"You figured it'd speak to the person who accused you of not understanding the male psyche in the meeting last night?"

"Well, yeah." Mark's feedback had jabbed at her, and she'd hoped choosing inspirational quotes from men would help prove she could appeal to them as well as women. "Do you think it'll work?"

What was he doing? Hadn't he decided he'd make limited appearances, as required, keep his head down, and just steer the ship?

Only he'd seen Danae standing there, worrying her lower lip with her teeth, and he'd been completely drawn in, even as warning bells rang through his head. "You say Michael Jordan, and I'm sold. I'm also the older demographic, so..." He shrugged.

Danae clicked her tongue. "You are not. Because that'd mean I'm getting close to that demo and I refuse to accept that. Mid-thirties is the new hip age, don't you know?"

Josh ran his fingers through his hair. Scattered strands of gray had begun popping up here and there, like hints of his dad shining through when he looked in the mirror. "Oh, great. Now I'm gonna need a new hip?"

Her giggle danced across the breeze and smacked him in the chest. She had a nice laugh. While her business exterior could be a bit prickly, underneath it were hints of a kind person who obviously hadn't laughed in far too long.

Naturally, Josh would recommend less work and more sea—knot-tying and all—but he doubted Danae would agree. Or appreciate the suggestion. Still, maybe he could sneak in a few fun activities without her realizing it.

Until she was already enjoying herself, and then he'd have sold her on his methods.

"What if I've left my thirties behind already?" Josh asked. "What does that mean?"

Danae turned to fully face him. "That depends. Have you ever yelled at kids to get off your lawn?"

A laugh burst free. "Not since my lawn turned into water. But I have been known to shake my fist at noisy waterskiers."

Danae's shoulders shook as she laughed,

and he wasn't sure if he'd moved closer or she had. Light freckles dotted the bridge of her nose. She'd worn her hair in loose waves today, and the silky strands framed her face and added a no doubt false sense of accessibility. "Then I'm afraid the word *hip* might not apply to you."

Josh let out an over-the-top gasp, as if it were the worst news he'd ever heard, before he went ahead and laughed with her. He suspected many a man had been lured in by Danae's beauty, only to discover the control freak resting under the surface. Then again, the jokes she'd made confirmed there was a lot more to her, and he found himself wanting to dig deeper.

Not a good idea. This next week could get complicated and uncomfortable fast if he attempted to cross lines and it went badly. Come to think of it, the mere idea of crossing the lines and doing anything that might be viewed as unprofessional would probably offend her.

And he wasn't interested in a relationship anyway, so why had his tired mind gone there?

Tired was the keyword. That was why he was noticing the way the sun lit up her profile. Why when the ship rocked and she gripped the forestay, all he could think about was how close his hand was to hers on the railing.

"Anyway, thanks for the help." After taking a second to steady herself, she flipped through her ever-present planner, peeled off a sticker, and placed it next to the Michael Jordan quote.

"Did you just give yourself a gold star?"

There was that amazing laugh again, making the blood in his veins zing faster. She haughtily lifted her head. "You're just jealous that you don't have one."

"I am. Where's my gold star?"

One honey-colored eyebrow arched, drawing attention to her hazel eyes, the whirlpool of green and brown sucking him right in. "Do a good enough job, and maybe you'll earn one by the end of the trip."

With that, she headed toward the cabin where the kitchen was located.

Leaving Josh to think up ways to make her happy enough to snag himself one of those fancy stars.

After breakfast, they took their steaming mugs of coffee and sat at the table on deck to start the morning's think tank session. The entire time, Danae struggled to make eye contact with Mark.

Yesterday's comments felt personal, especially the remark about using Google calendar to run their lives, which was something they'd disagreed on while dating. She'd simply wanted to have a shared calendar, so she knew what was going on and when. Instead of seeing how convenient it'd be for the both of them, he'd told her that she didn't need to micromanage his life.

Not what she'd been trying to do, for the record. Silly her, she'd thought it would bring them closer, instead of being the final straw.

Even though she and Mark had promised to continue to support each other, and that they wouldn't let the promotion change anything, things were different. By accusing her of putting too much emphasis on the wrong market, he also seemed to be implying she didn't deserve to be the Chief Marketing Officer.

His verbal jabs during meetings might become an issue she would have to address—one he'd probably dodge while accusing her of being too sensitive—but since she'd just delivered the inspirational quote, she was focusing on staying upbeat.

"This morning I want to mix things up and do something fun," Danae said. Clearly her team needed to climb aboard the optimism train, because their skepticism was palpable. "Let's split into teams of two and come up with out-of-the-box ways to market our boats. Then we're going to shuffle our papers and have other teams present them as their ideas on how to make it work.

"Everyone remember how you want your own ideas to be received. Remember to be open-minded and brainstorm ways to implement the idea before making a snap judgment or declaring it impossible or unproductive."

Her gaze automatically flickered to Mark, conveying to him that she'd heard his silent critique yesterday, and she was working on it. The residual sting radiated through her, Mr. Barton's similar feedback pushing it that much deeper.

Mark gave her a tiny nod, and the pressure in her chest eased. She could learn and change. It'd only make her better at the job she fully intended to keep.

They worked for twenty minutes, shuffled the papers, and then created presentations for the concepts they'd received.

The wind had kicked up after breakfast, and it swirled Danae's hair around her face as she and Vanessa stood to give their mini presentation. As luck would have it, they'd ended up with Mark's idea. That was easy enough to figure out, thanks to his suggestion, and she recognized his scrawling handwriting besides.

Across the deck, she caught sight of Josh. He flashed her a smile. His skin was sun-kissed from the hours he spent outdoors, and those eye crinkles took charming to an unfair level.

"Danae," Vanessa shout-whispered at

her side, and she glanced at her partner, who raised her eyebrows even higher.

Right. She was in the midst of a presentation, and how in the world had she allowed herself to be distracted? "So, what we would like to do is show that it's not solely about getting the woman, so to speak. It's about getting the *right* woman."

"One who'll let you go sailing on a whim," Mark helpfully added, and Danae found she didn't even have to work to maintain her smile. Mostly because Josh had used his hand to stifle his.

"Exactly. The perfect lifestyle, right?"

Vanessa chimed in. "But then we'll also have that amazing, powerful woman on the boat sipping *wine*, because she deserves a perfect lifestyle with the man—or woman—she cares for, too." She'd come up with that twist at the last minute. Neither she nor Danae had been comfortable with the idea of objectifying a woman, even if it helped sell boats. Danae didn't truly think Mark intended his idea to come off that way, either. He simply wasn't as sensitive to it as women who'd grown up seeing it done in advertising way too often.

Mark ran his fingers along his freshly shaven jaw. "I'm sure no one will be surprised that I wrote that pitch. And I like what you two have done with it."

He gave Danae a nod that she returned. As soon as this meeting was over, there would be checkmarks, and she definitely deserved a gold star.

She glanced at Josh, remembering how he'd teased her about her stickers. Some people had gone bug-eyed over her organization skills and detailed planner, while others wished aloud they could be that on top of life. There had been condescension and eye rolls over the supplies required as well, but Josh had managed to joke without insinuating that her system made her uptight or kooky, feedback she'd gotten before.

"Whoa," Paige said, putting a hand on her stomach. "Is it going to be this rocky for the rest of the trip?"

The gray clouds overhead had been gradually dimming the light of the sun, bringing along with them the scent of rain. As they thickened, the water turned choppy and the swaying of the boat intensified. The sail whipped in the wind, the snap of the fabric loud. Sizzling energy hung in the air, signaling a looming storm.

"Looks like we're going to get some rain," Danae said. "I'm sure it'll be fine, but if anyone wants to go down into the kitchen cabin, feel free. Paige, there are some of those pressure point bracelets and motion sickness pills on the counter if you need them. The cooler is stocked with water and soda, if anyone needs a cold drink."

"I need more coffee," Mark said, standing.

He gripped the backrest of the bench seat as the boat rocked. "Would you like a refill?"

Danae glanced around, because he couldn't possibly be talking to her. But Vanessa had already headed into the cabin. "Water would be great, actually. I'm going to go see what our captain thinks about the storm and how long it'll be before it passes."

Mark nodded, and Danae gripped the railing and walked toward the helm, where Josh stood at the wheel.

"Hey," she called, and the wind blew the word back in her face.

"Remember, don't shoot the driver. Your beef is with Mother Nature, not me."

"It *was* with Mother Nature, until you implied I might take it out on you," she shouted over the roar of the flapping sails, hoping the volume she used to deliver the joke didn't make him think she was serious. "Any idea how long this storm is going to last? I know that's a stupid question, since it hasn't started raining yet, but even a ballpark—"

"Would help you schedule out our delay?"

Warmth trickled through her, fighting the cool air nipping at her skin. Even though they'd just met and hardly saw eye to eye, Josh understood how anxious getting off track left her. "Basically, yeah. If you're within fifteen minutes, I'll totally give you a gold star."

Josh ducked his head as a swell hit and water sprayed both of them. "It should pass soon, but it's heading the same way we are, so if we keep sailing along this path, we'll remain in it the entire time. I'm thinking we heave to and wait it out."

Heave to. Now there was a phrase she hadn't heard in a while, but memories flickered through her mind. Basically it meant parking in the ocean without having to drop the anchor, and it came in handy when fixing a part on the boat or dealing with a contrary wind or a storm.

"I'm gonna tack the boat." Josh began to spin the wheel, turning so the headsail was set against the wind. "Then I'll—"

"...let out some of the mainsheet. I'm on it."

Satisfaction swelled in her at the surprised look on his face. It was nice to know she could impress the guy, and she took a quick beat to enjoy it before rushing along the starboard side, ducking under the mast, and going to work.

With the headsail turned to catch the backwind and keep the boat in place, easing out the mainsail reduced the ship's forward drive. With that done, the boat slowed, and Danae felt Josh turning the rudder to windward.

Fat drops of rain trickled down, and then the clouds opened up and released more and more, faster and faster. Her job done, Danae returned to the helm.

Josh locked the wheel, and they managed to park, so to speak. The ship lightly bobbed in a seesaw motion, but they were no longer at the mercy of the choppy waves.

"Let's make our way into the cabin." Josh extended a hand. "Careful, it's slippery."

Danae was pretty sure she could manage, but there was his open palm and when it came to not slipping and falling into the icy ocean, employing the safety-first method seemed like the best course of action.

Her palm hit his, and he clamped onto her hand as they hurried toward the main cabin. His strides were twice as long as hers, and she worked to keep up, a flutter going through her as he maneuvered her around the deck of the ship with such ease.

Then they were in the entryway of the cabin, the closed door muffling the sound of the wind and lashing rain.

Droplets clung to Danae's glasses, obscuring and blurring everything. She slipped them off and wiped them on her damp blouse, her breaths sawing in and out faster than usual.

"That was impressive," Josh said, and she met his blue eyes, her heart thumping harder at his praise. "This isn't your first time sailing. Not even your second or third."

"You caught me. I'm a spy who's been sent to see how good a sailor you truly are."

"Are we sinking?" Paige asked, poking her head through the open doorway and wringing her hands together. "I knew this was a bad idea. I should've stayed home with my fiancé, with the solid ground beneath my feet."

Danae quickly assured her they'd be okay. "Storms happen all the time, and remember the specs on our ship? We use only the strongest materials at Barton Boats." Sure, she sort of sounded like an infomercial, but as team leader, she needed to make certain that no one panicked or did something as drastic as leave the trip early. She glanced at Josh, silently pleading for him to help.

"Danae's right. I've been through way worse storms. This'll pass soon, and it'll be much smoother sailing."

"Soon?" Danae tried to raise one eyebrow, but both of them came along for the ride. "Are you purposely using a vague term? Because I clearly remember mentioning you had to be accurate within fifteen minutes to earn a gold star."

His laugh filled the entryway. "How about I just tell you whether or not I was right once we get to shore? Spoiler alert: I'm gonna be."

She snorted at that, and they entered the kitchen cabin to find all eyes on them.

Mark slowly extended a water bottle her way. Right. She'd asked for one of those.

"Thank you." Danae twisted off the lid

and gulped it down. Funny how you could be soaking wet and still ridiculously thirsty.

Josh shook out his hair like some kind of overgrown puppy. Danae flinched and brought up her shoulders to block the water, despite the fact that it was too late and she was already wet. "Dude."

Since everyone was still studying them, and she realized she'd accidentally-on-purpose leaned into Josh slightly, she decided she should move away from him before people got the wrong idea.

Before *she* got the wrong idea.

"Did you find the snacks?" she asked, as she stepped into the center of the kitchenette and peered inside grocery bags.

"Not a whole lot of places to search," Vanessa teased as she boosted herself up on the tiny counter. "But we managed."

Danae dug out the pretzels, and since Josh had to be thirsty, too, she grabbed a bottle of water. As she handed it to him, a shiver racked her body.

"You guys have to be freezing," Vanessa said. She crawled inside the cabin she was using and yanked the comforter off the bed. She wrapped one side around Danae, the other side around Josh, and nudged them toward the table. "You two sit, and I'll make some hot cocoa."

"Oh, it's okay." Danae had never been great at accepting help. She was far more comfortable giving it. But the stern mom-type glare Vanessa gave her and Josh was enough to make Danae follow instructions. She sat at the rectangular wooden table, which had a piecework compass symbol in the center, and then scooted across the royal blue bench cushions so Josh could have a seat, too. When she failed to suppress another shiver, he reached across and tucked the blanket more firmly around her.

In order to fully warm up, she should probably get out of her wet clothes. But as the blanket and being next to Josh did their job of returning heat to her body, her motivation to move became nonexistent.

"So, where'd you learn those mad sailing skills?" Josh asked.

The sentimental emotions that had been her constant companions since climbing aboard the ship the first time crested once again. It was a bit like the tide, showing up in a huge surge, only to recede and return in intervals. "My dad. From the time I was a little girl, he used to take me out on the boat with him. Every so often my younger sister and brother would tag along, but they took a lot of looking after and weren't great at following instructions, so he and I both preferred it when my mom sent us on alone. He taught me everything I know about sailing and the sea."

Vanessa placed two mugs of steaming hot cocoa in front of them, and Danae decided she lived here now. After all, what more could a person ask for than sipping chocolatey goodness next to a guy who could turn her insides melty with nothing more than a smile?

Only then did she consider that her entire team was in the kitchen area, and she was getting way too cuddly with Josh. Another sip and she began to scoot away from him. "I'm, uh, going to go change my clothes. Then we should probably use this time stuck inside to get our work done."

Chapter Seven

"I MISS MY FIANCÉ," PAIGE SAID, sweeping her red locks over one shoulder while she drummed her fingers on the kitchen table they'd crowded around to avoid the rain. "It feels like we've been apart for a week already."

Vanessa rolled her eyes. "It feels like you've been talking about how much you miss him for a week already."

Danae pinched the bridge of her nose, taking a second so she could intercede in a calm, kind manner. "We all miss things, whether it's people or pets or our own beds. But we have to remember what a great opportunity we have to check out beautiful locations while doing our work."

"I've already been to most of the places we're going, though," Paige said with a sigh, and Vanessa opened her mouth.

Working to cut off a bickering match before it grew out of control, Danae spoke over whatever retort Vanessa had on the tip of her tongue. "Not only do publicity and social media go hand in hand, I need both of your incredible brains right now in order to make this new campaign as successful as possible." She flipped the pages in her binder to find the other teamwork quote—the Michael Jordan one had been aimed mostly at Mark anyway. "'Great things in business are never done by one person. They're done by a team of people.' Let's be that team."

There. Powerful. Motivational. Everyone's important.

It desperately needed to work, because being cooped up inside seemed to make everyone shorter-tempered. Thanks to how tightly packed they were around the table, Danae had accidentally elbowed Vanessa and Franco, who were on either side of her, several times.

Vanessa twisted her wrist and studied the large bejeweled watch that hung from her golden charm bracelet. "By my calculations, we should be reaching Block Island soon. If we work really hard for the next fifteen minutes, we could get a rough draft of our publicity and social media strategy hammered out before we dock."

"I love that idea," Danae said, and she was about to suggest they go outside to do so since the windows overhead were brightening up.

But Vanessa wasn't done. "*I've* never been to most of the places we'll be stopping at, and personally, I'm grateful to Mr. Barton for providing us the opportunity to check them out in style."

Oh, boy. The passive aggressive was strong with this one.

"It's okay to miss my fiancé. When people don't understand that, it makes it hard to feel like a team." Paige tossed her notebook on the table. "I have a headache. I'm going to head to my cabin and find an ibuprofen."

As soon Paige left, the rest of the team's attention scattered, and there was a zero percent chance Danae would manage to get it back. Since she wanted to maintain at least a semblance of control, she lowered her own notebook. "As Vanessa said, we'll be docking shortly, so we might as well break and prepare for our tour of the lighthouse."

Mark headed upstairs to the deck, and Franco scooted over, giving the three of them who were left more room. "Don't get me wrong, I think Paige likes saying the word *fiancé* a little too much, but I miss Justin, too. And my dogs."

Danae patted his arm. "They'll be there waiting for you when we return to Newport, and I bet Jack is going to slobber over every inch of you to show how much he missed you. Rose as well."

Franco wrinkled his nose. "Thank you for the visual. That makes it easier to wait."

"Liar," she said with a laugh, and he chuckled.

"Fine. I'm going to FaceTime all three of them when we get a chance to sit on the sandy shore. Is that what you want to hear?"

Danae flashed him a grin. "Say hi to everyone for me."

Franco climbed out from behind the table, stood, and stretched. "Guess I'll go grab my bag." At least he seemed less hurt about the team's reception of the beta version of the website, although she suspected he'd buried his feelings down deep.

A pang went through her as she thought about how hard it must've been for him to show off a project he'd been so excited about, only for everyone to pick it apart. He hadn't even gotten to go home and get away from those people for a night, either. Part of her new job was to give critical feedback, but the fact that Franco was her closest friend in the office made it that much harder.

Mark didn't have any qualms voicing his regular disapproval, and then there were Vanessa and Paige. So far, they were squabbling more than ever, unable to agree on even what their departments were responsible for, much less an overall marketing plan.

A pit formed in the center of Danae's stomach. *I'm totally failing at bringing the team together.*

Vanessa loudly sighed and propped her sandaled feet on the part of the bench kitty-corner to her. "I swear, Paige is getting on my last nerve. She won't let me take the lead on anything, but she's also too busy talking about her *fiancé* to focus. As if that's not frustrating enough, she doesn't even realize how good she has it. I've worked for a lot of people, and Mr. Barton is the best boss I've ever had."

Being in the middle while trying to be respectful and encouraging to both people was always a tricky position, one Danae didn't feel that she had a handle on. "He is a great boss, and I'm sure Paige realizes she's lucky. Or at least she would if she took a moment to think about it. She's also in that exciting phase of love when it's hard to think of anything else. Honestly, I'm a little jealous. I've never hit that level in any of my relationships."

"That's because you're a strong, independent woman," Vanessa said.

"As are you. Please don't take this the wrong way, but you and I have also had a few more years to get there."

Vanessa closed her eyes and exhaled a long breath. "The idea of going back to my mid-twenties is literally the stuff of nightmares, so I hear you. But I'll still be glad to get off this ship and put some extra space between us."

Looked like as far as the Paige and Vanessa situation was concerned, Danae would be heading back to the drawing board.

The afternoon sun cast a golden sheen on Danae's curls and highlighted her cheeks when she smiled.

She'd been smiling a lot today. Josh was semi-tempted to ask if she'd put "smile more" in her planner, but she didn't always understand his jokes and he wanted the happy vibes to continue.

He was so focused on Danae that he nearly ran into Vanessa, who'd stopped without warning. She lifted her phone and swiped through several filters as she snapped pictures of the reddish-orange brick house and adjoining lighthouse. The A-frame part of the building had three floors, and a white porch added a welcoming touch. Like *Come on in for a lemonade, and later we'll save ships from crashing.*

"It's beautiful. Not as elegant as the mansions we planned on filming, but if men don't feel like men when they see the craftsmanship of buildings and lighthouses that've withstood the test of time, that's not our problem." Vanessa nudged Danae. "Right?"

"Hear, hear!" Danae added, lifting her fist in the air.

Josh surreptitiously checked the time on his watch. They were forty minutes late for their tour of the Block Island lighthouse, but Danae hadn't mentioned the fact that they were behind schedule. *Maybe there's hope for her yet.*

The tour guide greeted the group and gave them a mini history lesson. Mariners had always given Block Island a wide berth, on account of the submerged rocks and sandy shoals. She also explained that though the tower was fairly short, its elevated location atop Mohegan Bluffs allowed its flashing green light to shine over two hundred feet above the water.

Due to the narrow stairway, they were going to have to climb to the top in shifts, and Josh purposely hung back so he could go at the same time as Danae.

While they waited for the first group, Josh, Danae, and Vanessa walked to the edge of the bluff and peered down at the shore.

"Wow, that's some drop," Danae said.

"About ten stories." Josh leaned farther to get a better look, and Danae grabbed his wrist. He glanced over his shoulder at her, and he hadn't realized before that a grimace could be cute, but on her it was.

"Sorry. But you're making me nervous."

"Aww. You worry about me?"

"About your judgment, yes."

He laughed, as did Vanessa. Danae, not so much.

"I figured to save time, we could just roll down to the shore instead of hiking it." He tested the bounds of her grip, leaning another inch or so, and her fingers dug in, nearing cutting-off-circulation territory. "I know how much you care about sticking to the itinerary."

Vanessa tried to hide her laugh with a cough, but Danae still shot her a look. "*Et tu, Brute*?"

"I can't help that he's funny," Vanessa said. "Or that he managed to figure out how you tick in only two days."

"Full disclosure: Thanks to a couple of days of lengthy emails, I had a head start."

"Very funny. I bet the other group is almost done, so if you guys can take a break from teasing me, we should head back to the entrance." With a grunt, Danae tugged him backward a foot or so. As soon as she let his wrist go, he immediately missed her touch.

It almost made him want to find other ways to be devious.

Since he didn't want to stress her out, he followed after. She must have had some internal sensor, because sure enough, the other group was exiting the building as they walked up to the red-brick lighthouse.

The inside smelled a bit musty, the way

old buildings near bodies of water often did. The small entryway led to the narrow staircase, and then the metallic *clink, clink* of footsteps filled the air as they began to climb.

Halfway to the top, Josh peered down at the inside of the cool spiral staircase. As a result of the humidity, the steps were a mixture of coppery blue and green shades. "It's like art."

Danae hugged the outer curve of the staircase. "It's also a century and a half old, so I hope you're not trusting that railing to hold you. I'm done trying to pull you back from danger."

"At least take a look at it." Josh held out a hand. "Here, I'll anchor you."

She studied his hand, and he tensed as she didn't make a move to take it. He shouldn't care either way, but he wanted her to experience the bird's-eye view. Wanted her to trust him.

Wanted to have her hand in his again, like earlier when they'd been rushing through the rain.

Just as he was about to charge up the stairs feeling like an idiot for putting himself out there, she stretched out her arm and placed her palm in his. "You have to be an anchor closer to the wall if I'm going to do this."

He bit back a smile. "Okay." As requested,

he hung near the wall, holding tight to her hand as she peeked over the railing.

"It does look amazing." Danae slipped her phone out of her pocket and, gripping her phone so securely her knuckles turned white, snapped a picture.

"Ooh, make sure to AirDrop that to me," Vanessa said, and Josh did a double take. He thought she'd gone on ahead, but she was parked only a handful of spiral steps away, taking pictures of her own.

Danae scuttled backward until her body hit the brick wall. Since she was on the step above his, they ended up at eye level.

Every cell in his body pricked up as their gazes locked together, her glasses superimposing his reflection over her hazel irises and dilated pupils. "You okay?" he asked, his voice coming out huskier than usual.

Her chest rose and fell with a deep breath, and then she nodded. "Thanks for helping me see that. Now let's keep going before I freak out."

"I'll be right behind you. I won't let you fall. Promise."

Another nod, and the she turned around to continue climbing, her fingers slowly pulling away from his. Which made sense. There wasn't room for them to walk side by side. Although for the record, he totally would've taken the scarier side. Once they made it to the top of the lighthouse, Vanessa headed to the far end to take videos, leaving him and Danae as alone as they might get for the rest of the day.

"Our earlier conversation got cut short since *someone* likes to focus too much on work."

Danae made a big show of glancing around. "That person sounds super cool, so maybe you can introduce me sometime."

"Ha ha," he said. "You were talking about how your dad used to take you sailing."

Her features softened as she scooted closer to the panes of glass that separated them from the outside world. "There's not much more to the conversation. Most every weekend we'd gather the fishing supplies and our boating gear and set sail at the crack of dawn."

"Dang, you fish, too? I'm seeing you in a whole new light."

"The lighthouse light?" she asked with a giggle.

Josh rested a hip against the rail, facing her instead of the rolling green hills and ultra-blue ocean. "Something like that."

She pushed her glasses up her nose. "We'd always lose track of the time, and then we'd be racing the sun home so my mom wouldn't get upset at us for being out so late. She'd say that I should spend more time playing with kids my age and keeping up with my homework. Then Dad would tell her that he was teaching me important life lessons—I wasn't exaggerating my knot knowledge, you know."

"You'll be ready for the pop quiz later, then?"

There was the smile he'd hoped for, although only one side of her mouth got in on it. "I'm much better at not-popped quizzes. Allowing people to prepare is only fair." Not a surprise. How endearing he found it, on the other hand...? A sensation he hadn't felt in a long time twisted through him. "My dad taught me to sail as well. We went every summer except the year my sister was born. I was ten, so there's quite an age gap. Around the time I turned sixteen, my parents decided to sell the boat and move to the suburbs. To say I was devastated would be an understatement.

"So after my divorce," he said, throwing it out there so he could get it out of the way and then move on, "I decided I needed a big life change. I thought back to what made me happy, and those summer days on the boat and sailing around Buzzard Bay popped into my mind."

"Summers as a kid are the best," she agreed. "They felt so magical. But when I was seventeen, my dad passed away." At the slight tremor in her voice, an ache formed in his own heart on her behalf. He couldn't imagine losing a parent at such a young age. "The problem with growing up—especially when it comes too early and you find yourself responsible for your entire family—is that you see the summers weren't so magical, at all."

"Explain," he said. Occasionally he felt like she was talking in code, leaving out pieces that made it impossible to complete the puzzle of who she truly was.

Danae rested her stomach against the rail, her cheek so close to his shoulder that several emotions thundered through him at once. "It was staggering to learn what the boat cost, and then to have to deal with the financial strain it put on my family after he passed away."

Josh opened his mouth in an attempt to come up with words that'd soothe the pain in her voice, but before he could, she cleared her throat and charged on.

"It was a long time ago. And I'm fine. But not only did my father live on the edge of his means, he was in debt. Creditors didn't care that he wasn't around anymore or that we were grieving. There wasn't any grace period. My mom and I just had to start working like crazy."

Danae glanced at the metal platform under their feet, sniffed, and attempted a smile that was on the watery side. "Anyway, that's why I have conflicting feelings about those memories of sailing out on the water with him, even though I wouldn't give them up for the world. And hey, they came in handy today, so..." She scraped at the rust on the railing with her thumbnail.

"I get that," Josh said. "I'm sorry about your dad."

"Thank you. I'm sorry about your divorce."

Somewhat naively, he'd been sure the statistic would never apply to him—not after witnessing his parents' happy relationship and being a big believer in romance himself. That was why it was dangerous to put too much into plans.

"It happens, I guess. It was years ago, so it's water under the bridge, as they say." Now he was the one fiddling, shifting his weight from one foot to the other. Searching for a subject change. "I've had a couple of co-captains who could learn sailing skills from you. Normally I have to do a lot of micromanaging. Possibly because I'm as controlling about my ship as you are about your planner. And your sticker collection."

She patted her bag. "Are you still fishing for a gold star, Mr. Wheeler?"

While he'd corrected Mark for calling him mister, he found he liked it more than he should when it came from Danae. "I'll get one yet."

Danae straightened and flipped her hair dramatically. "We'll see."

Yes. Yes, they would.

Chapter Eight

"I DON'T UNDERSTAND WHY IT'S CALLED deep-sea fishing when it's technically deep-*ocean* fishing," Danae said to Josh, as he handed her a fishing pole. She'd told him to go ahead and get everyone else started. Not because she was super benevolent or anything. They'd just had such a nice afternoon, so she was delaying the moment when Josh would discover that her fishing skills weren't nearly as impressive as her sailing skills.

Josh squatted and unlatched his tackle box. "I don't understand how you think you're gonna catch dinner if you keep yapping instead of casting. And *technically*, we're in the spot where the Atlantic meets

Buzzards Bay, and they refer to it as a saltwater fisherman's paradise. Now"—Josh waved a hand across the top row of segmented squares, like a model on TV who showed audience members what they could win—"what bait would you like to use?"

"The floral-scented kind. Ooh, do you have any that are pink and sparkly?"

Josh gave her an unamused glower that amused her to no end.

She squatted next to him and studied the funky lures. "Ew. Those squid look too real."

"That's because they are—I picked them up on the island. Don't they smell like actual squid?"

Danae pinched her nose shut and breathed out her mouth. "Yes, yes they do."

"I thought you were an avid fisherman."

The ponytail she'd pulled her hair into after climbing back onboard swished from side to side as she shook her head.

"I have fished." She placed a hand on her chest and transitioned into her narrator voice for reasons she couldn't explain. "Many moons ago, when it meant sitting next to my dad, fishing line in the water as we went through a six-pack." She flashed Josh a smile. "Of soda. But I'm much better at sailing—I'd actually leap at the chance to adjust the sails so that I didn't have to watch my pole for a while. I've never had the patience to be an avid fisherwoman."

"Let me guess. It bothers you that fish don't keep a tight schedule."

The insanely handsome fisherman in front of her got the scowl he deserved. "I mean if one of them has 'get caught' in their planner and needs to check it off, I'd love to help them out. But considering paper disintegrates in water..."

Josh snagged the end of her line and swung in front of his face. Then he formed a loop. "That's it. You get a deep diving crank." He fastened a plastic fish to the end of her line. "Tonight, I'm going to teach you patience."

"Doubtful. Also, your threat about needing to catch my own dinner doesn't scare me, FYI. Not only do I have the fridge stocked with groceries, frankly, I don't like fish."

The lure hit the top of the tackle box as Josh gaped at her like she'd sprouted a unicorn horn. "How can you be a Newport native and not like fish?"

Since she didn't have a great explanation for her off-kilter taste buds, she simply shrugged.

"Unacceptable. Obviously you've never had one cooked the right way. Now we *have* to catch one so I can grill you the best fish dinner you've ever had."

"Or maybe I just don't like fish, and I know what I want."

"You said maybe." Josh stood and extended her the handle, his large hand wrapped around the maroon rod. "So just maybe you'll like the way I make it."

With a huff, Danae took the offered pole. "Fine, I'll try it. Fishing and..." She shuddered. "But when I don't like it, don't take it personally."

Sorting through dozens of memories stored in her brain, she searched for the day Dad had taught her how to cast.

Hold that button down until you whip the pole forward, NaeNae. The faster and harder you fling it, the farther it'll go.

She drew back the pole and cast out her line. Pride streaked through her when the plunk of the hook landed way out in the midnight-blue water. "Did you see that? I thought for sure I'd snag the sail or my own clothes or something equally as disastrous. Turns out I still got it. The casting part, anyway."

Thanks, Dad.

"Farthest cast I've seen all day." Josh's fingertips brushed her forearm and Danae's surprised inhale gave her an extra dose of fresh air. "You good? I thought I'd do another sweep and see how the rest of the crew are faring. Then I'll circle back around."

"Totally," she said. "Do whatever you need to."

A tiny string in the center of her chest tugged, as if it were attached to Josh. Then he practically melted into the inky sky, his dark profile blending in with the others until she could no longer tell who was who.

A handful of minutes passed in silence. Danae tipped onto her toes, attempting to see over the cabin to the other side of the ship.

It was no use, though. She wasn't tall enough in her flats—might not even be tall enough in her heels. She reeled in her line and recast, simply for something to do. Then she paced back and forth a yard or so, idly wondering how long it would take to form a groove in the pale wood.

At the ten-minute mark, she added some dance moves to her pacing, tapping out a rhythm with the soles of her shoes as she did her best to convince herself she didn't miss Josh. How could she, when he hadn't been gone that long and she barely knew the guy?

Still, something had shifted between them this afternoon. First, when he'd teased her about rolling down the bluffs to save time, and again in the lighthouse, as they'd discussed her dad and the stress his passing had caused, and he'd mentioned his divorce. A big part of what had made it easy to be that open was their mini adventure in the stairwell.

Once you reached adulthood, there weren't many magic moments to seize hold of. Having Josh there to anchor her so she could get a prime view of the multicolored swirl and timeless beauty of the architecture involved in the staircase had left her in awe. Of how people had done so much with simpler tools, and that thanks to his encouragement and strong grip, she'd done something risky. For her anyway.

"How you doing?"

Danae jumped, then rolled her eyes at her flighty reaction. It was the second time Josh had scared her.

He snickered, and she tightened her grip on the pole in her right hand and smacked his arm with her left. Considering the stretch, it hardly had anything behind it—not that she wanted to hurt him.

His solid shoulder made her doubt she could.

"Has anyone had any luck?" she asked, fiddling with the handle on the reel. The end was loose, so she'd have to find a screwdriver later, but right now, she was enjoying spinning it round and around.

"A couple of nibbles. I think Paige and Vanessa are both determined to show one another up. They were both asking for the best tactics and bait and all sorts of questions, rapid-fire-style, until I felt like I was being interrogated." The chuckle that came out at the end of the sentence made it clear he'd found it entertaining.

"As long as a fight doesn't break out when one of them does catch a fish, I'll consider it a fortuitous turn of events."

"Don't worry. I used to play basketball and football, not to mention I follow the pros, so I've seen a lot of refs in action." He lifted an imaginary whistle, blew it, and gave his invisible players a ten-yard penalty.

"Well, I'm here to burst your bubble and say seeing is not the same as doing."

He rested his forearms on the railing, mere inches from her fishing pole, and spoke in a low voice, his mouth not far from her ear. "Which is why I'm making you fish instead of having you watch how many I could expertly reel in."

A shiver of awareness tiptoed up her spine, and goose bumps spread across her skin.

"Are you cold?"

Danae was about to tell him that if he'd hold her pole, she'd go grab one of her cardigans. But then he shucked off his green army jacket and held it out to her. She considered refusing it, but she *was* getting cold.

She slipped her arm in the too-long sleeve, basking in Josh's leftover body heat. He wrapped it around her and guided her other arm through the hole. As he swept her hair out from underneath the jacket, his fingers grazed the sensitive skin on the nape of her neck, and her lungs forgot how to function.

"Better?" he asked.

Her tongue stuck to the roof of her mouth, foiling her attempt to speak, so she went with a nod. Her hand trembled as she zipped up the jacket, and she wanted to bury her nose in the fabric and take another whiff so she could soak in the intoxicating combination of ocean and the woodsy cologne Josh wore.

The moonlight lit up his profile, and her heart *thump, thump, thumped*. The tingly sensation she'd experienced earlier intensified, whispering that there was something between them. While she wasn't sure it was a good idea, she couldn't help but want to explore their connection—after all, she hadn't felt like this in months.

Maybe longer, if she factored in never feeling so immediately drawn to anyone before.

With her pulse hammering away, it took a couple of seconds to realize the thump in her palm was a different sensation. "Josh, I feel something."

His Adam's apple bobbed up and down, and he placed his hand over hers. "I think I do, too."

"That means I have a bite, right? It's been almost two decades, and I don't remember much, besides my dad having to help me out a few times because the fish were so strong. But I was a lot young—"

The next jerk nearly wrenched the pole right out of her hands. She clasped the grippy handle and yanked back in an attempt to set the hook. The end of her pole bowed, to the point it almost hit the water.

"Must be a big one," Josh yelled, excitement ringing through the phrase and echoing through her core.

"Now what?" Her mind went blank, leaving her scrambling to recall the tips she'd stored away for what she assumed would be...never. Honestly, she'd never expected to catch anything.

"Reel it in!" Josh reached around her to tap the handle attached to the spool.

Right. Of course. Danae cranked it as quickly as she could, doing her best not to get distracted by the solid body directly behind her and his warm breath on her cheek. "You got it, you got it."

"It's either huge or fighting me. Oh, no," she said, her stomach plummeting to the ground. "What if it's both?"

Her shoulder and arm muscles burned as she continued to reel with all her might. In the background, she heard someone ask if she'd caught one. As her coworkers rushed their way, Josh took a giant step back.

"You've got this, Danae," Vanessa said. Not to be outdone, Paige yelled her encouragement, as did Mark.

One quick glance at the group, and determination flooded her. She pushed past the burning in her arm, and then she heard the jingle of the lure and the slapping of fins on the surface of the water.

Another tug, and she would've fallen on her bum if Josh hadn't braced a firm hand on her lower back to steady her.

Water splashed her face and hands as she lifted the fish and swung it into the boat, but thanks to Josh's jacket, her arms were nice and dry.

Everyone gathered to check out the black sea bass.

"That's a nice sized one, D," Mark said, and she did a double take. He hadn't called her D in a very long time. Like, since their breakup. She blinked at him but didn't see any clues as to why.

Not that she'd expected to.

Or maybe she had. Her adrenaline flowed in overwhelming spurts, and a surreal haze hung over the evening. Then a blip of a memory rose to her mind—Dad congratulating her, shouting and jumping with such gusto that they attracted the attention of a nearby fisherman who'd come to see the catch of the day.

After he quickly and humanely dispatched it, Danae shoved the pole into Josh's hands and squatted to see her fish. Vanessa turned on her phone's light so she could take pictures, and the blue and black scales glimmered in the bright glow.

If Danae didn't stand soon, her burning thighs would give out on her, but she quite liked the view from down here. From this angle, their captain's beard was extra rugged, and the line of muscle in his forearm stood out as he gripped the fishing pole she'd used. "Okay," he said, "so now you have to get the hook out of its mouth."

That got her to her feet. "Um, that's okay. I'll hold the pole. You do the gross stuff."

"Lucky me," he said lightly, and the smile he aimed her way gave her that fresh-from-the-roller-coaster swirl. Perhaps she should've set a nice strong example for her team by doing it herself, but what mattered was they were all gathered to celebrate their freshly caught dinner. Along with the fact that at least in the here and now, everyone was getting along.

Except where was Franco? She didn't see him, and she crossed her fingers that it didn't mean he was retreating from the group.

With her fishing win, the rest of the team were encouraged and returned to their poles. Whenever one of them got a bite, they all gathered to cheer that person on. As they were wrapping up their fishing session—it was getting so dark they could hardly see—Danae glanced at the time. "Whoa."

While her blood pressure spiked for a moment, she expelled a long breath and told herself it was okay they were an hour behind schedule. Dinner was the only thing left for the day, and that made it easier to be okay with it.

The guy proudly holding up their catches also helped tremendously.

Josh walked up to her, and she put her hands up to block, in case he thought throwing fish at her would be funny—it absolutely wouldn't be, even if she had his jacket to wipe off the slimy scales. Which she would totally do.

"Are you ready to be impressed by a fish dinner?" he asked.

"As long as you remember you're fighting a losing battle."

His left side brushed her arm and shoulder as he passed by. Instead of continuing on his way, though, he leaned in and said, "The odds have been stacked against me before. And it doesn't scare me—I'm one of those never-say-die guys."

She arched an eyebrow. "You honestly think you could out-stubborn me?"

"I think we'll both have fun trying." He gave her shoulder a light squeeze, and she didn't care that his hands probably had fish scales and squid slime on them. Every ounce of her blood rushed to that spot, and she could say with a surety that today had absolutely been a better day.

There was just one more thing she needed to handle.

Chapter Nine

After washing her hands so they were as fish-free as possible, Danae found Franco seated at the outside table where they usually held their meetings.

"Hey," she said, sitting next to him on the bench seat. The padding underneath the creamy vinyl was thinner than her office chair, and she'd sat down hard enough that her bones experienced a mini jolt. "Deep-sea fishing not your thing? I didn't think it was mine until I caught what Josh insists is gonna be our dinner. Mark and Paige each caught one, too."

"I don't mind it, but I was exhausted after all our hiking. Guess I'm not in as good a shape as I thought."

"You and me both. I was wheezing by the time we made it down those stairs to the beach—I almost decided Josh's suggestion to roll down the bluffs instead wasn't crazy."

Franco laughed. "I'd definitely end up breaking an ankle or something."

"Nobody's going to get hurt on my watch."

"Not sure you can be in control of that," Franco said.

"You underestimate my power," she joked, adopting an evil-villain voice. "But for reals, we need everyone to stay at full capacity."

Now that she'd gotten a moment alone with Franco, she hesitated to ruin it by talking shop. She worried that the longer they went without addressing last night, though, the bigger a deal it would seem. Given that Franco was the one she'd leaned on at the office post-Mark-breakup, it made it harder to balance being in a management position and maintaining their office friendship. "As you know, I'm new to leading meetings. What I should've started with last night was what I liked about the website—the color scheme and the photos, for instance."

Franco rolled his eyes. "That's what the web designer picked out."

"Oh. So you're saying my pep talk is already severely lacking."

That earned her half a smile. "It's okay, Danae. Do you think that's the first time I've shown off a beta version of a website only to hear everything wrong with it? In the moment, it's always hard not to be upset if people aren't declaring it sheer genius, but after some time to process and brainstorm, I'm sure I can build a stronger site that appeals to everyone. Most everyone, anyway, because you can't please 'em all."

How ironic, because pleasing everyone was more or less Mr. Barton's challenge to her in order to keep her promotion. The pressure that had gripped her yesterday returned, quickening her pulse until her temples throbbed with it. Since right now wasn't about her, she'd have to pencil in her panic attack for later. "Wait. That means the font probably wasn't your pick, either."

"Nope. I also thought the words were hard to read, which is why I didn't put much copy on the homepage. But I often get so focused on functionality that I'm not always the best judge of those types of artistic touches. I figured the web designer had a reason for going that way."

"Why didn't you say anything when Paige mentioned it?"

Franco shrugged. "Didn't see the point. It's on me to fix it anyway. I did send the designer an email asking for some tweaks this morning, though."

"But you're okay?"

"I'm fine. If anything, the fact that people didn't like the animated ships made me realize why I'm on the tech end and not the design end. I also got too caught up in trying to show off all the cool things I could make our website do, instead of keeping our key demographic in mind."

Danae tucked a leg underneath her and propped an elbow on the back of the bench seat. "As Mark pointed out at the meeting, I also struggle with that. Sometimes who we cater to gets in the way of the big ideas I have for other target markets."

"I hear you," Franco said, granting her one of his signature toothy smiles, and relief tumbled through her, allowing for easier breaths and looser posture. The fun moments with Josh had helped distract her, but accidentally offending Franco had loomed in the back of her mind. She'd worried that she might return home to lose not only the promotion she'd worked months to attain, but a good friendship, too.

She tugged the sides of Josh's army jacket tighter, crossing one over the other. Hopefully Josh wouldn't mind her keeping the borrowed jacket a tad longer, since he was in the kitchen and it got super toasty between the oven and the extra bodies.

"You like wearing that jacket, don't you?" Franco asked. The knowing gleam in his eyes caught her off guard.

"Well, sure. It's chilly out here." But her cheeks suddenly felt warm.

Franco lowered his voice. "Right. And it has nothing to do with the handsome sea captain it belongs to."

"I don't know what you're insinuating."

"All right." Franco shrugged, clearly not in the least convinced.

A loud throat-clearing made both her and Franco glance up. Mark strolled over. Had he overheard that last bit of conversation? If so, he gave no indication of it as he took a seat across from them

"I've been thinking, and I..." He raked his fingers through his sandy-colored hair. "I owe both of you an apology."

Cold air filtered in through Danae's open mouth, enough to give her momentary brain freeze. Everything freeze, really.

"In my attempt to make my point about our target demographic, I'm afraid I implied that your opinion isn't valid, Franco. And it is. You've helped me with coding glitches and computer crashes—not to mention how every time I've needed a form for our newsletter or a marketing poll created, you come up with amazing options to get us more accurate data. All I can say is that I let my ego get in the way. Guess that makes me the caveman that Danae's occasionally accused me of being."

Mark winked at her, and if she wasn't seated next to Franco, she might've checked to see if the guy had turned into a robot. He'd never been forthcoming with his feelings. Never voluntarily discussed them.

Then again, she vaguely remembered this version of him. The kindness and intelligence that had initially attracted her to him.

"And, Danae, I've been practically throwing a tantrum since you got the promotion over me. Again, it was my bruised ego, and I'm sorry. I've been working up the courage to apologize all day, and figured it'd be easiest in the semi-dark." He gave a self-deprecating chuckle, and Danae scooted to the edge of her seat.

"Thank you, Mark. I appreciate that." Even after dating for nearly a year, she'd felt like she'd only managed to scratch the surface of who he was and what made him tick. Her attempts to dive deeper had been a big part of what broke them apart. He'd thought she wanted to micromanage him, but she'd merely been trying to find a way to get through. Now here he was, offering up an apology she hadn't asked for or expected.

"That's really big of you," Franco said. "I think it's important we have a lot of different perspectives in order for the new campaign to be as strong as possible, and I'm sure you'll agree."

Mark nodded. "I do."

Franco's stomach grumbled, and he put a hand over it. "Wow. Evidently I'm hungrier than I realized. Guess we'd better head to the kitchen and try out that fish."

Josh flipped the fish and salted the other side. He'd melted butter in the pan and browned the garlic. After that was done, he'd drizzled lemon juice over the top and added rosemary, salt, parsley, and black pepper, seasoning it to perfection.

Every few seconds, his gaze drifted to the doorway. Danae still hadn't come down, and Mark had mumbled something about going to find her and Franco.

Which was fine.

Regardless of whether or not the idea of Mark talking to Danae caused a toxic churn in his gut. He didn't have any right to be jealous. Although he couldn't stop replaying their moments from today. Her pitching in on the boat. The bluffs. The lighthouse.

When she'd said she felt something, he'd thought she'd been confessing to a mutual attraction. Or *her* attraction, anyway, since he couldn't stop looking at her. Talking to her. Eyeing her hand and twitching with the urge to hold it again.

He'd thought *Oh good, a woman who's gonna shoot straight and avoid playing games.*

The joke was on him, because she'd felt a fish nipping at her line. Still, surely the interest went both ways. Otherwise, it wouldn't be slowly consuming him. Right?

He heard movement near the door and, so he wouldn't appear as eager as he felt, grabbed a fork. Using the tines, he confirmed that the fish was cooked to flaky, melt-in-your-mouth tenderness.

Perfect.

The chatter grew louder, and then there she was. Standing between Mark and Franco, smiling and laughing the way she had earlier, with him.

Which is allowed, hello. Josh must be tired, because normally he could control his thoughts without so much effort. It had been a long day. He'd also tossed and turned last night, the foreign room around him throwing him off.

Danae split from the guys, moving over to the stove instead of the table where everyone was passing around plates. Vanessa had sliced a loaf of crusty bread and put it in the center of the table, along with a garden salad and a few bottles of dressing.

Danae studied the fish, her forehead wrinkling and smoothing as if she wasn't sure what to make of their dinner. "It smells better than most fish. I'll give you that."

"I figured you were going to go with *something smells fishy around here*," Josh joked, and there was the laugh that echoed through him and stirred up joy.

"I wish I'd thought of that. It was my way of saying I'm trying to keep an open mind."

"Hey, don't do me any favors. I want the truth."

Tipping onto her toes, Danae opened a cupboard door and withdrew a white ceramic platter. "Well, hand it over then, and I'll start passing it around."

He did as requested, using a spatula to transfer the two large fish from the pan to the platter. A large bass could feed several people, and since they didn't want to waste food, they had put one in the fridge for later, and released one.

The entire group crowded around the table, the mood far more jovial than it had been during last night's dinner, and Josh wanted to take at least partial credit for Danae's carefree demeanor. She hadn't mentioned the schedule or their project since before the lighthouse trip.

"Um, don't everyone look at me," she said a minute or so later, after everyone had taken a bite and declared the fish to be delicious. "It makes me paranoid to eat while people watch."

"Seriously, just try it already," Franco said. "I'm extra picky about seafood, and it's better than anything I've ordered at a five-star restaurant."

Josh nodded at the guy. "Thank you, Franco. I don't have a lot of specialty dishes, but fish happens to be one of them."

"Try it, try it, try it," the group began chanting, until Danae's skin reddened and she ducked her head.

Finally, she scooped up a bite and shoved it in her mouth. Her hand lifted to shield her face as she chewed. The fork clattered against her plate as she let it go, and Josh's stomach dropped.

She hated it.

Which again, was fine.

"Oh my gosh, if that's what I've been missing for years, I'm all regret." A close-lipped smile spread across her face. "It's so good."

Everyone cheered, as if they also had a stake in the dare he'd given Danae, and a floaty frenetic sensation buzzed through his body. It had been a long time since he'd experienced anything akin to camaraderie.

Danae dug into her food again, leaving Josh in danger of bursting with pride. She might've been able to fake a positive reaction to one bite, but she cleared her plate along with everyone else.

As people jumped up and pitched in to fill the dishwasher, Josh excused himself. With their fishing lesson over and dinner coming to a close, it was time to sail the ship back to the island so they could dock for the night. He'd heard Paige mention wanting to get a hotel so she didn't have to spend another night on the ship, but during dinner, the sour mood she'd been in earlier seemed to have dissipated.

Light footsteps alerted him that someone was coming, and his pulse skittered, hoping it was Danae, while telling himself it would be greedy to want more time with her.

Then the very woman he couldn't get off his mind came around the corner. Josh went to turn the wheel and completely missed, forgetting that this ship had a smooth metal steering wheel instead of wooden spokes that were easier to grip. Then again, since he'd also leaned forward to get a better look at Danae, he still would've ended up with a knob to the ribcage if they'd been on *Solitude*.

Danae Danvers turned his insides into a mushy mess, and he found he kind of liked it.

"Hey," she said. The tip of her nose and

cheeks were rosy and wind-whipped, and she still wore his jacket. "I just wanted to say thank you."

"For proving you wrong? Most people don't thank me for that, but I'll take it anyway."

She laughed, and he took that as a sign she finally understood his humor. "I meant more for..." She tucked her hair behind her ear, suddenly shy. "The whole day. The lighthouse and the hike on Cuttyhunk afterward. For making sure that Vanessa got pictures of that mansion, and for helping everyone with fishing."

"Everyone?" he repeated, unsure why.

Her eyes lifted to his and the air between them crackled, charged with a day that had felt like one amazing, multi-location date. With extra people, sure. But those amazing moments when they had ended up alone—mostly because he'd finagled his way next to her, unable to get enough—had felt like the best date ever.

"Well, as the ambassador of the group, so to speak, I don't want to leave anyone out." She took a few more steps until the toes of her shoes nearly met his. "But of course I'm extra grateful for my fishing lesson. And for the ability to talk about my dad. It helped me concentrate on the good memories. I've been guilty of focusing on the aftermath and forgetting the allure of the sea, and why he spent so much time and money there."

"Happy to help." This time he took a step. He reached up and snagged the runaway strand of hair that kept sticking to the glossy stuff on her lips.

Which left him studying her mouth, thinking about how soft and silky her hair was.

How beautiful she was, inside and out. He could tell she cared about her team and her goals, and he could only imagine how hard it had been for her to step up after her father passed away and become a responsible adult at such a young age. He swallowed, hard, as he tucked her hair behind her ear the same way she had.

Electricity flowed from him to her, or from her to him. His fingertips lingered on the shell of her ear. "Speaking of the fish... You honestly liked it?"

She licked her lips and her voice came out slightly breathless. "I honestly did."

"Care to admit defeat?"

"Discovering I actually like fish if it's been seasoned and cooked right can hardly be called a defeat. It's all win." She reached into her pocket and withdrew a tiny slip of paper. "But you definitely earned that gold star you've had your eye on."

As she lifted it, more details stood out. Sure enough, a glittery gold star caught the light coming from the control panel. They weren't like the stickers he'd very occasionally received in elementary—he'd had trouble sitting still, his gaze forever drifting out the window. This star was about the size of a quarter and completely over-the-top, much like the woman in front of him.

If anyone had asked him earlier, he would've said Danae wasn't his type. After talking to her about sailing and her father, and spending some time getting to know the real Danae, he found her drive and determination completely alluring.

"I don't know if you want to save it, or—"

"No way. I'm wearing that bad boy with pride." He peeled it off and almost placed it on his shirt. But he'd change his shirt.

I've officially lost my mind, stressing out over the longevity of a sticker. It was more than that, though. So much more.

After a moment of deliberation, he stuck it on his jacket—the one currently on Danae. He pressed it to the spot where a police officer would wear their badge. "Now I won't lose it," he whispered.

The smile she bestowed upon him lit him up inside like the fireworks at the big 4th of July show.

She began shucking the coat. "Right. Here, I'll get this back to you. Mine's in my cabin, and you've got to be cold."

Josh placed his hands on her shoulders, preventing her from removing the jacket. "I'm not cold." With Danae so close and his heart pumping like crazy, he could hardly imagine ever being cold again. "You keep it for tonight. I don't want you to shiver on your way back to the cabin, and you can just bring it to me tomorrow morning."

Danae rubbed the sticker, securing it to the fabric. "Okay."

Yes, he would give her the coat anyway, because he was a gentleman, but he also wanted her to stay. If she was cold, she'd want to leave.

With land approaching, Josh gestured to the wheel. "Want to park it?"

"Since I was only ever the co-captain and mostly in charge of the sails, it's been a while since I've steered. And I've never parked before."

"I'll be right here to help you. Just like with the fish." Josh placed his hand on Danae's lower back and maneuvered her in front of him.

Ever so slowly, she wrapped her fingers around the wheel. He helped her guide the sailboat into the marina, showing her how to accelerate and decelerate and line it up. One thing was clear: she was a natural sailor through and through.

"I need you to do me another favor," he said, his lips close enough to her ear that he caught a whiff of vanilla perfume or shampoo or whatever women used that smelled so incredible. Something Danae definitely took to the next level.

She glanced over her shoulder at him,

the lights around the dock dancing in the reflection of her glasses. "What?"

"Once you get back to your cabin, make sure you dig out another gold star, because you earned it."

"What if I prefer pink?" One corner of her mouth twisted up, the happiness radiating from her transferring to him.

"What if I'm not surprised?"

"Oh, you think you know me already?"

"No," he said. "But I'm figuring it out. Well enough to realize that I judged the sender of the emails a little harshly."

"Full disclosure: I judged the non-answerer of the emails a little harshly too."

Josh cut the engine, and other noises from the marina filtered in—someone hadn't secured their halyards, leaving a hank clanking against the mast. Under other circumstances he'd grumble about people not knowing how to properly button up their boat, but right now he was grateful for the sounds that jerked him back to reality.

What on earth was he doing? While it might be fun to forget for a while that he didn't date anymore, flirting with a client was an epically bad idea.

After his divorce shattered any romantic notion he'd ever had, he'd sworn off attachments to anything besides his boat and carefree lifestyle. Sworn off anything that would cause future pain.

While he knew nothing could happen

between him and Danae—not really—he didn't want to give her the wrong idea. "I'd better go tie up the ship and get us secured for the night."

"Need help?"

"No, thanks," he said, resolving to be more reserved around her for the rest of the trip. "I'm used to doing things alone."

Chapter Ten

"SO, YOU'VE PROBABLY VISITED HERE a whole bunch of times," Danae said to Josh as they exited the Oak Bluffs Marina and headed to check out the north end of Martha's Vineyard. She'd worn her contacts today, and while both with and without glasses were a win in his book, he enjoyed the unobscured view of her eyes. She also had on a blue-and-white striped shirt and blue pants with a bow, making her look like the cutest sailor he'd ever seen.

An observation he was going to tamp down in order to stick to the vow he'd made last night. Instead, Josh let his many trips to Martha's Vineyard flicker through his brain. "It's a popular destination, so enough times I can't even count."

Honestly, this side of the island was busier and more touristy than he preferred, but beautiful, with old-timey shops that lined the streets. Since everyone here seemed to be in vacation mode, both visitors and locals alike, things ran at a slower pace that suited him.

"Tell the truth..." Danae leaned in conspiratorially, as if she were about to confess something. Josh held his breath, an ill-advised surge of adrenaline rumbling through his veins. "Do you know Martha?"

"Martha?"

Vanessa giggled, signaling she'd overheard. "She means Martha of Martha's Vineyard."

Danae skipped more than walked, as if her energy had been cranked to high, and he'd thought she was plenty zippy before. Must've had a good meeting this morning as they'd sailed from Cuttyhunk to the vineyard.

"Hate to break it to you," Josh said, "but Bartholomew Gosnold named it in the sixteen hundreds, which is just a wee bit before my time."

"You weren't around then?" Danae asked, having the audacity to act surprised by that news. "Are you sure? Because yesterday you told me you were in the older demographic."

He raised an eyebrow that only made

her grin spread into the canary-eating range.

"Sorry. What I meant was"—she tapped a pensive finger to her lips—"go on."

His first instinct was to tease her back, but that would only lead to conversations that would get him in over his head. Facts were his friends; being an uber-professional tour guide his new rule of thumb. "While its namesake isn't definitively known, his mother-in-law and his daughter were both named Martha."

"That leads me to believe it was for his daughter." Vanessa gathered her thick head of hair into a loose curly bun and then re-adjusted her sunglasses. "I don't know many guys who like their mothers-in-law well enough to name an island after them."

Mark sniggered. "I'm glad she said it so I didn't have to." His gaze drifted to Danae and the amusement in his features faded to something softer. "Although, for the record, Danae's mother is lovely. Wanted to put that out there so no one assumed otherwise."

"Aww, thank you, Mark. You know she adores you, too."

Wait. *What?* Were Danae and Mark...?

Obviously they weren't married any-more, or he would've picked up on it. Or Da-nae would've surely mentioned it. Someone would've said *something*. If Josh had wit-nessed a guy helping his wife—or even girl-friend—reel in a fish, arms wrapped around her, he certainly would've given the dude a heads up.

Of course, he had noticed a weird vibe, but it was more like they tiptoed around each other. They didn't sit next to one another, and there was a competitive spirit crowding the air whenever they discussed business.

That would fit if they'd gotten divorced, he supposed, although he couldn't imagine working with Olivia after everything had fallen apart.

Josh hadn't realized he'd stopped walking along until Danae spun around. "Is something wrong? You're coming along, right?"

He shook his head, attempting to dislodge the whir of thoughts. "Sorry. I was just..." If he said thinking about his ex-wife and former mother-in-law, that would lead down a strange path, one he didn't want to discuss. Although for the record, he'd had good experiences with Olivia's mother. Her father, on the other hand, had heaped on the pressure, demanding that Josh provide a better life for his daughter. Which made it hard not to feel like a failure, even back in the days when he'd been going as hard and as fast as he could.

A few long strides caught him up to the group. "Where to first?"

"Are you saying you didn't look at the itinerary?" Danae clicked her tongue, but the smile she aimed his way made it clear she was teasing. Mostly, anyway. "The Flying Horses Carousel. Vanessa scheduled this stop, hoping to get some awesome videos for... the app that I'm totally going to download."

"You already forgot the name?" Vanessa placed her fists on her hips and addressed the entire group, her narrowed eyes flicking from face to face. "Did anyone finish their registration on Trendster yet? I haven't gotten any follow requests."

Vanessa lifted her phone and shook it at the team. Then she sighed and tapped the screen. "I'll check myself and Barton in on Trendster, but the app I want everyone using today is actually a different one. It's called Quest Obsessed. Danae, you'll love it. You get stickers for everything you check off."

That piqued Danae's interest, and her eyes widened as she studied the screen. "Ooh. You have so many stickers, too."

Vanessa mimicked a hair flip, in spite of the fact that she'd pulled up her curls. "It's part of my job, darling."

The two of them grinned at each other. They seemed to be growing closer by the day. Apparently not as close as Danae and Mark used to be, and Josh needed to scrub that out of his head. It wouldn't do any good. In the long run, it didn't even matter.

His memory had been jogged, flooding his brain with the countless complications that came along with relationships and marriage. All the compromising and hard work and hurt feelings on both sides, only for it to end in divorce. For a while it had been hard to imagine a happy life without Olivia and the belongings they'd spent years acquiring.

Eventually, though, it became harder to imagine a life that included anyone but himself, his sailboat, and the water.

I was perfectly happy before Danae came along. She'd reminded him of how nice it could be to laugh and talk and be open with someone else. Then there was that enticing pull of the possibility of more, and the interest that tugged at your gut the entire time you were around the person who sparked it.

Getting involved with anyone required risk, and he just wasn't willing to gamble any more of himself away.

A giant red building that resembled a barn loomed in front of them, the sign declaring it America's oldest carousel.

"When I moved from the West Coast to the East Coast," Vanessa said, "Martha's Vineyard and this carousel were on the top of my to-do list. I added them to my list of places on Quest Obsessed long before this trip was a twinkle in Mr. Barton's eye."

Since Danae and Vanessa had practically raced to the entrance, they were waiting for the rest of the team.

"You look fabulous, by the way." Danae swept her arm up and down her colleague's asymmetrical jumpsuit with a slit in the sleeve. It showed off Vanessa's toned arms, and the white fabric complemented her bronze skin. If Danae attempted that outfit, she'd look like Casper the Friendly Ghost.

"Aww, thank you." The bangles on Vanessa's wrist clanged together as she swept a corkscrew curl out of her eyes.

"White is a bold choice, too. I'd definitely spill food or drink on myself if I wore an ensemble like that."

Vanessa laughed. "I think you're being too hard on yourself."

"I think you're new enough not to have seen some of my disasters. Once—I don't even know how it happened—the coffee pot exploded on me. Like I lifted it to pour myself a cup of joe and the next thing I know, shattered glass and steaming coffee down my shirt and pants. I'd worn light pink that day."

Vanessa brought up her hands to cover her mouth. "No."

"Oh yes. Bonus, it was my second week of work. I didn't know what to do. Mark came in while I was on my hands and knees doing damage control and helped me clean up the mess."

The rest of the team caught up, and while their looky-loo pace was sometimes hard for Danae to deal with, she was in a good-enough mood that she was happy for them to look their fill. Perhaps she didn't have to power walk everywhere on this trip. Maybe. If they were on schedule.

The group entered the building together and walked over to where the carousel was spinning, the vintage organ providing the soundtrack. The period artwork painted across the top added to the classic feel, as if they'd stepped back in time.

"Aww, look at all the happy kids," Danae said.

"See how they're reaching for that mechanical arm?" Vanessa pointed, raising her voice and addressing the entire team. "There are these brass rings you try to snag, and if you get one, you win a free ride."

"Along with bragging rights," Mark added with a smile. He scuffed his shoe against the wooden floor. "I might've been the reigning champ of my family when I was a kid. My parents brought us here a lot during our summer trips with our cousins. There were six boys, so as you can imagine, we got a bit rowdy, despite threats from our parents."

Danae cocked her head and studied Mark. He could be opinionated and stubborn—traits she also had in spades—and don't even get her started on how he said he would add items to his calendar and immediately forget, but she could hardly imagine him as a rowdy boy. She found she liked the image of little Mark and all his cousins, so carefree, their eyes wide with adventure.

At least Dad let me run wild on the sailboat. Her childhood might've ended earlier than expected, but those days building sandcastles and pretending to be a fierce female pirate at sea had allowed her to fully be a kid. They had spurred her imagination and enriched her childhood. Thanks to Dad's always referring to her ideas as brilliant, she wasn't scared to take risks, either, which had served her well when it came to out-of-the-box marketing ideas.

The person running the carousel stopped the ride, waiting for the kids to climb off so the next group could go, and Paige yelled, "I call the dragon with the rainbow wings!"

"Not if I get there first," Franco yelled, and the two of them took off at a sprint, faster than Danae could scold them.

Then she was glad she hadn't, because she hadn't seen the two of them that excited for anything on this trip. If they could capture some of that childlike magic she'd just been fondly recalling, they should go for it.

As long as they didn't shout out the company name.

"This looks amazing on film," Vanessa said as she clicked away on her phone. Naturally she had cool filters to experiment with, adding more old-timey effects before switching to one with color pops. "The shorter the films, the better these days, so I'll take a mix of pictures and videos." She pocketed her phone and backpedaled toward the carousel entrance. "Do me a favor? Can you take a few pictures and videos of me so I can share them on Quest Obsessed and earn my stickers?"

"Of course." Danae moved closer to the white picket fence that bordered the carousel. Several members of her team climbed atop horses, including Mark. Danae took several pictures, snapping extra of Vanessa for her innumerable apps.

She sensed Josh at her side, and a flutter careened through her. She pressed her forearm against her tummy, as if that would help it calm down. Sure, the guy standing next to her evoked a thrill similar to a carnival ride, but his moods also had as many ups and downs, as last night had attested. Plus, this was a short trip, and a work one at that. Clearly, her self-control needed to get its act together.

"Come on, Danae." Franco beckoned to her. "You, too, Josh."

Paige parroted his request. Even though she hadn't won the race, Franco had let her take the first ride on the colorful dragon. Vanessa and Mark, on two buckskin horses, added their pleas for her to "come on already."

"It's for kids," she shouted back, earning a mock dirty look from Vanessa.

"Don't give me that lame excuse. I'm older and therefore wiser..."

Luckily, the carousel carried Vanessa too far away to continue the discussion.

"I'll go if you go," Josh said, his voice drifting into her ear and vibrating its way to the center of her chest. "Destiny awaits. I'm pretty sure that's the horse's name, by the way."

An unexpected laugh slipped free. "I'd hate to mess with Destiny. I hear she's an ornery one." If putting space between them required a spin on the carousel, Danae supposed it was the lesser of the two complexities. "Fine. I'm in."

Josh led her to the end of the short line to wait for the next turn. The ride slowed, and the conductor told them to go ahead and pick out their horses. Franco and Paige were switching seats so that he could get a turn on the dragon.

Unlike previous carousels Danae had ridden when she was a girl, several of the horses had realistic hair instead of painted manes. The conductor announced that the ride was about to start, and the two of them rushed to mount their noble plastic steeds. As she climbed atop her horse and glanced at Josh, the childlike excitement she'd been reminiscing about ignited and spread until her entire body tingled with it.

Usually she did a better job at resisting dares, but the way Josh issued them, with a combination of encouragement and witty taunting, made her want to oblige. If anyone asked, though, she'd be going with "team bonding" as her reason for giving in.

The kid a couple of horses in front of her tipped to the side, far enough that she was afraid he'd topple over. She opened her mouth to call to Mark for help, since he was astride the horse beside the young boy. Then she realized that the kid was reaching for one of the rings on the mechanical arm.

Danae squinted one eye closed, afraid to watch, and afraid not to. The boy's finger barely nicked the edge of the ring...and came up empty. She didn't have to see his face to imagine his disappointment.

The younger girl behind her shouted in victory as she snagged one of the rings. She had three piled on top of her horse's ear, and while Danae knew that life wasn't fair, it still dug at her.

During the next turn, she watched the kid again, silently urging him to snag a brass ring without getting bucked off, so to speak. She didn't trust the flimsy "seat belt" to hold him.

He stretched out his arm, his stubby fingers grasping and grasping...

Get it, get it.

"Dang it," she said when he missed for the second time.

"Everything okay?" Josh asked. "Or is Destiny acting up?"

Danae patted her horse's neck. "Not with me. I know how to grab hold of destiny and make it work for me."

"Let me guess, with a ten-point plan."

As they rounded the bend, the mechanical arm in sight, she stood in the stirrups, hoping they could hold her despite the fact that she was well beyond kid age, height, and weight.

"See that boy a few rows in front of us? He's been trying to get that brass ring, and he's already missed twice. I feel so bad."

Sure enough, he stretched out his fingers once again, and she leaned to the side of her own horse, as if that would help.

The kid's mom was trying to assist him this time, but she was also struggling to keep a hand on a toddler with golden curls on the horse in front of him.

Mark climbed off his own horse in a flash. He asked the mom and the kid a question, and when they both nodded, he gripped the kid around the waist and gave him the few inches' boost. The boy's happy shout bounced over to her, and happiness pinged her insides.

"You got it!" she shouted, adding a clap, and the boy twisted in the plastic saddle and held up his brass ring trophy.

Danae smiled at Mark, who ensured the boy was securely on his horse and then returned her smile. Instead of climbing back on, Mark simply leaned against his horse and gripped the pole as the ride began slowing.

After the breakup, she'd purposely focused on her frustrations with Mark so she wouldn't miss him so much. Between the way he'd apologized last night, his remark about her mom, and how he'd noticed the kid struggling and jumped to help, she was remembering everything that had drawn her to him in the first place.

Even the story she'd told Vanessa about the coffee pot. Mark had come in, and she'd launched into a rambling explanation. Before she'd even finished her spiel, he'd squatted next to her, placed his hand on her shoulder, and told her it wasn't a big deal.

Then he'd grabbed a roll of paper towels, told her to be careful so she wouldn't cut her fingers, and helped her clean it up. That'd been the first glimmer of attraction, and things had blossomed from there.

She'd doubted her instincts when it came to dating and relationships since the breakup, but maybe she hadn't been *completely* wrong about Mark, even if it hadn't worked out.

As they climbed off the carousel, she quickened her pace so she could talk to Mark. "That was very nice of you."

"I couldn't handle watching him miss one last time. Everyone deserves bragging rights and a free ride."

"Guess that rowdy boy grew up to be a generous gentleman."

As they went to step off the carousel, Mark extended a hand and helped her down. "That means a lot coming from you, considering you've seen some of my not-so-generous moments."

"Not true. Even with"—unexpected emotion clotted her throat—"everything that happened with us, you've remained courteous and professional, and I appreciate it. Even if I might not have at first."

"Trust me, it wasn't easy. And sometimes—"

"That was amazing," Vanessa said, hooking her arm in Danae's. "The pictures and the videos, and *ahh*, I feel like a kid again."

Mere steps in front of them, Franco glanced over his shoulder and then loudly faux-whispered to Paige, "What's next? I'd ask Danae, but I'm afraid she'll yell at me for not reading the itinerary." The entire team laughed. After a few days of wondering if she could pull off team bonding, it buoyed Danae's already happy mood to the next level.

She turned to Paige and Vanessa, crossing her fingers that they were feeling the bonding vibes as well. "Any publicity and marketing opportunities there? Even if it's just networking?"

"I'll look into it," Paige said.

"Awesome. Next up is a short walk down Circuit Street, and then we'll cut across Tabernacle Avenue and check out the real-life gingerbread houses. From there, it's only a three-minute walk to The Sweet Life Café, where I've booked us a late lunch. Not only is it one of the top-rated restaurants in town, I called ahead and made sure they had vegetarian options for Paige, gluten-free dishes for Franco, and that they'd consider opening an hour early to accommodate our group."

Then she'd present the five-year plan she'd worked so hard on to everyone. The nerves she'd kept at bay rose up, even as she assured herself that it would be fine. The last few meetings had gone much better than the first.

It was just that this one was the big one. The high she'd experienced from today's bonding time slowly leaked out of her, every breath tightening instead of expanding her lungs.

To combat her apprehension, Danae did what she did best. She dug her planner out of her bag and began studying the notes she'd made for her presentation while silently chanting, *Please,* please *let it go well.*

Chapter Eleven

When it came to getting through to Danae about living in the moment, it felt like one step forward and two steps back. Having every minute of a day arranged made Josh scratch at his throat, but she obviously found it comforting. Currently she had her nose buried so far in her planner that she was missing out on the little shops buzzing with tourists, the blue sky overhead, and the leafy green trees that provided welcome patches of shade.

Maybe the houses and businesses they were passing weren't the "gingerbread houses" she had on her bullet-pointed list, but there was a lot of beautiful architecture. For instance, the charming inn to their right, with its balconies and turret and greenery climbing up the sides.

"Hey, look," Josh said, stepping closer to her so that the family of four would go through the gap he'd opened up instead of slam into Danae, who probably wouldn't even notice. "It's the Lazy Frog. Danae, maybe you want to stop in and see if you can find tips on how to take some extra leisure time—it says 'dedicated to leisure' right there."

Several members of her team chuckled. Unfortunately, he didn't get so much as a glance from Danae, much less the smile he'd hoped for. Already he'd failed at remaining uber professional. It wasn't really his style anyway. Plus, they'd connected yesterday, and he couldn't just throw that away. Instead, he was attempting to walk closer to the friendly line rather than the flirty one. Vetoing the latter didn't mean he didn't want to continue to chat or push her to have more fun on their outings.

Danae's brow furrowed as she glanced up, as if she were surprised to find other people nearby. "Did someone say something to me? I'm just brushing up on my notes for my presentation, so I..." Her lips moved as she continued to skim down the page, lost in her planner yet again.

Evidently, Josh's powers of persuasion needed to be recharged—or maybe he'd used them all up getting her on the carousel. So he zipped his lips and continued walking along. Only problem was, frustration churned through him, growing stronger with each step.

Was it his imagination, or had things changed once she'd gone after Mark at the end of their carousel ride?

Worse, why did it matter so much to him?

With their cluster bobbing and weaving their way through the crowd, Josh ended up next to Franco at the tail end of the group. He opened his mouth, only to shut it. By the third time he'd almost spoken, only to think better of it, he rebuked himself for being a wimp and asked the question he'd been dying to ask since their walk to the Flying Horse Carousel.

"Hey," Josh said, keeping his voice low. "Did Mark and Danae used to be...?" The words snagged in his throat. "Were they married? Earlier he said something about her mom when we were joking about mothers-in-law." He shrugged, stopping short of saying he'd caught a strange energy between them, but not one that quite fit ex-spouses. After all, he and Olivia very rarely spoke, and while they could now be civil when their paths crossed, he couldn't imagine working in the same office. "I was going to ask Danae, but..."

Franco's eyebrows arched so high they blended into his dark hair. Then he glanced at the woman Josh had just inquired about. "But she's studying her planner like it's a playbook and her team's in the Super Bowl."

"Exactly."

"Well, they weren't married. But they did date for the better part of a year. At first it was hush-hush, although most of us at the office suspected it—that was back before Vanessa was part of the team. Anyway, a lot of us thought they would get married eventually, but about six months ago, things seemed super tense. Finally, they admitted they'd broken things off, but were determined to remain professional, and I've been impressed at how well they've pulled it off. That whole friends-with-your-ex thing so rarely works out."

Considering Mark kept finding ways to be near Danae, Josh wondered if the guy didn't want to be more than friends again.

Which was fine. Even if Josh were willing to attempt a relationship—which was a big if—he could never be in one that didn't allow room for spontaneity or adventure.

As everyone was finishing what had been an amazing lunch, Danae wiped her fingers on the white cloth napkin draped across her lap, and then placed it over her plate. The café was as incredible as the reviews claimed, its dark wooden floors, blue-and-copper floral wallpaper and matching blue trim creating a charming atmosphere that gave her a much-needed boost.

So far, the day was on the right, positive trajectory. Now to keep it going. "While everyone's finishing up, I wanted to dive into the subject of increasing sales this coming year." She shifted her plate aside and withdrew her trusty planner. Instead of diving right into her presentation, she was doing as Mr. Barton suggested and listening to her team, too. "Anyone have any ideas they'd like to share?"

"Get the website updated as soon as possible," Franco said. "I toyed with it first thing this morning and will have another version for you all to look at soon. I've heard everyone loud and clear, and after taking some time to process, I realized you were right. I'm working to make it chic and streamlined, with Danae's slogan in mind." He raised his voice, the same way she'd done when she originally pitched it in the meeting. "Barton Boats. Not just a boat, but a lifestyle."

She returned his smile, her mood getting another upsurge. "Thank you, Franco. I can't wait to see what that genius brain of yours comes up with."

"I was thinking we should analyze where we're spending our ad money," Paige said. "Places that used to work aren't performing as well for us, and I've found three more boating magazines to try. I've already emailed their ad departments and inquired about the cost."

Vanessa made a skeptical *hmm* noise that caused Danae's blood pressure to soar. "I'm all for trying out new places, but I'm not sure we're going to gain new buyers from magazines, no matter how many ads we run. For one, who even reads magazines anymore?" She ticked off other ideas on her fingers. "How about website banners? Travel sites, social media platforms?

"Or..." Vanessa hesitated in that way she did to build momentum, and Danae pricked up her ears, determined to be more open than she'd been in the past. "A lot of influencers run in the same circles, and thanks to my connections in the beauty blogger world, I can reach out to people with travel blogs. We can invite them to come take a cruise and document how fabulous it is. They'll be sure to mention Barton Boats."

Paige cocked her head. "Um, don't you

remember what Mark said about our target market demographic? Speaking of older, who even reads blogs anymore?"

"Okay," Danae said. "Let's—"

"It's a billion-dollar industry," Vanessa said. "Most of the blogging is done via pictures that show off beautiful locales and captions that are only two to three paragraphs these days. They still reach thousands of people."

"I appreciate your enthusiasm, but you still won't find *our* demographic among their subscribers. The idea is just a little too out there for us."

Well, at least Paige had added the "appreciate" remark. Surely that was at least a modicum of progress?

Vanessa crossed her forearms on the edge of the table. "Well, I'm afraid boring and conventional isn't going to move the meter. Not anymore."

Oh, great. Now Paige was going to think Vanessa was implying her ideas were boring, and Danae felt the need to take the train's controls before it jumped the tracks and wrecked their progress. "Thank you both for your input and giving me ideas to think about. While we mull them over, I'm going to set up my mini projector and go over my five-year plan. I think it'll provide us with a strong foundation, and then we can discuss ways to tweak it." She stuck her flash drive into the small machine and fired it up.

The presentation flashed on a blank space on the wall, complete with colorful headings, bullet points, charts, and statistics. She'd been working on it before she got the promotion, thinking she'd either present it as the CMO, or just as someone who cared a lot about the company she worked for.

"Wow," Mark said, when the presentation was over. She steeled herself for his criticism. While she appreciated their truce, it didn't mean they'd automatically agree. "You're usually detailed, D, but you've outdone yourself."

The stress that had been filling her for the past hour or so began to seep out of her, like a balloon that had been poked with a pin. The entire team was silent, contemplative expressions on their faces, and for about thirty seconds, it seemed like someone had hit the pause button.

Then Mark leaned back in his chair, two grooves forming between his eyebrows, kick-starting her nerves all over again. "But what if we get through the first year of this campaign and learn that we have to switch tactics?"

"Most of the columns and amounts can be tweaked. For instance, the ad budget is based on a percentage of our profit, and if you change it..." Danae went to type on her keyboard out of habit, her curled fingers hovering over the table for a beat before she straightened. "Well, I can show you later, once I have my laptop. But it's a formula, so it would automatically recalculate it."

Danae ran her palms down the thighs of the lightweight linen pants she'd picked up at Banana Republic. They felt a bit too casual for this presentation, but they were on a sunny island and she hadn't wanted to overheat or appear too rigid, especially with the rest of the team—save Vanessa of course—in shorts. "Anyone else? This is a safe place, where feedback is welcome."

"A formula is a good idea," Mark said. "However, I'm still wondering if there's enough flexibility. Say one department outperforms the others. Shouldn't they get a boost instead of having to redistribute their budget to other areas?"

"Okay. Thank you, Mark." Danae scribbled herself a few notes. She could handle this. Criticism that would benefit the company's strategy, just like Franco with the website.

Vanessa shifted in her seat. "I do like that you're projecting growth among the female demographic. More than that, I think with a few of the right placements, we can get there."

"Where's the wiggle room?" The question came from Josh, and she glanced at him, a strange buzzing noise invading her mind as she blinked at him. "Think about sailing. It's about reacting to changes and improvising and enjoying the journey. Shouldn't you have more of that kind of flexibility in your marketing plan?"

Uh-oh.

Josh immediately knew he shouldn't have jumped in, and the firm line of Danae's jaw confirmed it. He'd gotten caught up in feeling like part of the group—a group that he'd grown to really like. Then he'd been thinking about how much he'd relished his time sailing Barton's Fortune 703 model, a sailboat that was speedy and comfortable, and took very little effort to manage. Any company that paid that much attention to craftsmanship and functionality deserved to do well.

More than that, he wanted Danae and her team to succeed.

"A five-year plan doesn't mean there's no wiggle room," Danae said. "It's a long-term goal. It's what we're working toward at Barton Boating Company. My goals don't just change with the wind, and when it comes to marketing a business, enjoyment isn't my top priority. That's for after we succeed on launching this campaign."

Awkwardness crept through the air, everyone glancing in other directions. Josh's tongue stuck to the roof of his mouth, waiting for him to figure out whether he should to try to explain himself further or attempt to soothe Danae's ruffled feathers.

Mark cleared his throat and pointed his fork at the projection on the wall. "I'm glad that newspaper ads are still in the budget. I was worried you'd rule them out, Danae, and our demographic still likes to drink their coffee while they read their paper, same way they've been doing for decades. But of course you'd take that into consideration, so I never should've doubted you." He sat forward in his chair, drawing Danae's gaze. "I've got a great partnership with several of the staff members of the local papers, and they give us a great rate, too, so we can do a lot more with a lot less."

"Honestly, I considered trimming it," Danae said, "but I thought about what you said during the meeting at the vineyard, and decided it was worth holding onto for a while more." She smiled at Mark, and he smiled right back.

Oh, sure. Mark had implied that she had no idea what men wanted, and suddenly *he* was the good guy?

It seemed like his suspicions about Mark trying to win Danae back were spot on, and her ex had just pulled ahead in their unspoken competition. Not that Danae was a prize to be won, but if she were comparing him to Mark now, Josh doubted he'd come out ahead.

For the rest of meeting, Josh sat silent, tuning out the business talk. He'd never wanted to be part of it again, so why had he gone and put his foot in it?

With the restaurant about to open up for normal hours, Danae took down her presentation, and used the company credit card to pay the bill—in spite of his insistence he pay for his own meal.

Obviously she didn't need his tour guide skills, since she hardly let him give any facts or took any of his advice. She could probably sail the boat herself if it came down to it, too, leaving him to wonder what he was even doing tagging along on every outing, getting involved. Throwing out ideas no one wanted to hear.

Maybe he should do his own thing from now on.

A cloud of tension hung over them as they made the ten-minute walk to the ship, starkly contrasting with the happy, carefree mood they'd felt on the way there. Vanessa and Paige spoke in clipped tones and one-word answers, and Danae charged down the street as if she were being timed and had a record to break.

Mark and Franco hung back, as if they were wary about getting caught in the crossfire, and a general grumpiness lingered. Why hadn't Josh's common sense kicked in sooner? Preferably *before* he'd given his input on Danae's plan.

About an hour later, he was on the boat, bent over and fiddling with one of the winches, when he heard someone approach. Call it pessimism or intuition, but foreboding tiptoed along his spine.

"We need to talk," Danae said.

Josh winced at the words every male dreaded. He'd heard the phrase way too many times before, the prequel to many a fight. It started off with Olivia telling him what he'd done wrong, and escalated to a screaming match.

He reluctantly straightened and turned to Danae, who stood about a yard away, arms crossed.

Yep. It was about to go down.

"You undermined me in front of my team," she said.

"I was only trying to help. I like you and your team and want you all to succeed. And you did say you were open to advice."

"To feedback. From my team."

That stung, a sharp prick to his heart. It was more than his ego. Even though they hadn't known each other long, surely she didn't think he'd been trying to sabotage her presentation.

Danae ran her fingers through her hair, switching the bulk of it from one side to the other. "Do you understand how hard it is to be firm enough that I don't get plowed over, but encouraging enough that all the departments will contribute ideas and get onboard? It's a tricky balance—one I'm struggling to hit, by the way. If our sailboat captain starts questioning me, it'll only be a matter of time before my entire team does the same. I can't lead if they don't have faith in me."

"Look, I get it, but I think you're reading *way* too much into it," Josh said, unable to resist the urge to defend himself. "You're overanalyzing it, same way you do with your tight schedules, goals, and your never-ending to-do list."

"Overanalyzing? Seriously?" Danae reached down and grabbed the end of the rope that kept snagging, as if she were on autopilot. "I can't believe you'd say that when you know what's at stake for me." Her chin quivered and hurt flickered through her eyes. "I confided in you about how important it was that I prove myself to my boss in order to hold on to my new position. Something not even my team knows, and I'd like to keep it that way."

Disappointment and frustration joined together and streaked through his veins, weighing down his limbs and his lungs. The charismatic, upbeat woman he'd spent yesterday with was gone. He'd thought he'd broken through to her, but she had reset overnight. She would undoubtedly do it again tomorrow, emerging from her cabin that much more determined to eliminate all risk, as if that were possible.

He'd tried it before. Lived that life. It only ended in stress and high blood pressure. He straightened and opened his mouth to tell her as much, but she wasn't done with her rant.

"The more in control I am, the more confident I come across, the more my team will follow my lead. That's why I like schedules and detailed objectives, and there's nothing wrong with accomplishing goals. In fact, not writing them down and working toward them would make them wishes. I have to work to make things happen—it's how I've gotten to where I am today." She crossed her arms, adopting the same pose she'd originally come to him with, and shook her head. "Next time I'm leading my team, do me a favor and butt. Out."

"No problem. I'll be keeping my thoughts to myself from now on, letting you attempt to schedule every second of everything until you drive yourself insane."

"Good." Danae whipped around, one stride into a dramatic exit.

"Great," he said, because he never did know when to keep his mouth shut.

She spun back around, jaw clenched. Unshed tears glistened in her eyes, and then he felt two feet tall.

"Danae—"

"Save it. I'll be going into town for dinner. Everyone's doing their own thing, so enjoy your unscheduled free time. I'll see you in the morning at nine sharp, when our rental bikes get delivered. As much as I hate to admit it, I don't know the trail. Although I'm sure I could figure it out if needed."

With that, she continued her retreat, leaving him standing there, completely flustered.

Bright side? It confirmed he'd made the right decision to pull back with Danae. His ex-wife had been all about a five-year plan, too, one that included a big house and a baby. And look how that had turned out. Grand plans like that only led to disappointment, and a big no thank you on his end.

Unfortunately, it didn't feel very bright, or make the churning in his gut go away.

One thing was for sure: his life had been a lot simpler before Danae Danvers came into it.

Chapter Twelve

At least the bike rental company Danae had booked knew how to be on time. This morning she had paced the cabin, worried that if she went above deck, she'd have to fill the awkward silence with their sailboat captain while pretending it wasn't awkward.

Danae sent a group text announcing that their Pedelecs—or electric-assist bikes—had arrived, and that they'd be taking off ASAP. Paige was first off the boat, her red hair up in a high ponytail similar to Danae's. They were both wearing yoga pants, breathable tank tops, and sneakers.

"Were you able to chat with your fiancé last night?" Danae asked Paige when she came over to claim a bike. Of all the people on the team, she'd spent the least time interacting with Paige. Since Danae had connected with Vanessa, she also didn't want Paige thinking she had picked sides.

"I did." A dreamy expression overtook Paige's features. "Neither one of us wanted to say goodbye, so we FaceTimed until we both fell asleep. I woke up to a text about how much he loves me."

The mushiness in Paige's voice touched Danae, and a hint of longing rose up. "Aww, that is really sweet." She'd always adored couples talking about how they fell in love, or how madly in love they were with each other. It gave her hope that one day, she would find that as well.

Once the campaign is officially launched, maybe I'll attempt to get serious about dating again. Josh's face flashed through her mind, and she quickly blocked it and peered at the water.

"Are you enjoying the trip? I know the beginning was slightly rocky for you, but I'm glad you're here. I'm hoping you're feeling better about things, too."

"For sure. During the storm, I was so seasick I thought I'd have to go home. But the bracelets helped—as have the calmer waters—and last night, I actually found the sway of the boat soothing."

"I'm so happy to hear that."

"Yeah, and in news that surprised me

and my fiancé, I kind of love fishing. Enough that he and I are going to plan a deep-sea fishing excursion of our own. Although I already told him he's doing all the icky stuff involved." Paige laughed, and Danae joined in.

"That's amazing. I hear you on the icky stuff—it's a no from me."

That made them both giggle. The rest of the group began streaming off the ship, and they turned in tandem to greet them.

Danae held her breath as Josh disembarked, a tornado of conflicting emotions wreaking havoc on her state of mind. Yesterday she'd been so furious, and she'd unleashed on him.

Then immediately regretted it, while assuring herself she'd been justified. Her promotion was at stake. Commanding authority was important in a managerial position. Even when she'd been calling creditors back in the day, if she didn't switch from polite to stern, no one would help her.

Admittedly, she probably hadn't needed to go full force with Josh, and she may had overreacted the tiniest bit, and *ugh*. Since they had an upcoming appointment and she refused to be late, she shoved her personal issues aside and assigned bikes to everyone. Then she handed out maps with the highlighted route they'd be taking to Island Alpaca Company.

The idea of the poofy animals and

their squishy faces elicited the enthusiasm she'd been missing since crawling into bed last night. Instead of falling asleep, she had tossed and turned and rehashed every moment of the trip so she could figure out how to do better. She was the team leader, and that meant she didn't have time to have a bad day or be annoyed at a handsome sailor who made her feel too many things at once.

Danae straddled her bike. "Does everyone have water bottles? It's a five-mile course, but it's fairly level. According to the map, it should take about thirty minutes. I've padded our ride with two five-minute breaks, so if you need to rest for a few minutes, let me know."

Once she'd confirmed everyone was ready to go, they were off, riding past the busier part of the town they'd walked yesterday.

As soon as the vehicle and foot traffic cleared, they found the bike trail that ran along the main road and headed to the heart of the island. The trail also allowed them to spread out and cluster in groups instead of having to remain in single file.

Mark biked up on her left side, and while she was huffing and puffing, he'd hardly broken a sweat. So unfair, but then again, he frequented the gym after work, whereas she cuddled up on her couch most evenings.

At least she had the electric-assist to

amplify her pedaling power, although her thighs were burning, her face heating with the effort. "I knew I should've reserved a regular pedal bike for you."

Mark chuckled. "And leave me wondering why I was falling behind while everyone else was so speedy?"

"Exactly," Danae panted. "Seriously, do you have some magic way to make it easier? I've never understood bike gears. I just fiddle with them and hope for the best."

Mark instructed her how to downshift into a low gear that would help her climb the hill, and while she was initially skeptical, it helped immensely.

"I keep meaning to tell you..." Mark's pause caused her to prick up her ears and pray this ride wasn't about to go downhill—well, metaphorically, because heading downhill would be a welcome reprieve right now. "I admire how you've handled things with Franco. I'm sure it's not easy to critique one of your friends, but he showed me a couple mockup pages last night, and they're gonna blow everyone away."

"Thank you. That means a lot. And I meant to tell you how much I admired you for helping that kid grab the brass ring. I was so worried he was going to fall, and then I was cheering for him to get it. The way his face lit up when he held up that ring said it all."

"Ah. No big deal."

"It was to him."

She could sense Josh behind them and couldn't help wondering what was going through his head. How he was feeling today.

If he was mad at her. If he'd given up on her.

If she should put him and the flutters she'd felt during the lighthouse tour and deep-sea fishing trip out of her mind. Just accept that they were vastly different people with conflicting life goals, and call meeting each other a learning experience. Same as with the rest of the team.

The idea scraped at her, not sitting right, although it made the most logical sense.

Pedaling and seeing alpacas. For the next couple hours, that's my focus. I'll worry about later, well, later.

A bike ride into the less-crowded part of the island should have been right up Josh's alley. While scheduled, it spoke to that side of him that craved the simple life, the breeze in his hair, and a new adventure.

Given that it wasn't one of the usual destinations included in chartered tours, Josh had forgotten about the alpaca farm. For all his talk of adventure and changing up his backyard, he'd fallen into a pattern of his own, visiting the same places and reciting the same spiel. Missing out on new destinations and experiences himself.

Yep, it would've been great if he hadn't had to watch Mark flirt with Danae the entire ride. The guy stuck close to her side, and as they parked their bikes, Danae gave him the smile Josh had prided himself on pulling out of her. Whatever had happened in the past, it was clear that Mark wanted to rekindle things.

Jealousy gnawed at Josh's gut, even as he reminded himself that last night, as he'd been pounding his pillow flat, only to plump it up, he'd decided that he was sticking to his simple, single life.

But then Danae glanced his way. Her smile changed into a sadder, tighter version that kicked him in the gut. Then she returned her attention to Mark and whatever he was saying, and boy, did he have a lot to say.

As hard as Josh tried to convince himself it wasn't a big deal—he and Danae barely even knew each other—it didn't hold water. It wasn't every day that someone managed to get past his walls. Not every day that a woman like Danae came along.

He'd screwed up.

Olivia's words from a long time ago came back to him. *Why can't you ever just apologize? It doesn't matter if you think I* should *be hurt. What matters is I am.* She had often pointed out his unwillingness to apologize, and he'd failed to truly hear her until it was too late. Until they'd done too much damage to their relationship and to each other.

Are you going to let your pride get in the way? To just let Mark woo her while you cling to your stubborn need to be right?

Resolve propelled him forward, but before he could reach Danae, she was talking to the staff, checking in their party. Once she turned around, she announced that they had ten minutes to kill before setting up for yoga.

Wait. Yoga? Somehow, he'd missed that. Surely she didn't expect *him* to participate.

As if she could read his mind, she plopped a mat in his hands.

"Oh, I'm not...I don't do yoga."

"You do today. After that bike ride, it'll feel good to stretch out." Amusement played along the curve of her mouth. "After all, we can't have our captain too sore to sail our ship."

Surprise and pleasure clattered through him, stumbling over the fact that the statement had come out sounding...Was she flirting with him? Or was she simply anticipating watching him struggle through yoga? Either way, he'd play along. "If I do that pretzel stretch stuff, that's exactly what'll happen."

Danae shrugged. "I'm not here to force you into anything. But there's a spot for you, and I thought you were all about trying out new things and living in the moment." A challenge, belied by the casual way she'd tossed it out, and he had to hand it to her, she'd found the right button to push.

She continued down the line, giving out mats and instructions. As she reached Mark, he aimed a lovestruck grin her way. Josh gritted his teeth and glanced down at the rubbery blue mat in his hands.

Looked like today, he was going to do yoga.

Chapter Thirteen

"OH MY GOSH," DANAE SAID as she fed a black-and-white alpaca a carrot. The creature ate in a seesaw sort of motion, not up and down like humans did, and the *crunch, crunch, crunch* permeated the air. "He's so cute."

Josh wasn't sure *cute* was the word he'd use. Funky-looking. Graceless. Needed to close its mouth when it chewed.

"Actually, all of these alpacas are female," the staff worker in charge of their group informed them. "Females only have their lower teeth for chewing grass, so they can't bite. Males have two upper pairs that are called fighting teeth."

"And yoga is no place for fighting." A

woman wearing tie-dye pants and a T-shirt with a cartoon alpaca giving the peace sign walked up to their group. The seashell bracelets on her wrist rattled as she waved a hand through the air. "Hi, I'm Jill, and I'll be your instructor for today. I suggest spending about five minutes getting to know these majestic creatures, and then I'll sprinkle grain around our mats and get started."

Seriously, was he still asleep? Had he wandered into an alternate dimension? He loved animals as much as anyone, but he kept waiting for Danae or one of the staff to let him in on the joke.

Vanessa let loose a squeaky noise as a brown baby alpaca with a black snout approached her. "Whoa, check out this one's eyelashes, Danae. They're ridiculous. They're even longer than my thirty-dollar lash extensions that all the beauty influencers rave about."

"That's Bitzy," the staff member informed her.

Danae giggled and told Bitzy "You're such a pretty girl. I bet you do an amazing downward dog."

"Or is your specialty tree pose?" Vanessa asked.

Once again, Josh was totally out of the loop on whatever they were talking about, but if he was going to do yoga, he was snagging the spot next to Danae instead of letting it go to Mark.

Jill sprinkled the grain around their mats, as promised. Then she sat in a cross-legged position up front and began reciting instructions in a calm, soothing voice. "Let go of all the tension in your body as you feel the breeze blowing through your hair..."

Josh exhaled, focused on the light breeze, and admittedly, his tension did begin to melt as he followed along.

But then the more complicated stretches started. He bent at the waist and lowered his hands. Which stopped at about knee height. No way was he going to get them to the mat without snapping his back or hamstrings.

A tan alpaca with a shaggy hairdo meandered between him and Danae, who had her palms down on the mat as if it didn't take any effort. She stretched out her fingers and let the tips run across the alpaca's side. "Good girl, Marcella. Way to breathe through your moves."

Marcella's wheezing sounded like a freaking freight train. One that was struggling to chug its way uphill.

Danae craned her neck and peered up at Josh's face, her ponytail swinging with the movement. "Come on, Josh. Bitzy's more flexible than you." She jerked her chin at the baby with the long eyelashes, who was ducking under one of the grown females.

"Bitzy walks on all fours, so that hardly counts." A grunt slipped out as he lowered his hands to dangle in front of his calves.

"Let's see how long she can walk on two legs," he said, and Danae giggled.

As they transitioned to their next move, three alpacas traipsed over, joining their fuzzy buddies and blocking the view of the instructor. "I can't see what we're supposed to be doing," Josh whispered. "Although I doubt I could do it anyway."

Chewpacca, the tall female of the group with an out-of-control mane, sniffed his neck.

"And exhale," Jill said, and warm, sickly-sweet breath that smelled vaguely like hay wafted over his cheek and nose.

Josh lifted his chin so he and Chewpacca were face to face. As he peered into her big, nearly black eyes, he swore she smiled, her two bottom teeth popping out.

"Fine. You're kinda cute."

Seemingly satisfied, the animal circled his mat and nibbled at the grain. Judging from the ripping noise, Chewpacca had moved onto nibbling grass, and she wouldn't eat his yoga mat, would she?

"Since we can't see Jill anymore," Danae said, popping to her feet, as the fluffy white creature at her side mimicked her stance, "It's freestyle time." She placed one foot on the inside of her other thigh and brought her hands together as if offering a prayer. "Hey, I guessed right. They're switching to tree pose."

Josh wobbled as he attempted to do

the move. What it had to do with a tree he had no idea. They should've called it clumsy flamingo. Finally, he managed to flatten his foot to his calf—the thigh so wasn't happening. *Okay, I can do this.*

Carefully, he pressed his palms together, working to maintain his balance...

Right as an animal nose goosed him from behind.

He yelped.

Danae burst out laughing.

Her eyes widened as she lost her balance, tipping too far to the right. Josh dove to catch her, but thanks to his shaky stance and too-slow reaction time, they crashed in the middle.

Down they went in a heap of tangled limbs, and then they were both laughing, which summoned every alpaca in the area to come and gawk at them.

"Everything okay back there?" Jill asked, ducking her head to see underneath his and Danae's furry, four-legged audience.

Danae slapped a hand over her mouth, attempting to silence the infectious laughter that rang in his ears and elevated his mood all the way up to the endlessly blue sky overhead.

Josh cleared his throat. "Yep. We're nice and relaxed. Really feeling the nature setting."

"Seriously. I think I ate some grass." Danae blew her breath past her lips, more on the spitting than exhaling side. The baby alpaca who had become obsessed with her nudged her shoulder, and Danae patted its neck. “Don’t worry, Bitzy. I saved some for you.”

That had him laughing again, and soon everyone was craning their necks, trying to see what was so funny.

Danae leapt up, far more agile than he, and extended a hand to help him stand. Josh slapped his palm in hers, and once she had tugged him to his feet, he reluctantly let go.

He lowered his voice so no one else would overhear. “Hey, I’m sorry about yesterday. I was out of line.”

She cast her eyes downward, and the world paused, each second grinding against the next. Then her gaze latched on to his and his heart expanded, testing the bounds of his rib cage. “I appreciate you saying that. And I might’ve overreacted the tiniest bit.” She wrapped the end of her ponytail around her finger. “As you pointed out, I did say I was open to feedback.”

“I should’ve known better. After all, you’re the captain of your crew. I’d be upset if anyone told me how to run my ship.”

The smile he’d been missing all day spread across her face—even brighter than any of the smiles her ex had gotten this morning—and a knot he hadn’t even realized had formed in his chest loosened.

"Everyone ready for our cool down?" Jill asked.

Thanks to being back in friendly territory, Josh would have preferred to chat with Danae. Satisfaction zinged through his veins when she seemed as hesitant as he was to return to her mat.

As they completed their last few poses while inhaling and exhaling, Josh thought that he might just become a fan of yoga yet.

Danae sat in the sand, her fingers sinking into the softness and soaking up the leftover warmth from the sun. After ten miles on a bike, her muscles were pleasantly tired, and sitting in the sand felt like falling into bed after a long day.

The scent of smoke and sound of crackling flames drifted over as Paige and Mark got the bonfire going. Now that the last rays of the day were on their way out, barely peeking over the horizon, they lit up the mottled clouds overhead, turning them purple and orange. With all the bright colors and the beautiful setting, it felt like she'd stepped into a stunning photograph that seemed too beautiful to be real.

Danae's heart quickened as Josh walked over, and she held her breath, hoping he'd choose the spot next to her, but not wanting to draw too much attention by saying so. They'd already created quite a spectacle during their yoga session, and while she wouldn't change a thing, she didn't want to come across as unprofessional.

Even if her thoughts about Josh Wheeler weren't strictly professional.

"Is this spot taken?" he asked, and she became acutely aware of everything about him. His whiskered jaw, the creases in his forehead, the way the sun lit up one side of his face while leaving the other in shadow.

"It's all yours."

As he crossed his legs and settled next to her, the glow from the flames caught the gold star on the jacket she'd had wrapped around her the other night. A second later, the bag of marshmallows nearly hit her in the face. She glanced over, and Franco winced.

"Sorry. I thought you heard me yell 'heads up.'"

Maybe she would have, if she hadn't been lost in all things Josh. Someone passed skewers around the circle, and then they scooted closer to the bonfire to roast their marshmallows.

The end of Josh's marshmallow caught on fire, and he jerked it away. He whipped it back and forth until the flames were extinguished and he was left with a half-blackened marshmallow. A minute later, Danae lifted her perfectly toasted marshmallow and waved it in front of him, taunting him with her crispy golden success.

Josh gripped the skewer in the middle, and his eyes met hers. A thunderstorm of hoofbeats pounded through her body and echoed through her head. He leaned closer, the orange flames reflecting in his blue eyes.

Then he peeled off her marshmallow and popped the entire thing in his mouth.

Danae lunged, but she was too late. "Ah! That was mine!"

Josh slung his arm around her shoulders. "Oh, I thought with the way you were waving it in my face," he said through a giant mouthful, "you wanted me to have it." He packed a whole heap of smugness in his grin. "That one was perfectly done."

"You're gonna pay for that. I'm not sure how yet, but mark my words."

He had the nerve not to appear the least bit worried about her threat. Perhaps if she hadn't delivered it with a smile...

The bag of marshmallows crinkled as he lifted it with his free hand and extended it her way. "I'll roast you another if you want, but I'm guessing I'll burn it. I save my patience for the sea."

Danae jabbed a marshmallow on the end of her skewer. As she held it over the fire, she fought the urge to lean into Josh, for warmth and stability, and because she wanted to. More and more, there was this thing building between them, growing and taking over her brain.

For a while, she'd considered giving up on dating, but there were other things besides dessert that were worth the wait.

Only she was trying not to get ahead of herself.

With sparks flying—and not just the ones from the fire—that was easier said than done.

"What's that necklace you always wear?" Josh pointed at it. "I noticed it the other day in the lighthouse and again while we were doing yoga."

Danae took the charm between her fingers. "My mom is obsessed with Greek mythology. It's where the name Danae came from, but since she's not as well-known, Mom gave me a necklace with Athena."

"Goddess of wisdom, courage, strategy, and a whole mess of other things. That fits—you do seem to balance it all."

Delight sang through her entire body, leaving her tingly and warm. She wasn't sure she deserved the praise, and since she'd never known how to take a compliment, she figured she'd throw in some self-deprecation for good measure. "Don't forget war. I suppose I encompass that sometimes, too, when I get a bit stubborn and set in my ways."

"You? Nah." Josh nudged her with his elbow. Then his expression became more serious. "You're doing a great job, Danae.

I've done several of these corporate bonding trips, and your team's really coming together. I have no doubt that your boss will see what an amazing job you've done and make your promotion permanent."

Just like that, her insides went squishy, her worries and cares lightening so much that they drifted away in the breeze. "Thank you. I needed to hear that."

He must've caught something out of the corner of his eye, because he did a double take. "Oh, uh. Your marshmallow is—"

She jerked it away from the firepit, and the flaming marshmallow slipped off the end of the stick and flung through the air.

"Watch out," she yelled, but luckily, no one was behind them. The melted goo blob landed in a clump of sand and fizzled out. She and Josh both stared at it for a few seconds before they burst into laughter. Then she lightly smacked his arm. "Someone was distracting me."

One corner of his mouth kicked up. "Same."

Her heart gave an excited leap in her chest.

"Now I feel extra bad for taking your perfectly toasted marshmallow," he said.

"I happen to know a way you could make it up to me." She wanted to show him that she could be flexible and do something that wasn't on the agenda. Well, semi-flexible-ish at least.

"Take me to see the lanterns? Yesterday during the tour of the gingerbread houses you mentioned how amazing they looked all lit up at night, and I've been thinking about how pretty that would be ever since." She'd just been too prideful to ask about it after their stupid squabble.

The corners of his eyes crinkled as a smile spread across his face, and if she could bottle the heady, exhilarating feelings running amok inside of her, she would. "Deal," he said. "As long as somewhere along the way, you also let me buy you dessert."

Chapter Fourteen

Evidently, the key to making Danae beyond happy was to take her for Thai ice cream. She bounced on the balls of her feet as she watched the shop's teenage employee pour the ice cream mixture and use metal spatulas to blend it together.

Once it was frozen, the girl rolled it into floral-looking slices. She arranged it in a cup and added the toppings Danae had chosen.

"Extra marshmallows, please," Josh said, winking at Danae. "I owe her."

Danae's eyes widened as the employee handed over the sugary concoction. "It's almost too pretty to eat."

Josh led her out of the shop so they could make the short, five-minute walk to the gingerbread houses. “Are you saying you need *me* to eat it?”

Danae squealed and swung the bowl away from him as he made a halfhearted grab at her spoon. She dug into the mix and brought a scoop of the cookies and cream with fudge, whipped cream, and marshmallows to her mouth. “*Mmm.* Nothing against toasted marshmallows, but I definitely won the dessert game tonight. Thank you.”

“My pleasure,” he said.

Several couples were out and about, strolling and enjoying the balmy weather. Josh steered Danae around the clusters of people so she could keep her attention where it should be: on her ice cream and reveling in the genial buzz that hung thick in the cool night air.

One minute she could be so fixated on schedules and itineraries, and the next, she was rambling on and on about the cool storefronts. She followed that up by asking if he thought there was anywhere for her to do alpaca yoga back in Newport.

“This might surprise you, but that was actually my first time doing alpaca yoga. Also, my first time doing yoga in general.”

“I am all surprise,” she said, heavy on the sarcasm. Like she had in the ice cream shop, she bounced in place, as if someone had turned her energy knob to high. “It was so much fun, though, right?”

He bit back a grin, and then went ahead

and let it loose. "I had a lot more fun than I expected to."

Mostly because of her. She'd moved so effortlessly, bending and stretching and flowing through moves that had been completely foreign to him. Then there was the way she smiled and laughed as the animals had flocked to her—not that he blamed them. Everything the woman did, she did on a grand scale, and while it occasionally drove him crazy, he admired her drive as well. It couldn't have been easy to take on so much responsibility so young.

Which was why he had pushed her to allow herself to live in the moment more often.

Now he'd learned his lesson, though. Danae wasn't the kind of woman you could push. Ice cream bribery was the way to go. She licked fudge off her upper lip, and he had trouble concentrating on anything but her mouth.

"Okay, you *have* to try this ice cream. It's, like, the best ever." She scooped some onto her spoon and extended it to him.

Josh dipped his head and ate the offered bite. She was right. The dessert was one of the best he'd ever had, but he supposed that also had something to do with who he was sharing it with.

Danae paused by a trash can, wiped her hands on the napkin that had been wrapped around the cardboard cup, and then dropped it and the dish inside. “Thanks again for the ice cream. I’ve never had it rolled like that before.”

“Sure thing. I’ve found ice cream is always a win on dates.” The second the words were out of his mouth, Josh wanted to snatch them out of the air and shove them back in—talk about awkward. “Not that this is a date.”

Wow. Not only was he rusty, he was hopeless. Possibly out of his league.

Enjoying the journey was the motto he lived by nowadays, but he wasn’t sure how to do that on this occasion. He’d just patched things up with Danae, and he didn’t want to do anything that would put their developing friendship—or the rest of the trip—in jeopardy.

Then again, he didn’t want to give her the wrong idea.

He kept reminding himself that he didn’t have time for dating, much less a relationship. He was married to the sea, and while Danae was smart, funny, and amazing in so many ways, it didn’t negate the fact that their lifestyles were worlds apart, save for this one week in time.

Which left him torn between savoring their limited time together and avoiding getting too close, so it wouldn’t be as difficult when the time came to say goodbye.

What a roller coaster this trip had been.

A week ago, she had stood in Mr. Barton's office, nervous and then excited as he'd informed her she had gotten the promotion. Then nervous once again once he'd dropped the "interim" bomb. She'd been so sure this retreat would be a disaster from day one, and now here she was, out on an evening stroll with a handsome sailor.

Not only that, the team was starting to band together. They had some great ideas to implement, and while there were still items that needed to be nailed down, she felt confident they'd get to where they needed to be.

Now she just had to work like crazy to ensure they reached that vital place by the time they returned to Newport. *We'll get there. We have to.*

"Wow," she said, almost tripping over her feet as they turned onto the street with the gingerbread houses. The colorful exteriors and decorative trim were almost eclipsed by the myriad of glowing lanterns. So many beacons in the dark, a kaleidoscope of colors and designs. It felt as if they'd stepped into a fairytale, and Danae sucked in an awestruck breath. "You were right. It's beautiful at night."

Instead of saying "I told you so" like he could've done, Josh simply smiled down at her. It lit her up from the inside out, giving the multicolored lanterns a run for their money.

They kept a casual pace as they strolled along, and Danae paused in front of a white house with scrolling pink trim and posts done up in pink-and-white candy cane stripes. "It's like we've stepped into Candy Land."

Josh groaned, and Danae scrunched up her eyebrows.

"Wow. I've never heard that kind of reaction to candy."

"It's more about the game," Josh said with a chuckle. "My sister Jane is ten years younger than I am, and she was *obsessed* with Candy Land. She'd demand I play with her, and naturally, if she didn't win, she'd have a meltdown, so I went along with every weird rule she came up with. Then, around the time she was in Kindergarten, she insisted we play Candy Land for real, draped candy necklaces on me, and declared me King Candy. I'd have to sit still while she fought every stuffed animal in her room to save me, and she had so, so many stuffed animals."

Affection swirled through Danae, and her heart went pitter patter. "That's pretty much the most adorable story I've ever heard."

Josh shook his head, but his features went soft and reminiscent. "I'd always get in trouble for eating the necklace before she"—he made air quotes—"'saved' me. Half the time it was just so I could breathe. Those things were tight."

Danae laughed, imagining a teenage Josh wearing a candy necklace and playing with his little sister. Seriously, how could she not swoon over that? "Does she live in Newport, too?"

"Basically—my entire family relocated to the suburbs, so they're not too far. I met with her the night before leaving for this trip, and she informed me I'm gonna be an uncle."

"Aww. Congratulations."

"As you saw with my marshmallow, patience isn't my strong suit. Seeing the baby will be cool and all, but I'm counting down the months until he or she is old enough to go sailing. It'll be nice to have a co-captain, so when I'm old, I can doze while they do all the work."

She was already psyched for how much fun that kid was going to have with their uncle. Being on this trip reminded her of the skills Dad had taught her on the boat: patience, and being able to react under pressure, and preparing for every scenario—at sea anyway—and gratitude filled her that Dad had taken her along.

Josh shifted into tour-guide mode, telling her about the tabernacle that had been built in the mid-1800s. People would come with tents so they could immerse themselves in a week of preaching and religion. Eventually, they erected the tiny cottages.

"A lot of these houses have been in their families for centuries," Josh said, "and most of the lanterns are handmade. Somc are a decade or two old."

Danae paused to study an illuminated blue umbrella with painted-on cherry blossoms. The couple on the porch greeted them from their rocking chairs, and Danae lifted her hand in a wave. "Your home and the lanterns are lovely." She stepped a bit closer so she wouldn't be in the way of people who wanted to continue down the sidewalk. "Do you get tired of lighting everything?"

"It's really just the summer and early fall," the woman said. "I look forward to it, actually—it's like a celebration every night. We get to connect with our neighbors and meet the tourists and newcomers to the island. It's always been a tight-knit community, and it draws us even closer together."

The cheeriness in the woman's voice transferred to Danae and settled in her soul. She wished the friendly couple a goodnight and strolled on, basking in the glow of the lights.

As they reached the end of the loop, she couldn't help taking one last glance. "I was thinking how nice it'd be if every community had something like this to bond them. Then it hit me that that's exactly what Mr. Barton wanted—it was all part of his grand scheme, or whatever. He was in the Navy and he said there was nothing like being in close quarters on a ship to learn about people and how to work with them."

"True. Even when I charter trips that are only a few days, I always discover interesting facts about the people onboard. Once you learn more about people and what makes them tick, it becomes easier to get along with them." He nudged her to the far edge of the sidewalk to avoid a group of boisterous college kids. "I still spend most of my days and nights alone on my own ship, though."

"And look how well you get along with yourself," Danae teased, and his laugh vibrated through the air and settled squarely in her solar plexus.

Josh ran his fingertips across his whiskered jaw. "I meant more that I'm not sure I could do it for months and months. I need my space and alone time."

She nodded, wondering how to take that. Was he hinting that he wasn't interested in a relationship? If that was the case, she needed to stifle the crush she was developing on him before it got out of control.

Logic had gone on a bit of a vacation, caught up as she was in the fairytale outing. As it reawakened, it dawned on her that she should be shutting those types of feelings down anyway. This was a business trip. Her entire marketing strategy needed tweaking and unanimous approval. She had big milestones to hit, such as keeping her job title and launching a new campaign, and that was only the tip of the iceberg as far as her goals for the year.

As it was, she had way too much to do in the next four days, and flirting with an unavailable sailor was so not in the plans.

Chapter Fifteen

DANAE STUDIED THE HALF-MADE SAILBOAT on the table in front of her. "Maybe if we tape a bunch of toothpicks together, it'd be enough to hold the sail?"

Josh happened to come down the cabin stairs as she'd posed her question. "Sounds like a puny mast."

Over breakfast, when she'd announced they were going to stray from her reworked itinerary to put one of the original team-building activities back in, everyone else on the boat had gaped at her.

"What?" she'd said. "I can be flexible. I figured we could use this time to do the 'Use what you have' challenge before our big meeting. It entails grabbing items we can find onboard to build our own sailboats. The only hard rules are that they have to have a sail, and they have to float. Oh, and naturally you can't use actual parts of the ship, because we'd like to keep ourselves afloat, too."

No one had uttered a word, and she'd been so sure the moment was going to go differently that she began rethinking her rethinking all over again. "But if everyone wants to have a meeting instead, I guess I'll grab my notebook and—"

"The challenge," her coworkers had yelled, practically in unison.

From there, they'd split into two groups—boys versus girls—and the ticking timer on the table signaled that Danae and her team only had four minutes left. Not enough time to banter with Josh right now, regardless of his being correct about the toothpicks being too puny.

Technically, she was still working out how talk to him, since last night she'd decided she should refrain from any activities that might lead to falling for him. Fun conversations were fine, but anything close to flirty was a no-go.

"Are you spying on us for the boys?" Paige asked, blocking Josh's view of their sailboat. Currently, their crafted-together vessel resembled something that would sink if someone looked at it the wrong way. "How's their boat coming along?"

Josh lifted his hands in the air. "I only came to grab a bottle of water. Since I'm the judge, I'm remaining nice and impartial."

Danae roused her competitive side, focusing on her desire to win until all cylinders were firing. "Come on, ladies. Surely we can find something that'd be sturdy enough to hold up a sail. Just remember, it has to float, or it won't count."

The bottom had been fashioned out of paper plates since, sadly, they'd used all of the paper bowls for cereal this morning. At least they were the sturdier kind, so they had a shot at it floating for a while before it got too soggy.

"Best of luck," Josh said, saluting them with two fingers before heading up to the deck.

"Where's the cork from the wine bottle?" Paige asked, and she began shuffling through the items in the kitchen. Then she held it up with a battle cry.

"Genius," Vanessa said, and if they hadn't been in a rush, Danae would have doled out stickers. So far, the two of them had been working together rather well, and a thrill went through her belly at all the camaraderie.

My plan is working! It was why she'd thrown out the "boys versus girls" suggestion, casual in tone but a deliberate stratagem she'd developed in advance. It left her to referee Paige and Vanessa while they worked together. Better yet, she hadn't even had to pull out her metaphorical whistle.

Paige cut the cork into fourths and glued one to each corner of their square ship.

For the mast, they used a plastic spoon, and for the sail, they chose foil. Danae found her summertime fun-pack of stickers and decorated the sail with rainbows, smiling suns, and sandcastles. The timer rang, so unfortunately, they didn't have a chance to test it in the sink as they'd hoped to do.

"Time," Mark yelled down. "Bring up the boat so we can see you're not still working on it."

"You think it'll float?" Vanessa asked.

Paige carefully lifted it, balancing it in her palm. "There's only one way to find out."

As they got ready to "sail" their boats, Josh couldn't stop glancing at Danae. Last night had been amazing, and after walking her to the doorway of her cabin, he hadn't wanted to say goodnight.

While he rarely slept well on his chartered trips, too much occupying his thoughts, he'd slept like a rock last night, Danae's smile the last image on his mind.

Water sloshed over the sides of the cooler as Mark maneuvered it to the center of the deck for their contest, a puddle forming underneath the blue plastic.

Danae's gaze drifted up and met Josh's, and it felt like someone had hooked him up to battery cables. A shock of electricity, followed by the purr of a motor—in this case, his galloping heart.

His emotions had been set to high all morning, even before she'd announced the itinerary change. The sun was brighter, the air fresher, and the sway of the ship added an extra bounce to his step. Josh had even sacrificed half his bagel to feed a flock of seagulls, and the entire time he'd hoped Danae might just happen across him—he knew she'd love watching the birds bob for crumbs.

While his skeptical side warned it might be a bad idea to get too caught up in Danae Danvers, the fact that she was willing to bend made him think that maybe he'd give her a call after they arrived back in Newport. Maybe even ask her on an official date.

It was the first time he'd been open to the idea since his divorce. Scary, yet exciting.

"You wanna do the honors?" Franco asked.

"Is that even a question?" Mark squatted next to the dish towel they'd placed over their craft and, with a flourish, revealed their makeshift sailboat. "Ta-da!"

"Whoa," Paige said. "Their boat is giant compared to ours."

Vanessa withdrew the ladies' vessel from behind her back, forgoing the big reveal route. Paige was right—their ship seemed extra tiny as they placed it next to the one the guys had made.

Franco and Mark had packed a discarded water bottle with batteries and a couple of other random odds and ends—presumably to add weight—along the bottom. Then they'd used wooden skewers from their marshmallow roast and a plastic bag to fashion a mast and sails. Josh had seen this challenge done several times, and their boat looked to be one of the best-engineered, as far as sailing went.

No surprise, the one Danae and her team had constructed was the flashiest, prettiest one he'd seen, although he was relatively sure it'd be top heavy.

"It's not the size of the ship in the fight, it's the size of the fight in the ship," Danae said, rallying her team.

Mark squatted next to the water bottle ship and adjusted the plastic-bag sails. "Hate to break it to you, but our ship is packed full of fight."

Mark and Paige placed their ships in the water. As soon as they straightened and stepped closer to their groups, the two teams yelled instructions to their boats, like football coaches to their teams on the field.

"Go, go, go," Mark shouted, while Danae encouraged their ship to "Be strong."

As Josh had privately predicted, the ladies' boat capsized.

Danae sighed, and then put one arm over Vanessa's shoulder and the other around Paige. "Well, crookedly or not, at least it floats."

"Are you saying I should sail our ship on its side like that?" Josh joked, and Danae raised an eyebrow that promised she'd get him back for that remark.

He could hardly wait.

The guys' boat floated serenely along, the sail catching the breeze and propelling it to the other end of the cooler. Mark crouched and blew a breath that filled the sail and sent it rushing to the other side.

Then he straightened and held his hand up to Franco for a high-five. "That was all you, man. Twisting that bag to form rope was genius."

"You're the one who pointed out that it needed extra weight to keep it from capsizing," Franco said.

"A tip that we could've used, clearly." Danae glanced at her team. "Our boat's beautiful, though, and I enjoyed building it."

"Me too," Vanessa said, and Paige echoed the sentiment.

Danae stepped between Mark and Franco, gripped their wrists, and lifted their arms in the air, as if they'd won a boxing match.

"Congratulations to Mark and Franco, the winners of the 'Use what you have' challenge."

The two men bowed before breaking into over-the-top celebratory gestures. Everyone cheered and laughed, the atmosphere happy and light, and best of all, vastly different than the first day.

"Do you mind if I tinker with your boat, ladies?" Mark asked, already reaching for the watercraft. "See if we can't get it to float?"

The three women agreed they were fine with it, as long as they also got to be part of it. Franco gathered the glue and crafting supplies, and the entire group plunked themselves down on the deck and worked until both boats could float.

Danae glanced up and cocked her head. "Josh, don't just stand there. Come build a boat so you'll have one to race, too."

Josh had seen his fair share of team-bonding activities during corporate retreats. He appreciated CEOs who rewarded their employees and pushed them to grow, but a lot of it came down to the people themselves and how willing they were to work.

On day one, he'd had his doubts about this group. Over the past couple of days, though, they'd cemented themselves as one of his favorites. Sure, it helped that he was becoming more and more taken with their CMO, but overall, they were a solid group of people.

Even Mark, as much as it bothered him to admit it.

If Josh had worked with a team like theirs, he might not have hated his cubicle days quite so much—not that he'd return to that life for all the money in the world.

Still, as he sat in the center of hubbub, creating boats out of what most people would consider garbage, he thought it'd been a while since he'd had this much fun on any of his chartered journeys.

Chapter Sixteen

Paige fiddled with the lens of the projector until the image on the wall opposite the kitchen table sharpened. Blurred letters and images took shape, including the bolded title: Five-Year Marketing Plan for Barton Boating Company. Not just a boat, but a lifestyle.

"As you can see, I've kept a lot of Danae's original structure and goals in place." Yesterday afternoon, Paige had asked Danae if she would be comfortable emailing her the five-year plan so she could fiddle with it. "The main thing I changed up was padding each item for more flexibility. Leaving us free to jump on an opportunity, regardless of whether it's one we've planned on for a year, a couple of months, or last minute."

The screen briefly went dark as Paige crossed in front of the projector. She walked over to the document on the wall, pointing as she continued explaining the edits she'd made. "I also created a category for each department, so that once every quarter, everyone can try something new. Whether it's an event, a new ad placement, or a social media push. That way, each department gets a chance to experiment, grow, and improve."

Pride bubbled up inside of Danae, along with a fervency she hadn't experienced when she'd been creating the original version. Paige's changes came from a viewpoint Danae never would've tapped into. "Wow. It's super impressive."

"Well, you provided the very detailed framework, and that made it much easier to work with. I've always been better at spinning and tweaking stories than creating them. Thus, the career in PR." A modest yet gleeful giggle escaped Paige, a new side of her emerging.

Mark added that he liked the flexibility, along with the idea of experimenting here and there. "Gives everyone some freedom within the structure."

Paige turned to Vanessa. Danae automatically flinched, hoping the progress they'd made building a miniature sailboat wasn't about to be undone. "As we were traveling around Martha's Vineyard, I spent a lot of time on Trendster and Quest Obsessed. The way the apps are set up is brilliant. I found myself rushing to check in at each place and upload videos so I could earn stickers."

Dang it, I totally forgot. Although I still prefer physical stickers.

Paige asked Franco if he would press the button to advance to the next slide, which showed a side-by-side comparison of the two apps and their lists of suggested activities. "Both apps have running bucket lists for places you *just have to go* and things you *have to see.* And I realized we could work that into our own marketing tactics."

At her signal, Franco moved to the next slide. A bucket list appeared on the wall, one that included family vacations, riding the oldest carousel in America, and deep-sea fishing. The very last bullet point said "own a Barton Boat."

"Then, we flip it." Another click, and the list onscreen changed so that "Own a Barton Boat" was the first bullet point. "Purchasing one of our boats is what will allow you to travel to these destinations and do these things."

"I love that," Vanessa said, and judging from the dropped jaws and raised eyebrows, Danae wasn't the only one surprised by her approval of something Paige had presented. "It'll also give more purpose to the images and videos I've been capturing to post online. A target, so to speak. Along with a call to action."

Franco chimed in to say he could set up a VIP membership on the website. "We can have running lists to send to those members, and a place where they can upload their own bucket items."

"We could also provide incentives for people who post about their adventures on our Barton boats," Vanessa said. "We'll cheer them on as they complete their bucket lists, and they'll be boosting our social media and publicity reach in a way that comes across as natural and effortless. The boats will essentially sell themselves to their families and friends."

Danae asked Franco to go back to the first slide again. Since she'd practically memorized the plan she'd proposed, it was easy enough to see the modifications. Whether or not Danae liked it, life and the pace people lived it was forever changing. Same as the market, and if she had her way, eventually their target demographic.

Not that she wasn't grateful for Barton's clientele, but if they widened their reach, they could unearth new consumers. She'd always viewed change and risk as enemies. If she could find a way to embrace them in a lower-risk way, it would help the business *and* her nerves. Win, win.

"Having everyone's perspective has made

this version so much stronger," Danae said. Relief also coursed through her, along with a silent plea that everyone might actually agree on this strategy. "Everyone in favor of going forward with this edition, say aye."

One by one, everyone added their ayes.

"Yay, I'm so excited!" In addition to bouncing in her seat, this time Danae added a quick golf clap. "Now that we have an approved five-year plan, we can really dig in and get the ball rolling on our new campaign."

Danae flipped to the page of stickers in her planners, searching for the perfect one. The multicolored HOORAY! caught her eye, so she peeled it off and placed it next to the meeting they'd just wrapped up.

Twenty minutes later, they had reached Nantucket Island and were seated on a gorgeous sandy beach, soaking up the sunshine and fresh air.

Danae handed out the sub sandwiches and salads she'd purchased at the market near the marina. She tossed a pile of condiment packets in the middle, along with bags of chips.

Ugh, pickles. The sandwiches had been wrapped in cellophane, so she'd snagged several and hoped for the best.

One by one, she picked off the offensive green circles. Biting into a sandwich or burger with pickles was like discovering that the brown bits in your cookie were raisins instead of chocolate chips.

"Wait. Are you...?" Josh frowned at the pile, and she thought maybe they offended him as much as they offended her. "You're removing the pickles?"

"Yeah, they're disgusting. I'm trying not to think about how they touched my food, or I'll go to take a bite, and that'll be all I taste."

"They're my favorite."

Danae made a sour face. "Ew."

"More for me, then." Josh opened up his sandwich and piled her pickles on top of the ones already covering the ham and cheese, while she added mayo to her sub and reassembled it. Then he took a giant bite and added an over-the-top *mmm*.

"Hey, maybe if you cook them a special way like you did the fish, Danae will eat them," Vanessa said with a laugh.

"Hard pass. It's not just the fermented cucumbers I object to. It's—"

"Vinegar," Mark supplied. "She can't stand the smell or the taste."

"Growing up, my mom used it as a cleaner. I'd come home and the entire house would reek."

Mark grabbed a napkin and wiped his mouth. "Remember when you refused to add it to your Easter egg dye, even though the instructions required it?" He chuckled. "Her eggs were so sad-looking because none of the colors took. They just looked dirty."

Danae laughed as well. "We went to Mark's parents' and none of the kids wanted to find, much less touch my eggs." She'd forgotten about that. Her distaste for vinegar, not so much.

After lunch, as they were cleaning up so they could head to their next destination, Vanessa stepped up to Danae and held open a trash bag. "So?" she whispered as Danae tossed the garbage inside the bag. "What's the deal with you and Josh?"

Unable to help herself, Danae glanced over her shoulder. Josh was shaking sand off the blanket they'd sat on, and a flutter went through her stomach as she took him in. As casually as she could, she shrugged one shoulder. "It's...I...There's not a deal. He's nice. A good sailor, too."

"There's nice, and then there's sharing a blanket and picking at each other's food. Seemed like a couple kind of move."

Oh no. Her stomach plummeted down to her toes. She was working so hard to stifle her attraction for Josh and remain professional, but if Vanessa had noticed...Was everyone else aware of it and speculating about them as well?

Hello, you both disappeared at the same time last night. Hardly a shock that people might assume there's something going on... "We like different things, so it worked out during lunch. That's all."

Vanessa's *mm-hmm* matched the skepticism in her features. She even propped a fist on her hip. "Okay, well then, how about the vibe between you and Mark?"

In spite of everyone else's being well out of earshot, Danae kept her voice low. "There's no vibe. He and I have a history, that's all. I'm sure you heard that we used to date."

"Yes, and I noticed the weird tension between you two in the office when I first arrived. But over the last few days, I've started to wonder if there's more to it than history. Something closer to interest."

Funny how many shared memories had come up on this trip. How well Mark knew her in a lot of ways. Josh might not know her as well, but he challenged her more than any other guy ever had. Whether that was a good or bad thing changed by the day, although after last night, they'd formed a sort of truce that—she crossed her fingers—might prevent future clashes.

Not that there was any reason to compare the two men, or that it was a competition. More like a casual observation that she would tuck in her pocket and ponder later. Possibly add to the list of what she would or would not want once she was in a better position to date.

Which is not right now, remember?

In order to keep herself from obsessing about Josh or Mark or anything else, she raised her voice and asked, "Who's ready to go see the seals?"

A cluster of seals lounged in the sun-dried sand, snoozing away. Some of them had their bellies up, while others cuddled together. A few still had their back ends in the tide, as if their upper halves had touched the warm sand and they couldn't make it any farther.

During his corporate days as a desk monkey, Josh would have experienced jealousy over the sea creatures' carefree lifestyle. Nowadays, he wanted to flash them a thumbs-up and tell them to keep on living the good life.

As they passed near one of the pods, a few of the seals began barking away, warning them that they were nearby, but not going to move. "You're a little sharp, buddy," Franco said to the closest seal, and Vanessa laughed. Evidently, the round, blubbery seal was a fan of the attention, because it barked even louder, to the ear-ringing point.

Vanessa flinched and covered the ear closest to the warbling, blubbery sea mammal. "I guess that's why they chose to have a mermaid sing instead of having Prince Eric fall in love with a seal. Although they did come in handy during that almost-wedding on the boat."

"Hey, if a crab can sing, who's to say a seal can't learn?" Franco joked.

The two of them laughed more, and began creating an entire musical. One of the seals was desperately in love with a killer whale who felt the same, but it was a whole Romeo and Juliet situation where their parents and society would never allow it.

Unable to help himself, Josh looked at Danae to see her reaction. As expected, she was beaming at her coworkers, and it sent pure liquid sunshine through him. The more he learned about Danae, the more he wanted to unearth. If only he could ignore the alarm ringing in the back of his head, warning him that going deeper would only result in drama and future pain.

"Do you see that?" Danae gestured to the duo in front of them. "With Vanessa and Franco weaving their tragic fairytale, every single person on my team has now connected."

Josh held up his fist. "Rock on."

Danae blinked at it for several seconds, as if she'd never seen a fist before. "Oh, um, didn't you hear? Fist bumps are out."

"Silly me, not keeping up with celebratory gestures." Slowly he lowered his arm. "So, how do I congratulate you, then?"

Danae frowned, and now he was wondering if her happiness was closer to deliriousness. Despite being the one who'd left *him* hanging, her expression implied she was upset about it. "Actually, I want a fist bump. I don't care what the cool kids are doing. I'd rather be an overly organized nerd any day. I'm pretty sure the window for us to be considered 'kids' passed a decade or so ago anyway."

Josh shook his head and clucked his tongue. "This just keeps getting worse and worse. First you imply I'm not cool, next you're implying I'm old. *Again.*" He firmly crossed his arms. "Last time I offer you congratulations."

"No, wait, I'm sorry." Danae jumped in front of him, blocking his way, and brought out the pouty lower lip. "I need a redo." She gave his arm a tug, loosening it from its crossed position.

After making her stew for a couple of seconds, he halfheartedly held out his fist.

"Like you mean it," she said with a tilt of her head.

He plastered a goofy grin on his face and repeated, "Rock on."

"Boom," she said, bumping her fist to his. Then she exploded it, eyeing him until he did the same.

Seemingly satisfied, she pivoted around, more skipping than walking. "I was so worried, but it's all coming together. It looks like I'm going to keep my promotion, which leaves me a teensy-weensy amount of wiggle room to breathe and relax and..." She exhaled like they had in yoga, one long whoosh of air.

"And improvise?"

"Let's not get too ahead of ourselves," she said, and while he didn't want to examine why too closely, he liked that she'd used "ourselves." Suddenly she came to a stop, her high-pitched squeal similar to the noise she'd made at the alpaca farm. Which keyed him into the fact that she'd come across something she considered cute.

Down the way, a speckled harbor seal wiggled across the sand, jigging the entire way, and settled next to a seal Josh assumed was its mom. Danae retrieved her phone and took several pictures, and Josh dug his own phone out of his pocket and snapped a couple as well. Something to show George and Nancy.

Just before he put away his phone, he lifted it higher and captured Danae's smiling profile. The sun hit just right, the cresting waves and seals providing a stunning backdrop.

Between last night's amazing stroll and her decision to do a challenge he'd put on the itinerary, a big old soft spot was forming. Problem was, he was getting sucked in by Danae. By her smile and her laugh and her swinging ponytail and...

Man, she's pretty.

Was it so bad that he wanted the ability to pull up her smile on his phone screen once in a while? To consider using the image to cheer him up during lonely nights and long trips?

"I really wish we could pet them," Danae said, yanking him out of his jumbled thoughts. "But don't worry, I'm a rule follower."

Josh bit back his laugh, so she wouldn't accuse him of mocking her, slightly accurate or not. "Pretty sure that last sentence was unnecessary."

Her jaw dropped. "Ah! We can't all be rebels like you."

Sure. That was him. A rebel. One who wanted to ignore the complications that would inevitably rise, grab her hand, and hold it.

He probably should've kept the distance he'd originally attempted to maintain on this walk. No worries, though. He could practice self-control.

"Aww, check out that one. His eyes are so big." Danae knelt down in the sand, several yards away. "Hi, dude. Or dudette."

As if the seal could understand her, it barked back.

Pretty soon, everyone on the beach had come to watch Danae talk to the chatty seal. She mimicked its movements, and a couple of other seals scoot-jiggled their way over to see what all the ruckus was about. Ironic that Franco and Vanessa had just been talking about *The Little Mermaid*, because right now, Danae seemed to be auditioning for the role.

Eventually they said goodbye to the seals, who'd abandoned chatting for snoozing. They reached the last stretch before the lighthouse, a narrow strip of land with the harbor on one side and the Atlantic Ocean stretching out on the other.

"Hey, new marketing idea," Danae said, pausing in front of the mansions that lined the beach. While Josh was all about ocean views, he'd be too afraid to build here. It was only a matter of time until the strip of land disappeared, the way it had in Martha's Vineyard a handful of years ago. "Door-to-door boat sales."

Mark, Vanessa, Paige, and Franco glanced at the houses and began discussing which boat they'd pitch based on the exterior design of their houses.

"Wow, check out that old sailboat," Vanessa said. "Looks like it washed ashore, and they left it to die."

"It just needs a bit of polish," Josh said.

Danae blinked at him. "A bit?"

Josh didn't want to violate any trespassing laws, but he wandered a few yards closer. "I bet it's a seventies model. I bought a similar boat a couple of years ago. *Solitude* was awfully beat up when I bought her, so I spent the last year restoring her. She turned out beautifully, if I do say so myself."

"*Solitude*? Sheesh, why didn't you just name it sadness?"

"Hey," he said with a laugh. "I like my private slice of heaven. If the whim hits me, I can head out onto the ocean for days or weeks. Leave my worries behind. Change my destination. Begin a new adventure."

Danae wrinkled her nose in that adorable way she did when she was processing. "I don't think I could handle that much quiet."

No, quiet wasn't a word he'd use to describe Danae. While he'd become accustomed to the peaceful silence of living on a ship by himself, he had a feeling that once this journey was over, he would miss the hubbub.

He might even miss Danae bouncing to her feet in the crowded kitchen to recite the itinerary for the day.

What a silly thought. He'd be fine. Same as always. There were other people at the marina if he did get lonely.

Although Danae wouldn't be one of them, and a pang thumped deep inside his chest at the thought. "Someday you'll have to come to the marina and check out my pride and joy." Josh realized everyone else was still around as well, and he hadn't meant to exclude them, so he tore his gaze off Danae and glanced around. "All of you."

The idea of five extra people onboard his tiny ship made air leak out of his lungs. Surely they wouldn't show up all at once, though.

Thinking of Danae aboard *Solitude*, pitching in with the sails as he steered, on the other hand, caused a flush of excitement. He'd like to take her for a quick sail on *Solitude* sometime. See how much fun they could have with absolutely no schedule whatsoever.

"When did you christen her?" Danae asked, and the entire group focused on him, waiting for the answer.

Josh swiped a hand through the air. "Eh. I didn't do the whole christening ceremony."

Danae gasped in horror, and she wasn't the only one. You would've thought he'd told them his ship had an enormous leak. "Josh, that's not okay," Danae said. "Not only is it tradition, you'll anger the sea gods. They'll think you have underhanded motives if you don't do the renaming ritual."

Vanessa's eyes flew wide. "Whoa, whoa, whoa. We can't have that. It's been a lovely trip, and I'd like for it to keep going that way."

"Danae's kidding," Josh said.

"Danae doesn't kid," Mark countered, and Josh had to work to not glare at the guy. All day, the entitled jerk had been making a point of showing how well he knew Danae. Mark wasn't the one she'd been out with last night, though, was he?

Instead of the sense of smugness Josh had expected, conflicting emotions tugged at him. As much as he'd enjoyed their time together and Danae's awe at the beauty he'd shown her, he still couldn't decide if spending time alone together had been a good idea.

"Not about this," Danae said. "You need to have a christening ceremony ASAP, Josh."

He was fairly sure she'd said his name more in the last few minutes than she had for the entire trip, and while he liked hearing it spilling from her lips, he was done being the center of attention. He also needed some of that space he'd mentioned to pull himself together. "It's not a big deal," he insisted, but Danae was already shaking her head.

"It's a huge deal. And we're gonna fix it."

Chapter Seventeen

As Mr. Barton had suggested before they left, Danae had made reservations at one of the fanciest restaurants in Nantucket Island to celebrate finalizing the business plan. She'd included instructions to bring a couple of nicer outfits, and everyone was all dressed up.

The overhead lights in the restaurant caught the silver overlay on Danae's pink dress as she led the group inside. Thanks to her hair having been in a ponytail earlier, she'd gone with an updo to hide the bump, although she'd loosened a couple curls to frame her face. She'd also switched from her regular bag to her clutch, because glitter. The ankle straps on her matching heels made her feel like a sparkly ballerina, and she barely refrained from doing a spin.

Vaguely she'd realized previously that they were an attractive group of people, inside and out, but tonight, they shone. Even Josh wore a black button-down shirt and a leather jacket, giving him a refined yet rugged edge that suited him. He'd mentioned he did have a tie if he *had* to wear one, and she'd responded that he looked nice enough without the tie. And he certainly did. She couldn't stop staring.

Once they were settled at their table, their drinks placed in front of them, it was time to choose entrees. Since the other side of the table knew what they wanted, Danae told them to go ahead, leaving her and Josh up last.

"Um..." Danae studied the two entrees she'd narrowed her options to. "I keep going back and forth between lobster or the filet mignon. Which do you recommend?"

"I was eyeing those as well," Josh said. "It's hard to beat a good steak, but the same could be said about lobster."

"Ah, you want the romantic meal." The waiter scribbled on his notepad, and Danae froze in place. She hadn't accidentally flirted with Josh, had she? She was struggling to draw lines. Even earlier, when he'd offered her a fist bump, she couldn't decide if it was the kind of move she should avoid. Then she'd felt like a jerk for rejecting it, and that was the perfect example of why she favored knowing what was going to happen in advance.

Danae skirted her fingers along the edge of the linen tablecloth at her thighs. "Oh, we're all on a work trip."

The waiter nodded. "Okay. I can put in an order for both of you to get that meal, but see this here?" He pointed at the last entree on the menu. "The romantic meal for two is less expensive, and you still get to try both."

"On two plates?" Danae asked, and the waiter scrunched his forehead.

"Yeah. Unless you want our chef to cram it on one."

Danae shook her head. "No. Two plates is good." Great. She could feel herself heating up, and her face was undoubtedly as pink as her dress.

In order to preserve what was left of her confidence, she changed the subject. "Okay, so let's talk guest list." She tapped her pen against her notebook, only halfway glancing at Josh. "Who do you want at your boat's christening party? Besides all of us, of course."

Once she'd explained the ceremony and how it ensured good fortune to the owner and crew, everyone helped convince Josh to perform one. So naturally they were coming, too.

Appetizers that included oysters, wild rice and smoked ricotta, and beef carpaccio—she wouldn't be touching that last one—arrived. They paused the conversation while two members of the waitstaff placed the plates on the table.

"You really don't need to go to all that trouble," Josh said.

"You probably don't know this about me, but I actually enjoy planning things."

A crooked smile slanted his lips. "Wow, I never would've guessed."

"Every improviser needs a planner. Someone to consider all the scenarios and be prepared, granting the impulsive person the freedom to change without ending up in trouble."

"I've survived so far."

"You're tempting the gods every day that ship's in the water without being properly christened. Someone back me up on this." Danae glanced around the table. Most everyone was nibbling on appetizers and sipping celebratory cocktails.

"I might not know much about the ceremony," Paige said. "But thanks to reading the *Odyssey*, I assure you that angering Poseidon is a bad idea. He didn't let that guy go home for so, so many years."

Danae placed her hand next to Josh's plate, drawing his attention away from his food. "Please let me do this for you. I won't be able to sleep worrying about you out there tempting fate."

Josh's features softened, and when his

eyes met hers, everything inside of her went gooey and warm. "You worry about me?"

"You are our captain. We should look at the calendar and choose a date." Danae flipped through her planner. "How's two weeks from tomorrow? Do you have any unprotected journeys scheduled before then?" The question hung in the air, time stuttering to a halt as she realized that setting up this event would mean seeing Josh even after this trip came to a close.

"Two weeks from tomorrow works for me."

Danae's stomach completed a full somersault. Before she could warn her brain not to get carried away, she was envisioning him standing on the deck of his restored boat, a crooked grin spreading across his face as she approached. "Don't you need to check your calendar first?" She twisted one of her curls around her finger, doing her best to not seem overeager.

"Oh, that's a good idea." Josh tapped a finger to his temple, and his eyes rolled toward the ceiling. "All clear."

She shook her head but couldn't hold back her smile. He could tease all he wanted. In fact, now she was picturing joking around as the two of them prepared his boat for the ceremony. Plus, she wasn't lying about how much she loved planning. "Does that work for everyone else?"

Everyone answered that it did, so Danae

penciled it in, along with the names Josh gave her.

Then she held out her open palm to him. "Hand me your phone, please." When he hesitated, she added a finger wiggle. "I just want to see for myself that it gets added to your calendar."

After acting like he was going to relinquish it, only to yank it away, at long last, he relented. She opened up his calendar, scheduled the christening, and set an alert the week before, two days before, and the day before.

One more for good measure. An alert for thirty minutes before, and she called it good and returned his phone to him. Her inner prankster laughed at how hard he'd roll his eyes and grumble during each and every alert.

Their entrées arrived, the aromas causing her mouth to water, and she slipped her planner in her bag so it wouldn't get food on it. No surprise, the many glowing reviews were spot on. The restaurant was every bit as good as they claimed.

After dinner, everyone split off to go sightseeing. Danae hung back to settle the check and enter it into her expense spreadsheet. She exited the restaurant, slightly disappointed that no one had waited for her.

Okay, mostly that Josh hadn't waited for her.

But then there he was, leaning against

the white railing. He straightened as she approached. "Hey," he said. "I figured it'd be best if we followed the buddy system. Even though you probably have at least three apps that could safely direct you back to the harbor."

"Is any app as safe as a personal guide who's familiar with the area, though?"

One side of his mouth kicked up. "Not if I'm the personal guide."

Together, they headed in the direction of the shore. With the sun dipping low in the horizon, the clouds were turning varying shades of orange and pink. Lights began clicking on across the city, a flash here and a glimmer there, tiny squares that glowed brighter the closer it got to dusk.

"For the record," Josh said, "Vanessa was going to wait for you until I informed her I would do the honors. Hope that's okay."

It meant Vanessa would be asking twenty questions tonight in their cabin, but too much happiness was coursing through Danae to care. "It's perfect."

Too late, she worried that had come out sounding too bold. She contemplated leaping into a discussion about the boat christening, but then her fingers and Josh's brushed together.

Her tongue stuck to the roof of her mouth, rendering her speechless.

With their arms loosely swinging and the narrow sidewalk, it wasn't like it was a big deal. Surely he wouldn't think she was making a move on him.

His fingers grazed hers again, and dozens of butterflies swirled inside her.

Josh curled her hand in his, nothing accidental about the move. In this moment, holding Josh's hand and nearing the beach around sunset, she wanted to be bold.

Her heart ticked out of control as she spread her fingers apart and laced them through his. It galloped faster as he tightened his grip so their palms perfectly aligned.

None of this had been in the plans. While it felt like free-falling, it was all thrill, that instant when you let go and give in to gravity and its pull. It didn't happen very often—especially in her life—so she shut off her overly analytical side in favor of embracing the here and now.

As they reached the beach and her pink heels sank into the sand, she bent, undid the ankle straps, and held the shoes in her free hand. Down shore, the light from the Brant Point Lighthouse flashed, nearly as pink as the sky behind it.

"Your dress matches the sky," Josh said. "It even glitters like the lights across the harbor."

For some reason, she lifted one side of her skirt and curtsied. Before she could try to explain the odd move, she caught sight of two glowing eyes. A few yards away, a cat prowled through clusters of white and pink flowers. An older woman stood at the edge of her lawn, shaking a box of treats and calling to the cat, who ran in her direction at the sound.

"Ooh, a black cat. Another good luck sign. Did you know that Irish sailors often adopted black cats for luck?" Danae paused, then rushed to fill the silence. "There were also all kinds of beliefs surrounding them. Like if they licked their fur against the grain, it meant a hailstorm. Sneezes meant rain, and if the feline was extra frisky that day, it meant wind." Obviously she was more nervous than she'd realized, because now she was rambling. Amusement filled Josh's expression, along with a dash of *aren't you adorable.* "Again, I'm not superstitious. People make their own luck. With hard work."

"For someone who's not superstitious, you sure have a lot of information stored in your brain about good and bad omens."

Danae dug her toes in the sand, and memories flooded her brain. "My dad was superstitious, especially about sailing." Fishing was a waiting game, one where it could often be hours between bites, so he'd recite folktales and fables, along with a few stories she was sure were urban legends. "He used to have this chant, too. Everyone thinks that 'yo, ho, ho,' came from pirates, but the *Song of the Volga Boatmen*, which includes the lyrics 'Yo, heave ho,' was originally a Russian folksong."

"Oh, I'm going to need to hear the chant."

She vehemently shook her head. "No way. I'm getting embarrassed just thinking about it. Luckily, when I was a little kid, I didn't think about people seeing or hearing."

"I think we could all use more of that attitude."

"Says the impulsive guy."

He shrugged, and she fiddled with the strap of her heels, looping them through her clutch so she only had to focus on carrying one thing. "I like to pretend to be above signs and omens, but apparently my brain stored them simply to mess with me."

"When clearly that's my job," Josh said, taking her hand again, and she flashed a smile at him.

"You're very good at it, by the way."

Josh removed his invisible hat and tipped it at her. "Happy to be of service."

The breeze caught her laugh and tossed it back at her, like a boomerang of joy, although had her laugh always been that high-pitched?

She breached the wet sand and waited as the water rushed forward to lap the shore. Although it seemed to want to stay for longer, it drifted away, taking sand and shell fragments with it, as if it were reluctant to say goodbye but couldn't stay any longer.

That was how she was beginning to feel every night when she had to say goodbye to Josh. How she felt about the fact that soon this trip would be over, and they'd have to part for even longer. At least now they would have the boat christening to look forward to.

"I wasn't so sure I believed in luck, either," Josh said, his voice quiet. Speculative. "But after this trip, I might reconsider my stance."

Optimism bubbled up, leaving her steps that much lighter. Regardless of how many times her brain told her it was a bad idea to cross lines with the handsome, funny and kind sailor, her heart refused to listen. "Then it's an extra good thing we scheduled your boat-christening ceremony. From there, your luck's only going to get better and better."

This time she got the wide smile with the crinkled eyes. Instead of continuing to question herself, she decided to go ahead and let her heart set the course.

As she'd learned in today's meeting, sometimes giving yourself room for risk meant a better, brighter plan, with an even more promising future.

Chapter Eighteen

FOR A GUY WHO WASN'T usually an overthinker, Josh was overthinking his head off.

If that was a thing that could be done. He'd ask Danae, but since she was the object of his hyperactive thoughts, it seemed like a conflict of interest.

Not to mention embarrassing. A grown man afraid of an attractive woman.

Which was ridiculous. What was there even to think about? Perfect nights like this one didn't come along very often, and much like sailing, they required reacting. Taking risks. Seizing the moment.

After their fingers had accidentally brushed, the urge to hold on had overwhelmed him. So he'd initiated the next contact, capturing her hand in his without fully thinking through the move. He supposed it meant that subconsciously, he'd ruled in favor of savoring the time they had left together on this trip.

After all, it wouldn't be as difficult to say goodbye now that they had plans to see each other again.

More than that, it was becoming more difficult to avoid his feelings for Danae than to face them. His pulse kicked up a notch as he dragged his thumb over Danae's knuckles. Her hand was so much smaller than his, her skin so soft. It had been a long time since he'd had a woman on his arm, and as they neared the wharf, longing looped itself around his heart.

Danae stopped just short of the wooden planks and pivoted to face him. The clouds behind her had turned more purple than pink, their rippled reflections gleaming across the surfacc of the water, until the entire place glittered as much as Danae's dress, earrings, shoes, and purse. "Tonight was fun. Thank you for being my escort."

"I agree, and you're welcome," Josh said. He stepped closer, eradicating the foot or so of space between them. "I just realized I never told you how beautiful you look, and that's completely unacceptable, because *wow*."

In the dim light, he could barely make out the pink that rose to her cheeks, but the slight smile and way she shyly dipped her chin was a dead giveaway. "Thank you. As I told you when we left the ship, you also look very nice. I'd go so far as to say handsome."

She sunk her teeth into her lower lip, and just like that, his nerves calmed, like the sea before the storm. If he held up a microphone to his heart, however, it'd sound like thunder, one clap after another, nothing placid about it. The entire walk along the shore had felt like a dream, as if he had one foot in the real world and one foot in fairyland.

With Danae standing in front of him, her hand still curled inside his, there was no doubt in his mind that luck existed. Tonight, he was feeling extremely lucky.

"Talking about my dad and his superstitions brought back a lot of good memories." Danae tipped back her head and blinked at the enormous sky overhead. There were certain places in the world where the sky seemed bigger, and near the ocean was one of them. Partially because away from populous cities, there weren't as many lights and skyscrapers to interrupt the view. "One of the other things that always stuck with me were his lessons on the stars. Whenever we sailed at night, or even walking or driving somewhere, my dad would ask me to find Polaris.

"When I was two or three, I'd tell him I found it, only to point at a plane. Or a streetlight." A soft laugh escaped, the exquisite sound hanging the air between them. "He'd always kindly correct me and turn me in the right direction. He often warned me that if I set my sights on the wrong star, I'd find myself going in the wrong direction."

The first time she'd mentioned her father, she'd used a different, slightly disappointed tone. Tonight there was a fondness and a bit of that childlike wonder that people lost far too early, thanks to the bumps that came along with life.

Josh tightened his grip on her hand, affection and attraction melding and strengthening her elemental pull. "Even before my sailing days, I always had a fascination with finding the North Star, too."

Danae's grin widened, and speaking of stars, it felt as if he'd been suffused with stardust. "I guess I just exchanged the actual stars for stickers."

"Hey, a gold star's a gold star as far as I'm concerned."

With a sigh, she tilted her head toward the wooden planked walkway. "I suppose we should make our way back to the ship." From the sound of it, she was as reluctant to end the evening as he was.

As they stepped onto the wharf, Danae nudged him toward the middle. "I'm always wary of piers that don't have fences or rails. I feel like I'll suddenly trip and fall into the water."

"Some of us like a little danger," he teased. "Or perhaps it just makes it easier to fish off the sides."

"Big surprise, Mr. Improviser doesn't want guidelines or rails, even if they make him safer. Let me guess, getting knocked off and ending up going for a lovely swim would only feed your spontaneous nature."

He burst out laughing. "Not quite. When it comes to swimming, I'm all for planning—at a minimum, five minutes in advance. Enough time to shed my shoes at the very least. But if anyone knocked you in, rest assured, I'd jump in, shoes, jacket, and all."

"You'd better," she said with a smile, and he tugged her to a stop. She swallowed, and her eyes widened as they met his. "What are you doing? I'm warning you, if you even think of pushing me i—"

Josh cupped her cheek, and the rest of her sentence died on her parted lips. He took a couple of seconds to soak in the way the harbor lights lit up her profile, her sharp intake of breath, and the endless stretch of water behind her.

Sometimes life gave you perfect moments.

It was up to you whether or not you did something with them.

"I'm improvising," he whispered, using his thumb to tip up her chin. Time slowed, and his entire body hummed with emotions he thought he'd rid himself of long ago.

He dipped his head, and then there was a mere inch of space between his lips and hers.

She gripped his elbows, her fingers wrapping around them as she angled closer, and Josh closed his eyes as he lowered his mouth to—

"Danae. Hey, I've been looking for you. I even called your phone, but..."

Of course it was Mark.

Danae's eyes flew open, going from fluttering to panic mode, and Josh cursed her ex-boyfriend's timing. He couldn't help wondering if it was happenstance or purposeful.

Josh's arms complained as he lowered them to his sides, his entire body protesting at putting space between him and Danae. He longed to collect every wasted second and pile them together until he had a handful for the kiss he hadn't gotten to follow through on.

Although he couldn't call any of tonight's seconds a waste, not when he'd been completely captivated. What did Mark want? *Too bad, so sad, you missed out,* he wanted to tell the guy. *Now it's my turn, so get lost.*

Danae tucked a loose curl behind her ear and cleared her throat as she turned to address her ex. "I'm right here. What did you need?"

Mark glanced between them, and Josh silently encouraged him to say whatever it was so they could get their moment back.

"I told everyone how great you were at charades, so we thought we'd have game night." Mark gave Josh a smile too smug for his liking—not that he'd be a fan of anything of Mark's right now. "You're free to join us, if you'd like. Everyone else is onboard already, eager to get started."

"Well, guess we'd better not keep them waiting," Danae said, her voice a pinch higher than usual.

Josh didn't mind if they waited all night. He was the one who only got Danae for a little while. They could play games at the office.

Not in a million years would Danae ever do that, but couldn't they give her a few more minutes?

Wait, that wasn't long enough. Twenty minutes. No, more like an hour.

The fact of the matter was, he'd beg for one more minute all night long. Stifling a groan, Josh nodded. "Sure. Yeah. We'll be right there."

As if he hadn't spoken, Mark stepped up to Danae. "Are you cold? You look cold."

Before she could answer, the guy took off his suit coat and draped it over her shoulders. As if he was trying to mark his territory. What a jerk move. For one, Danae wasn't anyone's territory, least of all Mark's.

It hit Josh that he'd done the exact same thing with his own jacket the night they'd gone fishing...which left him without a leg to stand on, dang it.

"Uh, thanks," Danae said, too polite to refuse the gesture. She cast Josh one last glance, and then the three of them headed down the wharf and climbed onto a boat where there were suddenly too many people.

For the first time in the past couple of days, Josh missed *Solitude*. Both his boat, and his privacy. Only, if he had his way, he'd make room for one extra person onboard. She had blond hair, a sharp wit, and an amazing laugh.

Unfortunately, she was also walking away from him seconds after he'd made a move.

What are you doing?

Who asked a question like that? Especially after a romantic stroll?

Evidently, she did. The instant she'd blurted it out, Danae wished she could stuff it back in. Then she'd winced at how easily she could ruin a moment. Until Josh had replied, *I'm improvising*, and her heart had taken off, soaring all the way up to the sherbet-colored clouds in the sky.

As they stepped aboard the Fortune 703 Model, she glanced over her shoulder at Josh, imagining what would've happened if they'd had a few more minutes to themselves. Since they were about to be around her coworkers, though, she put on her best game face.

She shrugged out of Mark's jacket, thanking him again, in spite of how not-cold she'd been on the wharf. With Josh so close, his lips a mere breath from hers, she'd been pleasantly toasty, and her blood was still firing hot with the idea of everything that could've been.

What might be.

After all, they still had two and a half more days during which a whole lot could happen.

The entire team cheered as the awkward trio entered the main cabin, and she told herself to focus on how close everyone had grown and how much they'd accomplished.

By the time her turn to act out a clue came around, she had to overact a bit, so that no one would catch on to the fact that she was *this close* to falling head over fabulous heels for the captain of their ship.

Chapter Nineteen

MOST DAYS, DANAE COULD HARDLY wait to disembark and get to their destination. Cape Cod was one of the places she'd been most looking forward to, too. Yet after their idyllic morning sail, when they'd seen two whales, a big part of her yearned to return to the Atlantic.

"You okay?" Josh asked. He paused at the mouth of the wharf, gripped one of the posts, and gave it a good shake. "Not only do they have railing here, it's sturdy."

Danae smiled at him. "I appreciate your testing it for me. Although thanks to my special skills, I could still trip and fall through the gaps in the rope." She cast one glance at the ocean and then continued down the wooden walkway. "It's just...In all my time sailing, I've never seen whales. To see one of them come out of the water like that was amazing."

"Do my ears deceive me, or are you saying that you're happy about an unplanned surprise?"

She flattened her lips and gave Josh her best glare.

He held up his hands in supplication. "Don't shoot the captain."

"That's not even a saying."

"It should be. How else would people get where they're going?"

"Um, hello. Experienced sailor right here." Danae lifted her thumbs and pointed at herself.

"Oh, so I'm totally replaceable? Is that what you're saying?"

She almost nodded and continued the teasing, but the thought of this trip—of being on the sailboat without him—scraped at her. "I'd never say that."

His smile faded, a tender expression taking its place.

"Come on, slowpokes," Vanessa called over her shoulder, adding a hurry-up gesture. "I've been waiting for this shopping excursion for six days! Trendster ranked the top ten boutiques in the nation, and one of them happens to be here. Perhaps none of you fully understands how cool that is, but I do."

"After you," Josh said, sweeping an arm in front of Danae, and she quickened her pace to catch up to Vanessa.

Mark gave her yet another strange look. There wasn't the twinge of animosity anymore. Over the past few days, it had veered closer to curiosity. He'd also stuck fairly close since interrupting her and Josh last night, and she wasn't sure what that meant.

Had he known he was interfering? Or had he put the almost-kiss together too late?

Worse, what if he was thinking it was unprofessional of her to go around kissing the ship's captain?

A likely option, since she was having that same internal debate. Granted, good guys like Josh, who were age-appropriate, funny, and handsome, didn't come around often. Still, what was she thinking, getting swept away like that?

Last night during their walk along the beach, she'd been experiencing far too many butterflies to think clearly. This morning, her anxieties had woken up before her body fully had. It wouldn't cast her in a very good light if it got back to Mr. Barton that she'd been flirting instead of doing her job. What if Mark tried to use the information to prove he'd be a better chief marketing officer?

Surely he wouldn't use that against her. They had their boundaries and their truce, and he'd never been vindictive. It wasn't like spending an evening with Josh left her incapable of doing her job, either.

"I seriously adore you, Danae," Vanessa said, interrupting her internal dilemma, "but don't think I won't leave you behind. Then, when I show up at the office in fabulous new duds, I'll remind you that you were moving too slow to snag all the amazing steals and deals." She swung her pointed finger in a vague circle. "That goes for everybody."

The entire group snickered, even Paige. But they also walked faster.

Most of the shops on Commercial Street were colorful two-story buildings with dozens of people peering through windows, checking out merchandise, and ordering food. From the looks of things, the businesses were on the ground floor and the owners lived in or rented out the second.

"I love old architecture," Danae said. "I can never tell whether they belong to the Victorian or Georgian era, or why we classify houses by monarchs in England in the first place."

The seashell shop to their right had giant, beautiful shells for sale, along with every type of jewelry that could be made from them. Next up was a yellow-and-green house where they made fudge. Another place, kitty corner from the intersection, had been painted in rainbow colors, almost as if the building had been tattooed from top to bottom. Just beyond that sat a shop with pale wood and giant windows.

Between the mishmash of styles and colors, the entire street felt as diverse as the people strolling along it.

Finally, they reached the boutique Vanessa had been excitedly jabbering on about. The guys in the group glanced inside and all pulled the same bitter face—good to know it was universal.

Danae stifled her laughter and then decided to keep on extending the olive branch, just to ensure things between her and her ex remained cordial. "Mark, did you see that puzzle shop? It's bright pink and just down the way."

Right in front of her eyes, he transformed into a kid. He swung his head from side to side, an excited gleam flickering when he spotted the store.

"Shall we take an hour to explore? Then we can meet up at a restaurant for lunch?"

Vanessa commented that she wasn't sure an hour would be long enough, before eventually agreeing to the plan, as well as a spot for lunch. With that checked off her list, Danae attempted to make eye contact with Josh. She still wasn't sure what to do about the burgeoning crush she had on him, yet she didn't want things to be weird or for him to think she was avoiding him.

Before she could figure out which expression could wordlessly convey all that,

Vanessa clamped onto her wrist. Next thing she knew, she was being propelled into the boutique.

"Did you find some steals and deals, then?" Josh jerked his chin at the bag hanging from Danae's bent elbow.

"I was told so, anyway. I was also told the clothes looked good on me, so..." Danae shrugged. "Guess we'll see."

"I said *amazing*." Vanessa peered at Danae over the top of her sunglasses, the four overflowing bags she was carrying crinkling together. "If you're gonna quote me, darling, quote me correctly." The two women shared a smile, and then Vanessa turned her grin on him. "I'm sure Josh would agree if he'd been there."

Josh had a feeling Danae didn't want her coworkers to know anything had happened between them, so he dodged. "Need me to take your bags, ladies?"

"You can save the chivalry for Danae. I'm reluctant to let go of my bags. Not that I don't trust you. It's just a lot to keep track of." Vanessa checked the time. "We have seven more minutes. I'm going to peek at that shop across the way really quick."

Josh watched her dart across the street

in case he needed to block cars, but she wove in and out like a New Yorker. Once she'd disappeared into the colorful old building, he turned to Danae. "Funny how she told me she trusted me, but not to keep track of a lot of bags."

A laugh spilled out of Danae, the sound soothing to his soul. He relieved her of her bag and offered his elbow. "Shall we stroll for seven minutes?"

She glanced around, confirming his theory about wanting to keep things on the down low, before hooking her hand in the crook of his arm. "Gotta burn off all the delicious food I've been eating somehow."

A couple of blocks down, they stumbled across a shop called Mad as a Hatter. "Ooh, this place seems promising," Danae said, squinting through the giant display window. There was an old bike, a chain curtain, and several logs. Each of those strange items had hats propped on or around them.

"You go ahead and I'll—"

Danae grabbed onto his wrist and tugged him toward the red door. "That's not how hat shops work."

As soon as they stepped inside, she scanned the shelves. She snagged a white fedora and plunked it on her head. "Thoughts?"

He tapped the brim. "I think Vanessa was right about you looking amazing."

Her resulting grin sent a jolt down his

spine. She hummed to herself as she continued to browse, and he followed after her like a smitten puppy.

"Ooh, I found the perfect one for you. Close your eyes." Using her body, she blocked the row of hats she'd been studying. When he didn't do as instructed, she lifted her hand in front of his face to block his view. "Seriously, Josh. You're gonna ruin the surprise."

Seriously, he didn't think he could get enough of hearing her say his name. Since he also was a fan of keeping her happy, he let his eyelids drift shut.

A moment later, he caught a whiff of her familiar perfume, and he cracked open an eye to see she'd stood on tiptoe to put a hat on his head. Flashes of light bounced off the wall and danced across Danae's skin. Judging from the fractured rainbows, whatever ridiculous hat she'd placed on his head resembled a disco ball.

"It's very Wild West hero." Danae nudged him toward the circular mirror on the wall.

Whoa. Silver sequins adorned the pink cowgirl hat. He gripped the brim and tipped it at her. "Hello, ma'am. A close friend recommended this hat, and if you run away screaming right now, I'll have to jump to the conclusion that she has questionable taste."

Danae giggled.

Josh draped an arm around her shoulders and squeezed her to his side so they could peer in the mirror. They grinned at their reflections and then at each other.

"While I'm man enough to rock sequins, this hat matches the dress you wore last night, so..." Josh snagged the fedora and switched their headwear so that she was the one sporting the pink atrocity.

She wrinkled her nose and then plucked a black fedora off a faceless mannequin. Instead of putting it on herself, she swapped it with the white hat atop his head. She studied him for a beat before giving him one sharp nod. "Better."

While it wasn't as goofy-looking as he'd assumed it would be, it was far from his style. "I think I'm more of a baseball cap guy."

Danae returned the fedoras to where she'd found them and they circled the store, trying one hat after another. She found a straw garden hat in the clearance bin with the widest brim he'd ever seen. Seconds after she tried it on, the brim flopped over, covering half her face.

Josh stepped closer and lifted it so he could see those big hazel eyes. She stuck her tongue out to the side, pulling a wacky face, and he'd honestly never had so much fun shopping for anything before.

Suddenly she patted her pockets. The enormous brim flopped down again as she pulled out her phone, and she batted at the floppy fabric as she read whatever was on the screen. “That’s my timer. Our seven minutes are up.”

On the way out, she ran her fingers along the sequined cowgirl hat. “Are you sure you don’t need this in your life? I don’t want to be sailing away, only for you to be full of regret.”

“I’m sure.” The charming woman who’d placed it on his head, on the other hand... Well, he was glad he’d taken a risk last night, because missing out on this was definitely something he would have regretted.

Chapter Twenty

After their late lunch, the group decided to pass the time until their candy-making lesson in the old map store next door.

"Anyone find Newport yet?" Danae asked as she continued to shuffle through the bins. In theory, they were alphabetized. In reality, she'd found Boston in the Ns. She glanced across the aisle at Josh, who was studying an old globe.

She mentally reviewed the fun they'd had that day, from whale-sighting to shopping and messing around in the hat store, her grin so wide her cheeks hurt. What if she'd finally found someone she could build a future with? Didn't she owe it to herself to at least see?

These days, women could supposedly have it all—it simply required balance. First and foremost, she'd ensure that her team was on track and her own work was getting done. At night during their free time, however, she could spend time getting to know Josh better.

Satisfied she'd found an acceptable solution for the predicament that had consumed her thoughts, she rounded the bins and headed over to the globe. Right as she was about to ask Josh where he'd visit if he could go anywhere, Mark stepped through the doorway to one of the side rooms.

"I found a giant map of Newport from 1910." Mark waved everyone inside, and they crowded around the table in the center of the room.

Mark carefully unfurled a rolled map on the nicked wooden surface of the table, unleashing a puff of stale, slightly dusty air. The faded colors and frayed edges reminded Danae of the old star charts Dad used to keep in his ship. "It'll be interesting to see how much Newport's changed in the last century."

Newspaper print and pastel colors emphasized the old-timey appearance, and the mapmaker had gone above and beyond on the title. They'd used different fonts for Newport, Rhode Island, and the title, which made it harder to read but looked cool.

It took Danae a handful of seconds to find enough familiar streets to get her bearings. Once she'd done so, the entire city took shape. "Check it out! There's my house. Back when she was just a young house, making her way in the big world."

"Okay, weirdo," Franco said, and when she turned to him, he added, "I mean that as a compliment. Weirdos are my favorite."

"Thank you?" she said with a laugh, and the others cracked up as well. "Okay, what about everyone else? Can you find your houses? Or at least where they'd be on the map?"

One by one, every member of her team pointed at the color-coded sections of Newport. Besides her cottage, the only building they found that had been there as long was Franco's parents' house. The condos Mark lived in were only a handful of years old, and Paige's and Vanessa's places were in the thirty to forty age range.

The novelty of finding their houses—or where they'd be on the older map—wore off, and her team roamed around the other areas of the room.

Danae glanced at Josh, who had hung back as they'd pointed out their neighborhoods. Wanting to include him, she asked, "What about you?"

His brow furrowed, and something about

the way he studied her generated a healthy dose of trepidation. "I live on my boat."

"Full time? Like, even in the winter?" How had they not covered this already? He'd talked about his boat and how hard he'd worked to restore it, sure. Come to think of it, he'd also mentioned his lawn was water.

"Yes, full time."

Plenty of people kept boats at the marina without living there, so for some reason, it just hadn't clicked. Although now she was kicking herself for not putting it together sooner, as well as causing the awkwardness crowding the air.

"Oh. I didn't realize, but that totally makes sense." She rubbed at her neck. "Soooo, where do you think you'll buy a house once you decide to settle down again? Is there a certain area that calls to you?"

The creases in his forehead deepened, and a muscle in his jaw flexed. "I don't plan on doing that ever again."

Now she was the one scrunching up her forehead. "Which part? Buying a house? Or settling down?"

"Both. Neither." He tapped the marina, the motion resolute. "That's where *Solitude* is, and that's where I plan on spending the rest of my days."

"But..." Words weren't coming out right, and plans that had been part daydream and an abundance of optimism began to crumble, like several of the cliffside hills they'd seen on this trip. Once one rock took a tumble, others followed, until what had once been a giant wall of stone became debris.

"I'm happy with what I have," Josh said. "My lifestyle suits my needs. I work when and where I want. I don't intend to dive back into the rat race and spend all my hours in some cubicle, just so I can buy a giant house I never get to spend any time at."

Tension gridlocked the space between them, making it impossible to move forward or backward, and she wished she could undo the last two minutes. "I'm sorry. I didn't mean to offend you. I'm surprised, is all."

How could he plan on living alone on his sailboat for the rest of his days? Did he really mean what he said about never settling down? If so, there was no point in trying to see where this thing forming between them led. Not when he'd just made it clear it would go nowhere.

"Away from the marina, I get that a lot." Josh leaned his palms on the table, his gaze on the map instead of her. "After seeing what it's like to be on the open ocean, I guess I'm surprised, too. It might not be for everyone, but I'm happy with my life. End of story."

Silence fell. The air, which earlier had felt so full of history she'd wanted to soak in it, now felt thick and stale, like it could suffocate her.

It wasn't just the history from the maps

in the shop, but also her past and Josh's. She needed stable and reliable. As unfair as it was, she was also reaching the age when she had to settle down and start a family if she wanted one, and she did. Always had.

"Check it out," Vanessa said, her loud voice slicing through the quiet. She'd roamed to the far side of the alcove and was pointing at one of the framed images on the wall. "It's a super old map of Cape Cod, but it tells you where to find food. But in the olden times, so it's like hunt for a deer here. Try the apple trees down there."

At the sound of Josh's retreating footsteps, every ounce of oxygen drained from Danae's lungs, along with the happiness that'd pumped through her mere minutes ago.

The phrase "Like a kid in a candy shop" would usually apply to Josh, but it was hard to feel excited, even surrounded by colorful candy in flavors of every kind.

In spite of all the signs that Danae favored a more conventional lifestyle, he'd still been caught off-guard when she'd made it clear that living on a boat full time wasn't something she considered acceptable.

It scraped a raw nerve, one that had

never healed after his divorce. It had also stung his pride to learn that she disapproved of his freewheeling lifestyle—one that would never be enough for her.

"The nice thing about taffy is that you can make it in so many flavors," the woman who owned the candy shop said as she guided their group into the kitchen area. "Along this wall are all the flavorings. Go ahead and pick your favorite and we'll get started."

Josh had considered sitting out this lesson so he could take a long walk and sort through his thoughts. Upon voicing that desire, Danae had objected with, "But I made the appointment for six people."

It only provided further proof that she couldn't let go of controlling every situation—and that it would always clash with his desire to go with the flow—but the anxiety in her features made it impossible to storm away.

Because, dang it, he still cared. Enough that he didn't want to hurt her feelings.

"They don't have pickle flavoring," Danae said. "I looked."

He snapped his fingers, added a "shucks," and moved around her. If he talked to her, he'd up and forget that she considered his lifestyle lesser than, and he wasn't going through that again. It was best to just power through this session and the rest of the day.

He picked up banana cream pie flavoring and returned to the large cooling table.

Cold water ran underneath the metal. That way, the shop owner explained, the temperature of the boiling taffy mixture would drop fast enough so they could pull it before it set.

At the last second, Danae switched places with Franco so that she was next to Josh instead. "What flavor did you end up getting?" she asked.

He held it up, and she squinted at the bottle.

Then she lifted a tiny vial. "Orange Creamsicle. I haven't had anything in this flavor in a long time, and it was my dad's favorite. It's like sailing stirred up all these memories I always felt like I needed to repress, and now I'm trying to embrace them."

"I think that's a good idea."

Her exhale made it clear she was frustrated, but he was, too. Plus, not everything could be fixed with small talk. He was starting to wonder if they weren't just destined to clash. Not that he held her desires against her. She wanted what most women did: security, stability, and a fancy house with all the amenities that kept a person tied to it; a nice wardrobe with plenty of pieces; and reliable WiFi.

The woman from the candy shop tipped the heated pot and used a rubber spatula to spread the mixture across the cooling table. Using a cutting tool, she divided it in six segments. "Okay, put in three drops of flavoring, and then you'll knead it. For a big batch, we use Rosie over there, which is our taffy-pulling machine."

She gestured to a large red machine with two arms and four metal spires. One of the other workers was using it, and it was mesmerizing to watch it swirl and twist. "But for these smaller batches, and so you get the authentic candy-making experience, let's get pulling."

They did as instructed, each holding their sugary blob high and letting it fall downward. Once it nearly hit the table, they folded it in half and did it again.

"Whoa, whoa, whoa," Mark said, and his chunk of—dough?—hit the floor. "Oops. I'm afraid mine is going to have a hint of dirt flavor. Please tell me that pairs nicely with s'mores flavoring."

The entire group chuckled, save Josh. He was grumpy, and Danae had laughed. Why did he care, since he'd concluded he and Danae were incompatible, anyway?

"I'm sorry, I can't let you eat that," the woman said.

"Oh, I was just kiddi—"

The shop owner took the blob from Mark and tossed it in a large trash bin, and the guy looked so embarrassed that now Josh felt bad for him.

Never before had he felt so temperamental, and it really needed to stop.

"Here." Danae split her blob in half and

handed it to Mark. "It's too big for me to manage anyway."

"Thank you," Mark said. "I swear I won't let this one touch the floor."

The candy shop owner paced behind them, giving them tips and tricks and occasionally correcting their methods. Gradually, the gooey mixture hardened to the point that Josh's arms burned with the pulling movements.

After they rolled the setting mixture into thin ropes, the woman came through and divided each into bite-sized pieces. She handed out wrappers and told them they were free to taste their creations and wrap any leftovers. "Then, since Amy is almost done with her large batch, we'll show you how it works when we feed it into Harriet, our wrapping machine."

"Oh wow. This is just like the kind my dad bought." Danae extended a large piece from her batch toward Josh. "Do you want to try it?"

The hope in her question made it impossible to say no. As he was chewing the piece of creamsicle taffy, Danae glanced around. Then she backed him into the corner of the kitchen, next to the sink. "Okay, so I wanted you to try it, but I also wanted to tell you something, and this way I can get it all out while you chew."

He tried to mutter a retort, but thanks to her honed planning skills, she was right.

Talking around the sticky candy wasn't exactly easy.

"I'm sorry about the house comment. I didn't mean to offend you. I honestly admire that you took an old boat and fixed it up, and that you enjoy being on your boat enough to live on it. I don't want you to be upset with me for the rest of our trip."

Finally, the bite in his mouth dissolved enough to speak. But her apology had taken the wind out of his irritated sails. He also suspected the words had hit him harder thanks to his past with Olivia, and the fact that he'd been judged by his material possessions—or lack thereof—before. He didn't want to get into all that now, though.

"There's something about this flavor that tastes like my childhood," he said, deflecting.

Danae cocked her head with a discontented frown. "Is that all you have to say?"

Fair point. "I accept your apology, and I don't want to end the trip on a bad note, either." If anything, their squabble served as a much-needed reminder of why he didn't get involved. In people's lives, with women. Just him and his boat and the water—the ocean might be moody, but at least he could easily adapt and manage his ship in a storm.

Relief flooded Danae's expression. "Okay, cool." She pressed her lips together, her gaze dropping to the floor, and his muscles tensed as he steeled himself for whatever was coming next. "Honestly, I was afraid mixing business with pleasure might muddle the trip. I think it'd be best if from here on out, we stick to being friends."

Her relief echoed through him, although a hint of misguided disappointment whirled into the mix as well. "I agree."

They shared a smile, and the heaviness in his chest eased.

Danae tilted her head toward the cooling table, where the rest of her team stood. "We should get back over there. I don't want to be rude."

The group crowded around to watch as the workers fed a roll of taffy into the machine that cut it into bite-sized pieces and placed them in wrappers, and then twisted both ends. At the end of the demonstration, they put some of it—along with the taffy they'd made themselves—in bags. Then they headed out front to browse the storefront.

Josh picked up a gift box of fudge for his parents; a bag of sea life gummies shaped like sharks, crabs, and seashells for Jane and Nathan; and a sugar-free assortment of chocolates for Nancy and George, since George's doctor had instructed him to cut down on sugar. Josh figured that if anyone could make that taste okay, it'd be the people in this shop.

He stepped outside to find Danae posted in front. She dug into her bag, lifted out an extra-long candy necklace and, as she had with the hats, stretched onto her tiptoes to loop it over his head. "For you, King Candy. I bought the big one so it wouldn't choke you."

Their discussion about how Jane used to make him play Candy Land seemed like a week ago instead of a couple of days. So much had happened, the close quarters and nonstop activities making each day feel longer, while also managing to fly right by.

"Thank you," he said, bringing the necklace up to his mouth and biting off a couple of the hard candies. Like the orange taffy, it was one of those time-travel flavors. It took him right back to Jane's bedroom, littered with stuffed animals, dolls, and the Candy Land board.

"You're welcome."

The rest of the group exited the store and they began their walk back to the boat. As they neared the wharf, Danae stepped closer and whispered, "FYI, I'm still counting on you to keep me from falling, railing notwithstanding."

Perhaps it wasn't the outcome he'd expected after their time together last night and the fun they'd had in the hat shop. What mattered was that it was for the best, and that thanks to sailing, he was a master of readjusting and finding another course. "I got you. What are friends for?"

Chapter Twenty-One

AFTER ONE OF THE CRAZIEST, busiest weeks ever, Danae had struggled to get out of bed that morning. With the launch of the new campaign, the next month was sure to be extra hectic, so she resolved to take advantage of every single minute of their last full day at sea.

As she pitched in to help Josh with the sails, every word, gesture, and smile caused a bittersweet sensation to swell within her. No doubt in her mind, their decision to stick to being friends was for the best. If only it had erased every spark that had ever flickered between them. Why did they continue to ignite, ignite, ignite? Especially knowing it would never work?

They sailed across Cape Cod Bay, through the canal that took them underneath Bourne Bridge, and down to Monument Beach. So far during their trip, they'd mostly strolled across the sandy beaches, always on their way to another destination. Today, they had two glorious hours blocked out for soaking in the sun, and the sand and water were calling their names.

Danae had just settled on her beach towel and kicked off her flip flops when a man-sized shadow blocked the light. Josh squatted next to her, and a tingle corkscrewed through her as his profile sharpened into relief. The blue eyes, the slant of his nose, and that slight dip above his lips that matched the dimple in his chin.

We're no longer noticing those things, remember?

"Hey," he said.

"Hey." The part of her brain that came up with clever responses was feeling as fried as her shoulders probably would be after today—regardless of the thick layer of sunscreen she'd applied to her fair skin.

"I have an idea. Don't shoot it down before hearing me out, okay?"

Danae mimicked zipping her lips, and his smile widened enough that those delicious eye crinkles showed up, too.

"I want to show you something."

"Okay," she said, and he chuckled.

"So much for the zipped lips."

"Here's the thing, they don't stay that way. From the time I was little, I've always been a chatter box. While I've worked on it, it's one of those things that are beyond my control."

"Something beyond Danae Danvers's control? That's a possibility?"

"Ha ha."

Josh sat in the sand, not bothering to stick to the towel. "There's this super cool spot nearby that I'd really like to show you, but it isn't easily accessible. We'd have to rent a two-person kayak and paddle over to it. The views and how untouched it is by the rest of the world are totally worth it, though."

Her two sides went to war, the larger, pragmatic percentage tempted to ask a dozen questions before she even considered it. Where exactly was this place? What if they didn't get back in time for their scheduled launch? How would it look, considering the fact that her coworkers didn't know they'd agreed not to cross the line?

Then there was the other part of her, and while it was much smaller, with Josh next to her, it was also noisier. She wanted to dive headfirst. Do that *carpe diem* thing he insisted was all the rage.

"Oh, sure. Now you choose the quiet route." He nudged her knee. "Come on. One last adventure."

Danae swallowed and then nodded. "Okay."

The joy that claimed his features zapped the last of her concerns. From a friendship standpoint, anything that elicited that much happiness was a win. In fact, it was the *least* she could do after he'd shown her so many amazing places she never would've experienced without him.

Danae explained to Vanessa that she and Josh were going kayaking and asked if she'd watch her stuff.

"I got you, girl," Vanessa said. "You two have fun." There was definitely implied eyebrow waggling, and Danae's reservations came rushing back. Did everyone think there was something going on? What about Mark? She didn't want to undo the progress she'd made with him.

Then again, she'd see him day in and day out at the office. This was her and Josh's last day together before everything changed. Yes, she'd see him at the boat-christening ceremony, but he'd have all his family and acquaintances there.

In an out-of-character move, she slammed the door on her conflicted thoughts—she'd deal with them later. Right now, she was going to jump on in and let herself enjoy the ride. She tugged her shorts over her swimsuit, slipped on her sandals, and followed Josh to the row of shops lining the boardwalk.

Twenty minutes later, Danae was settling into the front seat of a kayak as Josh pushed it away from the shore. He walked far enough into the water that the bottom of his shorts got wet. The kayak wobbled as he climbed in, and Danae flinched, worried they were about to flip the small vessel.

"Okay, sailor," Josh said from behind her, and she cracked open an eye to discover they were still dry, as well as drifting away from the shore. "Let's see how you are with a paddle instead of a sail."

Danae started to row and smacked the side of the kayak with her oar, the noise loud enough that she jumped. Josh burst out laughing, and she grimaced. "Oops. I'm sure that answers your question."

Over the next few minutes, Josh demonstrated where to grip her paddle, how to stroke for going forward and backward, and how to turn. "Paddling in tandem will yield the best, fastest results, but if you get tired, let me know, and I'll take over for a while."

"What if I can't paddle at all? Will we get stuck in the middle of the water and end up stranded?"

"Those were the kind of questions I expected earlier from you."

She twisted as much as her seat allowed. "You told me I couldn't ask them."

"As I recall, I requested you hear me out *before* you asked them. Never said anything about them not being allowed."

"Then maybe we should head back to shore—that way I can get them all out."

Apparently he thought she was kidding, because he continued to paddle *away* from the safety of the beach.

Nothing else to be done, she began paddling as well. "I prefer a few extra feet of boat between me and the ocean."

"Technically, this is Phinneys Harbor. We'd have to paddle all the way across Buzzards Bay to get to the Atlantic Ocean. Instead we're just gonna cruise around this tiny island."

"If I wasn't afraid that smacking you with this paddle would dump both of us into the water, that's what I'd do with your 'technically.'"

Josh laughed again, and another glance backward showed him completely at home. He'd put on his baseball cap and insisted on buying her one from the kayak rental shop, so she was now advertising boat rentals to the marine life underneath them. *I'm sure all the fishies will be so impressed they'll swim right over.*

As they circled a strip of land covered with trees and a handful of houses, Danae found her rhythm. Her muscles burned with the effort, but each stroke gave her a sense of accomplishment.

After a while, her arms turned into wet noodles, her strokes off enough that her oar smacked into Josh's paddle.

"I got it," he said, and she was going to protest, but her tired body spoke louder.

"Just for a quick breather."

If anything, it felt like they glided through the water faster—she suspected Josh had been paddling slower to match her pace.

Since she couldn't do much else, she kept peeking at the guy behind her. He caught her staring and winked, and her heart soared way up to the sky, executing moves similar to the seagull overhead. Flapping, gliding, and dipping, before flying higher to do it all again.

Suddenly, a spray of water arced over her, the stream going right down the back of her life vest.

The snicker behind her clued her in to the fact that the dousing was far from accidental. Out of the corner of her eye, she caught sight of the shore. Josh pivoted them in that direction, leading her to believe that was their destination. Since they were well within swimming distance, she decided to rock the boat. Literally.

Using her paddle, she scooped as much water as she could and flung it over her shoulder at Josh.

"Oh, it's on," Josh said. They slapped water at each other, laughing and dodging the cold sprays, gasping whenever one slammed into them.

Tall grass skimmed the bottom and

sides of the boat, and then the front hit the sand. Josh climbed out to tow them ashore and, assuming he'd use his advantageous position to drench her, Danae stood to jump ship.

Only her foot caught on the edge of the kayak's seat. "No, ahhh—" The weight of her body propelled her forward, face-first toward the water, and she had the fleeting thought she was about to lose this water fight to herself.

But then Josh was there, catching her around the waist and steadying her. The kayak bumped into his shins, which had to sting, but he remained firm. Their eyes met, and her breath lodged in her throat.

He readjusted his grip, swung her around, and lowered her onto the wet sand. "You good?" he asked, still holding her in place, and she managed to nod.

"Yeah. Thanks for catching me."

"Anytime," he said, his voice low and husky. Goose bumps skated across her skin, and she reconsidered the mental pats on the back she'd given herself earlier for straying from the itinerary. She'd taken safety precautions, but now that she was away from her coworkers, she worried that she hadn't taken nearly enough. The life vest strapped around her might prevent her from sinking underneath the water's surface, but she was still drowning, one wrong move away from falling for a guy she'd agreed to remain just friends with.

"Watch this low branch," Josh said as he dodged it himself.

Danae followed after him, short enough to duck underneath the branch instead of going around it like he'd had to do.

A few more strides, and they reached the highest point on the trail. Instead of surveying the landscape, he watched for Danae's reaction.

Her eyes glittered as she peered down the hill. Leafy green trees with moss-covered trunks stretched high into the sky on all sides, the cleared-out trail providing an ideal view of the sparkling bay and the tiny island they'd passed. "Wow. It's breathtaking."

Josh towed her a few steps backward, to sit on the weathered wooden bench on which he'd spent countless hours throughout his life. He'd grabbed her hand without thinking, but now he was thinking far too much about not letting it go. Sticking to friends when it came to Danae was a lot harder than he'd expected.

As soon as he released her hand, he curled his into a fist so he wouldn't be tempted to reach for it again. "Little Bay

Conservation Area has managed to stay almost hidden. It's off the beaten path, and you can go from beach to forest in a manner of minutes. You can even see upper Buzzards Bay in the distance."

He'd wanted to share this slice of heaven with Danae, certain she'd appreciate it. But, another thing he'd underestimated...? How intimate it would feel. They were already here, though, and words he hadn't planned on speaking began to flow. "After my divorce, I came out here and sat on this bench to figure out what I truly wanted out of life. I watched all the different boats gliding in and out of the canal and thought about how much I used to love sailing. How much more I enjoyed my life before it got so busy."

Something about Danae made it easier to talk about subjects he normally couldn't discuss with anyone else. That was part of friendship, right? Saying things you'd held in for far too long because it finally felt safe to voice them? "That's when it hit me. You only get one life. Right then and there, I vowed to make the most of mine."

Danae turned away from the stunning scenery to study him instead. It should be illegal to look that cute in a baseball cap. Only problem was, the brim shaded her eyes. He dipped his head enough to view those windows into her soul and get a better read on her.

"I totally understand how you'd feel

that way," she said, "but when my dad died, all I could focus on was how uncertain so much of life is, and how I never wanted to experience having the rug jerked out from underneath me ever again. If I can minimize future pain for myself and my loved ones, why wouldn't I take those steps?"

Obviously a rhetorical question. Judging from the twist of her lips and the lines creasing her brow, the wheels in her brain were spinning in that way they often did.

She surprised him by placing a hand on the center of his chest, and his heart threw itself at her mercy, beating away against his inner walls as if it longed to get closer to her. "My dad poured tons of cash into a sinking ship. He did his best, but he wasn't as knowledgeable about repairs and renovation as you are. I think all that work you've put into *Solitude* is truly impressive. You're a great sailor and captain, and your job totally suits you. I can tell how much you love it."

"I sense a *but*," he said, placing his hand over hers and securing it tighter to his chest. It felt so right there. How could he possibly let go now?

"Not really. I'm merely letting you know that I hear you and understand where you're coming from. I enjoy my job, too. Hard work and determination got me to where I am today. My top priority is doing everything I can to secure my future, especially financially. That way, if anything were to happen to me, it wouldn't be as much of a burden to my family."

"If you live your life thinking about the end of it, though, that's not really living."

Her eyebrows knit together as she processed. "I'm not sure I can just let go of that need."

"The beauty is we don't have to agree on some grand life philosophy. My reason for telling you this isn't to convince you to let go of your goals. Maybe just allow a little more room for fun and spontaneity in your life."

"I'll definitely consider it." She blew out a breath, and her hand trembled as she withdrew it from his to reach up and fiddle with the charm on her necklace. "Okay, here goes my attempt at being spontaneous and taking a risk, in spite of being afraid everything's about to go down in flames."

All he could do was stare, his heart thumping harder as he waited to see what she said next.

"We've tried the friends thing, for...what? A day now?"

Now Josh was the one knitting his eyebrows as he tried to figure out what was going to come out of her mouth next. "Yeah."

"Is it working for you? Because it's not really working for me," she said, and his stomach bottomed out. She didn't want to associate with him anymore? Her face pinkened. "I know I'm the one who suggested we stick to friends, but I like you, Josh. The kayak ride and being up here with you—it's all emphasized just how much. Once this trip is over, maybe we could go on a date. But if that's not something you're interested in, please stop me before I embarrass myself any further."

He gently cupped her chin, tipping her face to his. Her expression was so open and vulnerable. It yanked at his heartstrings, so strongly he almost expected them to snap in half. "Of course I like you, Danae. If you haven't noticed, I can't seem to stay away from you."

"You've tried, though?"

He huffed a laugh. "I did. I just had some trouble with the follow-through."

"Me, too," she said, the barest of smiles touching her lips.

Pressure built beneath his sternum. In another life, he might dive headfirst and kiss her without thinking things through. But the last thing he wanted to do was hurt her, and a tiny voice whispered that they still didn't want the same things. That they might be too different to pull off a full-blown relationship.

"Look, I'm glad we have the boat christening to look forward to, but..." Josh slowly lowered his hand, everything inside him protesting at letting go instead of leaning closer. "I'm asking that when it comes to this thing between us, you don't insist on planning it all out. Let's catch up at the ceremony and just see where it goes from there."

"I... But what if...?" Her nose wrinkled, and reluctance drenched her words. "I can try. I think. Yeah. Maybe."

It wasn't the answer he'd hoped for, but better than the one he'd feared, where she insisted on more, and he had to admit he couldn't give it to her. He lowered his forehead to hers and closed his eyes, soaking in the moment in case she wasn't willing to take a risk with him. "Let me know when you have a firm answer."

Chapter Twenty-Two

JOSH HADN'T BEEN WRONG WHEN he'd taken her hand and said, "Guess we'd better hike back to the kayak before you get anxious about how long we've been gone."

It had been on her mind as they'd been hiking, sure, and she'd glanced at the time once after taking in the gorgeous view.

As for their intimate chat and the moment when she'd been sure he was going to finally kiss her...? Well, in that instant, she hadn't been thinking or worrying about anything.

She'd just been a girl who really wanted to kiss a boy.

Of course I like you, Danae. The words,

along with the gentle way he'd cupped her chin, had robbed her of breath and short-circuited her brain. Residual butterflies rose as she glanced at Josh now, kneeling in the sand on the other side of Franco. Both guys were pitching in to help Paige pack up her umbrella and beach mat.

If only there hadn't been that added *but*. The one he'd sensed was going to come from her but somehow ended up in her lap.

Let's catch up at the ceremony and just see where it goes from there.

Like most real-life plot twists, she wasn't a fan of being taken off-guard. Vague had never been her thing, either.

"So, we were talking," Vanessa said, and Danae jerked her attention off the guy and the situation she couldn't stop obsessing about.

Danae finished cramming her towel in her beach bag and scanned the faces of her team, who were all staring at the two of them. Why did she suddenly have the feeling that Vanessa had drawn the short straw? "You're freaking me out. What's going on?"

Her coworkers shared glances, and a pit formed in her stomach. What had happened? They'd come so far and grown so close. Why did it feel like there was about to be a coup d'état? She was hardly a dictator, so that seemed wildly unfair.

Danae stood and crossed her arms, afraid she'd need the protection.

"We don't care about the Forbes mansion," Vanessa said.

Paige advanced a step. "Yeah, we can see it when we sail by it tomorrow."

Danae moved to adjust her glasses before remembering she wasn't wearing them today. "But it's on the schedule for today. That's why we're gathering our stuff to head back to the boat."

"Right," Paige said. "We were all talking, and it's been such a busy trip, and relaxing on the beach has been so nice..."

"And Josh says there's this hidden gem of a restaurant here where we can have a nice relaxing dinner," Vanessa finished.

Danae's gaze shot to Josh.

Josh held up his hands, as if he were facing down a mugger in an alley. "Don't bring me into this, guys. I told you about the place as a fun fact, not so you could pull me into this battle. I'm fighting one of my own."

One of his own? As in whether or not she was open to a willy-nilly type of relationship that could very well lead to a dead end?

Both frustrations stacked on each other, causing them to feel that much bigger. "Let me get this straight. You all want to stay here and then just sort of glance at the Elizabeth Islands as we sail past them and head back to Newport? Is that what I'm hearing?"

After looking at one another yet again,

they all nodded and gave answers that boiled down to *yes*.

Then Vanessa gave Franco a shove, nudging him to the forefront of the group.

"Doesn't a nice evening with good food, where we can relish our last night instead of rushing to our next destination, sound nice?" he asked.

Danae curled her hand around the bill of her baseball cap as she considered it. "If that's what the entire team wants, then..."

Team. She blinked at the group, which had been full of mostly solo artists at the launch of their voyage, each person doing their own thing. Not anymore. They compromised and harmonized, and in the end, that was her main goal. "As long as we get into Newport early enough tomorrow, I'm okay with it."

The entire group erupted in joyous shouts and hoorays, so clearly they hadn't thought she'd agree to the switch-up.

"I'm so proud," a familiar deep voice said next to her ear, and she turned to gaze into ocean-blue eyes.

Yes, she'd learned to adapt and change on this trip, too. To at least consider the flow, if not go along with it. While the slight shift would require a big sticker to blot out her planner entry for the day, she had full confidence that Josh would sail them to where they needed to be, and that it would all work out.

More than that, this change made sense. The team needed an evening off. It would only help their productivity come Tuesday morning at the office, and they did deserve it.

"What's the name of this restaurant?" Danae lifted her phone. "I'll call and make arrangements."

"It's a secret." Josh clapped her on the back, as if she were some dude on his ball team. "But I'll make sure they can accommodate us."

"Right, but what about Fr—"

"Franco's gluten allergy and Paige's vegan diet? The owner and I are old acquaintances, and I'm sure he'll gladly whip up a few options."

No checking out the menu? No calling ahead to ensure they wouldn't have a long wait? No finding the best, most efficient route there?

"You're getting this cute little eye twitch." Josh pointed at her eye, as if otherwise she'd be lost as to what he meant.

Danae slung her bag over her shoulder. "If I didn't know better, I'd say you're enjoying this."

"I'm afraid you might not know as much as you think." His smug expression stirred up a frenzy of emotions and made her rehash their conversation on that wooden bench again.

There was so much promise permeating the air between them. Yet how could she possibly give Josh a firm answer when her brain insisted she needed assurance?

If he were truly interested, wouldn't he have agreed to a date? Or at least made a semi-sorta plan?

No, because he felt about plans the way she felt about the lack of them. Perhaps that meant they were too different, their lives destined to head in opposite directions.

That thought turned her butterflies into pebbles that rattled her insides before settling in one large lump. Then she was questioning every single thing all over again.

As he had earlier, Josh watched Danae's reaction as they walked into the restaurant. The exterior was gray brick with faded blue-and green awnings, so she'd gotten a hint it wasn't anything fancy.

A seascape was painted on the far wall, and a plastic marlin with a long pointy nose hung from the ceiling. The place had booths, which wasn't abnormal for him, but he'd noticed that the group had avoided vinyl benches in eating establishments thus far.

Simon the third, who upheld his father and grandfather's legacy, glanced up from the cash register, then grinned with pleasure. "Josh Wheeler." He rounded the counter and pulled Josh into a big, fried fish-scented hug. Then he raised his voice. "Hey, Linda! Get out here and see who's finally come to visit."

Linda exited the kitchen through the big open archway and gave Josh a slightly less bone-crushing hug.

"I've been sailing with this group for a week now, and I told them they couldn't head back to Newport without trying your food first." Josh introduced everyone, and Simon informed them they were going to get the red-carpet treatment.

The group ordered large plates of fried clam strips, shrimp and scallops and oysters, fries, and coleslaw. Then they ate picnic-style, each of them scooping up a bit of this and a bit of that.

When Danae's salmon cakes—which Josh had insisted she try—arrived, she skewered the pickle that had come on the side and dropped it onto his plate. Then she bit into her food. Her eyebrows rose as she chewed, and while Simon deserved the praise, Josh gladly took credit for the astonished gleam in her eye.

"This might be the best thing I've ever eaten. *Ever.*"

Simon showed up right then and placed a platter of onion rings on the table. "Aww, I appreciate that. Family secret, that one."

Danae lifted a napkin to wipe her

mouth. "It's so good. I can't believe I almost missed out. Do you happen to deliver to Newport?"

Simon chuckled, giving Josh's shoulder a quick squeeze before moving on.

"So, how do you know Simon?"

"My parents used to visit Borne every summer. It was a nice quick sailing trip, and my grandparents owned a timeshare. Most people head to the north part of Cape Cod, but we always came to this southeast end. A lot of my best childhood memories took place here. And as I mentioned earlier, it's my get-away-from-the-world place. Unfortunately, my grandparents sold their timeshare, so nowadays my parents stay in a hotel. If it's just me, it's easy enough to stay on my boat."

Danae nodded, and then nodded some more. Something was going on in that head of hers. He was so curious as to what, but he'd have to ask her later, if they got a chance to be alone again.

Everyone remarked on how good the food was, and then Josh caught sight of Simon and Linda, who waved him over.

"Excuse me." Josh wiped his fingers on his napkin and headed over to chat.

Out of the corner of his eye, he caught Mark gesturing to Danae's salmon cakes, and then she extended the plate to him for a taste.

It's not a big deal. I'm the one she's been spending her free time with.

Simon wrapped an arm around his wife and bent his head, forming a three-person huddle. "Linda asked me if there's something between you and the blond, and I told her she'd have to ask you."

"Don't let him fool you," Linda whispered. "He wants to know as badly as I do."

They glared at one another as if they couldn't believe the other had outed them, and Josh hid his grin behind his fist.

"I'm still figuring it out, honestly. There's interest. I'm just afraid we might be too different to make it work."

"Oh, sugar, you're going about it the wrong way." Linda sandwiched his hand between both of hers. "Different works. You think me and this guy at my side are similar?"

Actually, he'd never thought much about it. Since they ran a restaurant together, he'd supposed they were. Hope flickered, doing its best to crowd out his doubts, but there were so many more of them. "What if we want completely different things, though?"

"That's trickier. It's also what compromise is made for." Linda craned her neck to see around him, and if Danae hadn't already suspected they were talking about her, she'd be aware of it now. "Who's that other fella? He seems to be interested, too."

Josh didn't have to look to know who they meant. "They used to date. A long time ago."

"Hmmm," Linda said. "Is he a jerk?"

"I thought so at first, but sadly, no. I mean, not sadly, but...Mark's a decent guy."

"Hmmm." For some reason, that one sounded graver than the last one.

"Why?"

"I'm calculating your odds." Linda patted his cheek, the way she'd done when he was a kid. "Of course I'd put my money on you. You're strong and handsome and kind, although you've attempted to hide the kindness since you and Olivia broke up."

Broke up sounded so simple. They'd promised to love each other forever, and then ripped their merged life apart, and it had been far from clean. He never wanted to go through that ever again. He wasn't sure he'd survive it.

"But that man looks like he's regretting losing her. You should learn from his mistakes. You hear me?"

"Yes, ma'am," he said, because his mother had taught him manners.

As he turned to read the situation for himself, Mark's longing was as plain as day. Josh imagined he wore a similar expression whenever he was talking to Danae.

This entire time he'd been so focused on getting her to take a risk, that he'd accidentally hesitated to take a real risk himself.

Chapter Twenty-Three

DANAE WAS COMING OUT OF her cabin, pink cardigan in hand, when she ran into Mark in the kitchen area.

She had planned on snagging the cupcakes she'd picked up at a bakery and returning to the helm of the boat. The theory being that if she could stretch out her final evening with Josh a while longer, it might help her come to a firmer decision.

"Hey, I've been thinking, and"—Mark tugged on his ear, a nervous tic of his that caused her to tense up as well—"I've actually been wanting to talk to you for a couple days. It just never seemed to be the right time. Not to mention it's been hard to find a moment alone. But I also don't want to wait until it's too late."

Various excuses to put off the conversation flitted through her head, the ticking countdown of this trip still at the forefront of her mind. If she put it off, though, she'd fret about what Mark had been going to say as she tried to fall asleep later, and whether or not it was a concern about the campaign.

To prevent herself from forgetting the cupcakes, Danae slid the box to the edge of the counter and then rested her hip next to it. "Yeah, it's been super busy, but lots of fun, too. Anyway, what's up?"

"Yes. To the fun." He laughed, an odd laugh she'd never heard from him before, and she shifted from foot to foot, the suspense killing her. "Guess I should just spit it out. I was hoping that I could take you out sometime. Like on a date." Mark scuffed the toe of his shoe on the floor, his eyes fixed on the movement. Slowly, he lifted his chin. "I'm a different person than I was six months ago. Spending all this time together in a more casual setting has reminded me of how many great memories we have. I was a fool to throw us away so easily."

To think that he had regrets—well, she couldn't help but be flattered. For months she'd wondered why he'd dumped her, her wounded ego craving closure. That part of her did a little leap for joy, a sense of justification coming along for the ride.

Still, if she put her feelings for Josh on one side of a scale and her feelings for Mark on the other, Josh's side would outweigh Mark's, no question about it.

Then again, Josh didn't want to make long-term plans. He wouldn't even commit to going out on a date. But that wasn't the only complication.

"I'm not sure if that's a good idea, Mark. After we broke up, I was pretty hurt, and it was hard to work together for a while. I just got this promotion, and I don't want to do anything that might mess up my job or the new campaign."

Mark exhaled, his shoulders deflating slightly. "I completely understand. But D, we're both in better places in our lives, and this trip has proven how well we can work together when we put our minds to it." He stepped closer and braced a hand on the counter as his eyes implored hers. "Promise me you'll think about it?"

Standing in the tiny kitchen, across from the guy she'd spent nearly a year with, she recalled how easy it had been to be with Mark. He was straightforward, driven, and put a lot of effort toward work, and they had similar goals when it came to the future.

"Thinking happens to be my middle name," she said with a smile, and Mark grinned back.

The blood in Josh's veins burned hotter with each sentence Mark spoke to Danae, intensifying the toxic churning in his gut. The temptation to be overdramatic and burst into the kitchen called to him, so contrary to his usual personality that he wondered who he'd become.

All because he'd met a woman who drove him crazy in every possible way.

In order to avoid doing anything he'd later regret, he backed away, climbing the stairs as quietly as he could and returning to the helm. He'd been waiting for Danae there, his head up in the clouds like he was a teenager instead of a grown man. When it had taken awhile for her to grab a sweater and "a surprise," he went to see if she needed assistance. Or if she couldn't find her jacket and needed to borrow his again. As absurd as it sounded, he almost wanted to ask her to wear his jacket instead, so he could see her in the oversized garment again.

So it would smell like her the next time he put it on.

Footsteps alerted him to the fact that he was about to have company. He smoothed his features into an emotionless mask, doing his best to prepare himself for the news that

Danae had decided to give her ex another shot. After all, Mark's goals were sure to be more in sync with hers. The guy could give her the conventional type of life Josh had no desire for.

Even though their course was already set, Josh gripped the wheel for something to do.

"Sorry," Danae said, rounding the corner of the cabin wearing her pink cardigan and holding a box that matched. "I got held up."

"Oh yeah?" He was proud of how evenly his voice came out, as if he were neither interested nor disinterested. Completely neutral, that was him.

"Yeah." The light from the full moon lit up the pale strands of hair around her face, casting her in a soft angelic glow.

Ironic that someone so sweet was about to crush his ego with so little effort.

"I'm not sure whether to...? Or if I should just...?" She sighed and set the pink box on the seat she'd been occupying earlier, before the breeze made her go in search of a sweater. She'd also exchanged her contacts in favor of her glasses. Since he didn't want to see his own reflection as she let him down easy, he craned his neck to see the bow of the ship, as if he needed to affirm they wouldn't run into anything in a whole lot of endless ocean.

Earlier they'd sorted through pictures from the trip, Vanessa collecting several of them for their social media. One by one, people had split off to head to their respective beds, until it had been just him and Danae above deck, alone at last.

Now he was tempted to call for everyone to come up and delay the inevitable. At least for another hour or two.

Then again, if she wasn't sure whether going on a date with Mark was a good or bad idea, Josh hadn't gotten through to her as much as he'd hoped.

Urgency surged as a voice in the back of his brain shouted for him to do *something*. Disappointment came on its heels, because there was nothing for it. Not with so much stacked against them as it was. This was exactly why he never should've crossed the line in the first place. He'd known it would end badly.

"Is something wrong?" Concern swam through Danae's eyes as she placed her hand on his forearm and studied his face. "Are you feeling okay?"

He tried to hold onto his irritation so he could use it as a shield, but it faded with her so close, her palm warming his bare skin.

Instead of playing dumb—a condition he feared might fit all too well right now—he figured he might as well come clean. "I went to check on you and heard the tail end of a conversation between you and Mark."

"Oh."

"Yeah. Oh."

"I, uh, didn't know he was interested in rekindling things. I'm as surprised as anyone."

Josh tilted his head. "Really? I'm not. He's been trying to get close to you this entire trip."

"Not very successfully. As you'll recall, I've spent most evenings with you." Her gaze locked onto his. "Josh, I've had so much fun with you this past week as we've been getting acquainted and hanging out."

Hanging out. Right.

"But you have a lot in common with Mark, including a history," Josh filled in for her, "and you want to give the relationship another shot."

"Not at all where I was going with that." Her hand slipped off his arm and fell to her side. "Wait. Are you saying you wouldn't care?"

"You're free to date him or whoever else you want."

The hurt on her face made him want to take it all back. "I thought you and I were going to see where this thing between us went."

He shrugged one shoulder. "When it comes down to it, you and I want different things. We were both just fooling ourselves anyway."

"I don't understand what's happening. I said I'd consider taking it a day at a time with you, even though that's not what I normally do. I'm not asking for some huge commitment, but I also don't want to sit around hoping you'll call, only to end up staring at the phone all night."

"That's not what I want, either."

"Then what *do* you want? You asked me to compromise, but it feels like you're unwilling to compromise anything in return." Danae brought her lower lip between her teeth and when she spoke, her voice quivered. "I was afraid to bring up the map shop because I said the wrong thing and accidentally offended you, and as I said in the candy shop, I never meant to do that."

Her chest rose with a giant inhale. "But you said something that day, something I can't get out of my head..."

Danae's words caught in her throat, the barbed edges skewering everything she'd been so sure about less than an hour ago.

It was the type of question she *had* to ask, regardless of whether or not she truly wanted the answer. She'd held back earlier on their hike, and that had obviously been a mistake because they weren't even close to being on the same page. She wasn't someone who could simply cross her fingers and hope for the best. If Josh never wanted to get married or have kids—if he truly planned on living alone on a boat forever—was there even room for her in his life?

Agony dug its claws into her heart, the hurt radiating deeper than it should, given that she'd only met the guy a week ago. "That day, you said you don't plan on settling down ever again. Has that changed? Say that you and I date, and things go amazingly well. Would you, under any circumstances, consider getting married again? What about having kids?"

The silence stretched until it snapped and whipped her in the face. Had she accidentally fallen for a guy who was incapable of committing?

"I don't see it happening, no. When I think of my future, the one thing I'm sure of is that it'll include living on my boat and taking chartered trips. I'm not going back to working day in and day out to barely scrape by."

"Not for anyone? Even if that person promised that the burden wouldn't rest all on your shoulders? That there'd be hard days, but there'd be far more happy days filled with—" Love. But she couldn't say that. Not when he was already accusing her of going too fast and wanting too much, and where had that thought even come from?

If they weren't in the middle of the ocean, she imagined Josh would've fled by now.

"This is what I'm talking about," he said. "You're so far in the future, and we haven't even settled the here and now. Or what will happen after we land."

A fissure formed in her heart, and the lump in her throat grew bigger and bigger. "I guess you were right about fooling ourselves. I suppose it's better that we found out now, before either of us wasted our time."

With that, she strode away, each step she put between them widening that crack in her heart.

At the doorway to the cabin, she paused and angled her face to the sky. Countless stars glittered away in the inky black. Her breaths came faster and faster, the stars blurring and streaking as tears filled her eyes.

Then, there it was. Polaris. The North Star.

Dad.

The dam holding her emotions at bay broke, rushing forward and spilling sorrow and regret and a bittersweet longing through her. For years, she'd ignored several things that Dad had taught her, thinking she knew better. That she wouldn't repeat his same mistakes.

During this trip, she'd realized she'd been much too harsh. No one got out of life for free. People made mistakes—she'd made plenty.

Daddy, I don't know what to do. Am I

wrong to want a secure future with a man who's capable of settling down? Who's willing to give his all to making us work, the way I'd do for him?

Maybe it was the angle or the moon or her imagination—or perhaps heaven had heard her pleas and her father knew she needed a sign. Because the unwavering, unrelenting star glowed brighter, a strong flash that affirmed she deserved to be with someone who wanted her back.

Chapter Twenty-Four

AFTER HOURS SPENT TOSSING AND turning, Josh finally abandoned the idea of sleep. He rubbed his gritty eyes and got dressed. Instead of bothering to comb his wild hair, he pulled on his hat and shrugged into his military jacket.

The sun hadn't even risen; it was the time referred to as nautical twilight. The horizon and brighter stars were visible, making it easier to navigate at sea. With so many instruments to guide the way nowadays, nautical twilight wasn't as vital as in the days before modern technology, but there was something captivating about it.

Dark blue gave way to rich purple and bright oranges as the sun neared the horizon, and out of habit, Josh sought the North Star.

Then he thought about Danae, and about how her father taught her to always search for Polaris. How he'd told her that if she set her sights on the wrong star, she'd go in the wrong direction.

Josh had used Polaris to get his bearings many times, so why did it feel like he might be going the wrong way?

Since last night, irritation had been his constant companion. Given that he was in no condition to be around people, he was extra glad for his current solitary state.

This is why I live alone on my boat.

No complications, no having to deal with the expectations of others, which inevitably led to disappointment on both ends. He hadn't been dissatisfied with his life before this trip, so he shouldn't have cause to be anything but content with it now.

It'd be good to get back home to the marina, where he belonged. With people who understood that living on a boat was a plentiful, perfectly acceptable life.

She didn't even try. She considered it for a few hours before rushing into her ex-boyfriend's arms.

Fine, that was an exaggeration. But she'd no doubt be there in the near future. Which was why, for once, Josh was in favor of rushing. He'd speed the rest of the way to Newport, say goodbye to the Barton Boats crew, and put this entire misadventure behind him. No more "what ifs" or attempting relationships. Instead, he'd enjoy his itinerary-free existence and pour his affection into his true soulmate: his ship.

Door hinges creaked, and then Danae stepped onto the deck. She fixed her gaze on the horizon and swiveled around, and he realized she was searching for the North Star, the same way he had.

His heart clenched so tightly that it hurt every time it attempted to beat. Nautical twilight gave way to civil twilight, and as the sun emerged, a flash caught his eye.

He looked down to figure out what had caused it, and his gut sank.

Right. The gold star sticker on his jacket. He started to peel it off, but the memory of Danae gifting it to him left his fingernail frozen in place. He should've stuck it on his T-shirt, but he'd had to go and put it on his jacket.

Which had been on Danae.

Now I won't lose it, he'd said.

Then he'd taught her to park the boat, and he didn't want to replay their good memories, so why had his brain gone there? Did it hate him? As he took in Danae's profile, his entire body protested at the idea of not going over to her, so apparently the rest of his traitorous organs were Team Danae as well.

We don't want the same things. She's

never gonna bend. Get it through your head or body or whatever needs to hear it. Great. Now he was talking to parts of his body. Yep, she'd made him lose his mind, and it might take him a few days to get it back, but he would.

There wasn't any other option.

Even though Danae told herself not to look, her eyes couldn't seem to help it.

There was Josh at the helm.

Their gazes met, and then he quickly turned away, acting super busy with the wheel. Considering there was no need to correct their preset course, the fruitless move indicated that he was still mad, and why did *he* get to be the mad one? In spite of being fully aware she wasn't the gambling type, he was upset that she didn't want to roll the dice on them.

Extra infuriating, taking into account that he wouldn't budge *at all.*

"Morning," she heard from behind her, and she spun around to face Mark as he stepped out of the cabin.

Danae did her best to give him a smile. "Good morning." While Mark had told her that he'd give her time to think about going on a date with him, the eager curiosity in his expression conveyed his hope that she'd have an answer for him now.

Luckily, Franco stepped onto the deck, allowing her to dodge a conversation she wasn't ready for. Not with Josh a handful of yards away, a tornado of emotions rearranging her insides.

Paige brought up a pot of fresh-brewed coffee, while Vanessa carried the stack of mugs. Franco and Mark began discussing the website, and as they filled their mugs with coffee, everyone gathered around Franco's computer to see the new mockups.

They all commented on how much they liked the concept, and when a few minor issues were raised, Franco took them in stride as he jotted notes. A bit of fine-tuning and the website would be good to go.

"Not to be cheesy," Vanessa said, spreading her arms wide and encompassing as many of them as she could. "But I'm so lucky to work with such talented, amazing people. Let's hold on to this trip forever."

"Even when someone forgets to make coffee after taking the last cup?" Franco asked with a laugh, and everyone joined in. Well, Danae couldn't quite manage laughter, but she smiled. The entire point of this trip had been to truly become a team, and they'd done that and then some.

"Josh, you want coffee?" Vanessa asked, her attention drifting over Danae's shoulder.

Danae's internal organs stretched taut,

unable to properly function with Josh's name hanging in the air.

"Sure. I didn't sleep very well, so I could use the jolt." Hearing the deep voice that had whispered in her ear only yesterday ached as badly as looking at him had. No saving herself now, so she dared the briefest glance.

"Lucky for you," Paige said, grabbing one of the mugs and holding it up so Vanessa could pour, "I made it, so it's extra strong."

Danae could feel every inch of space between her and Josh, and she detested each one. He reached past her to grab the offered cup, and her already-struggling spirit crashed to the wooden floor.

She couldn't tell if she was the only one suffocating from the despondence, but she never could handle tense silence. "So, uh, how long before we dock?"

The guy who turned to her wasn't the same Josh she'd spent time with this past week. He wasn't even as civil as the cute-but-vexing sailor she'd met the first day, and that guy had been about as cuddly as a cactus. While she'd waved it off that day, the lack of his warm, joking personality jabbed at her. She wanted to make it better even though she knew she couldn't, and that frustrated her, too.

"It'll take as long as it takes," he said.

Vanessa blinked at Josh and then regarded Danae, hinting that she wanted an explanation of the shift in mood between them. One Danae didn't have, and she tried to convey that with the tiniest shake of her head.

Vanessa picked up her phone and opened her notes app. "Well, since it sounds like we have a few minutes to kill, why don't we finish hammering out some of the details for your boat-christening ceremony? I've got a contact who can get us supplies at a discount."

Josh lowered the steaming mug from his lips. "You know, I appreciate you guys getting excited about it, but it's just a foolish tradition. I'll take my chances."

"Foolish traditions make the world more fun. Plus, I have this whole plan to livestream it. We can mention Barton Boats and get potential clients thinking of their own christening ceremony. We'll also add that you're available for chartered trips, so it'll be mutually beneficial." Again, Vanessa looked at Danae, as if she could help convince Josh to go for it, the same way she had before.

Little did Vanessa know that everything had changed. It was all messy and ruined, and Danae clung to that moment last night when Polaris flashed extra bright, because she was one wrong word away from tears.

She spoke past the tightness clogging her throat. "Honestly, I don't have time to plan a boat christening anyway. I'll be too focused on putting the new campaign together. All of us will be extra busy with that during the next couple of weeks."

"Sure," Vanessa said, not getting the hint, "but we can take a Saturday to support our captain and his ship."

Josh took a large gulp of coffee and cast Danae the tiniest glance. "It's too late anyway. It's been renovated for months, and I don't want to deal with scrubbing off the old name and putting on the new one."

"You haven't done that yet?" The question burst out of Danae before she could stop it. Then she shook her head. "Never mind. It's none of my business."

"Anyway, it's about time to pack up. It shouldn't be too much longer before we dock, and I'm sure everyone's ready to get home." Josh thanked Paige and Vanessa for the coffee and returned to the helm.

Danae meant to head toward the cabin, but her heavy limbs weren't cooperating, so she plopped onto the bench seat and stared at a twisted gnarl in the wood grain.

Paige sighed as she sat beside her. "Well, that's a bummer. I've never been to a boat christening before, and I was looking forward to it."

"Me, too," Franco said. "I even told Justin about it, and he was excited to meet Josh and chat with the rest of you about our trip."

They continued to talk about trip highlights and what they were anticipating doing once they got home. Meanwhile, Danae tried to avoid thinking about the fact that she probably wouldn't see Josh ever again after they disembarked. While she told herself it was for the best, it didn't quite ring true. Not to her gut, which was tied in knots, or her aching heart.

Eventually, they headed toward their cabins and packed them up, along with the kitchen. When the familiar Newport shore came into view, Danae concentrated on all they'd accomplished during the past week.

As they disembarked, Danae foolishly cast one last glance at the helm of the gorgeous sailboat, only to find it forlorn and empty. A tight band constricted her chest, and her feet cemented themselves to the ground for a handful of seconds.

So that she could put one foot in front of the other instead of sprinting back to find Josh and apologize, she shifted her consciousness to where she would be six months from now. Secure in her job, her financial future cemented, a handful of short-term and long-term goals crossed off on the front page of her planner.

This trip would be but a blip—one she'd fondly recall—and she'd be farther down the pathway to checking off more goals.

Chapter Twenty-Five

Nancy beamed at him from the open doorway of her and George's boat. "Josh! When did you get home?"

"On Monday," he said, and shame that he hadn't come over that night catching in his throat. "But I left again shortly before sunrise on Tuesday and spent another week at sea." In an effort to convince himself that he was happy alone on a boat—although he'd keep that tidbit to himself.

"Well, come on in." Nancy waved him inside, and George greeted him by patting the couch cushion beside him.

"I brought you fudge from this little candy shop in Cape Cod. It's sugar free, so safe to eat, and delicious, I hope." Josh extended the box toward Nancy, but George intercepted it, cracked it open, and shoved one of the chocolate squares in his mouth.

The smile on Josh's face felt strange enough that it took him a second to realize he was still capable of smiling. Laughing.

That was something he hadn't done a whole lot of alone on his boat.

"How was your visit with your grandkids?" he asked, doing his best to keep his thoughts from straying into remorseful territory.

Nancy mentioned how fun the birthday party had been, while George grumbled about noisy teenagers. But he added that he'd enjoyed seeing his daughter and her family. "Missed the marina, though."

See. The marina was where it was at.

Now you're justifying your actions because George missed the marina?

Still, Josh would be George's age one day, and he'd be living out his golden years on his boat.

His boat that had been so quiet his ears rang from the silence.

"So, tell us about who was on the trip with you," Nancy said as she settled in her worn recliner.

Danae's face flashed in his mind, setting off the sledgehammer that hit him square in the chest every time his brain betrayed him like that.

"Just some company on a corporate

retreat." The white design on the purple and green rug under their feet blurred and sharpened as Josh inspected it. Over the past several days, he had hyper-focused on the inane so he wouldn't picture a blond woman with a smile that lit up his insides like the stars in the sky.

Don't think about stars, either.

"I'm going to need more details than that, young man." Nancy's chair creaked as she leaned forward to grab a piece of fudge. "Come on, regale me with tales of your adventures."

This past week's aimless journey didn't feel like an adventure. Something must be wrong with him, because he missed having Danae around, waving the itinerary at him. Missed her smile and laugh and doing bizarre activities like alpaca yoga.

Now that he'd experienced a trip with Danae by his side, not having her around emphasized the loneliness he'd occasionally felt before.

"I know that look," George said, squinting at Josh. Then he gave one sharp nod. "He's lovesick."

"You met someone." The words came out high-pitched and laced with excitement. Such joy shone in Nancy's features that he hated to confess it was already over. "That's the kind of news you start with."

"I...There was a woman..." Josh dragged a hand over his face. "It's a long story."

"Well, George and I have nothing but time." Nancy patted her husband's knee, drawing his attention and then speaking loud enough to be heard over the TV. "Don't we?"

At the knock on the door, they all glanced up.

Nancy stood to answer it, and as soon as she opened the door, Tinsley's voice carried over to them. "Hello, Nancy." Tinsley waved at George and Josh. "Hey, guys."

"Come on in," Nancy said. "Josh was about to tell us a story about a woman he met."

"Ooh." Tinsley clapped. "I love stories like this." She skipped the few steps to the couch—making him think of Danae because every dang thing managed to—and flopped down on the cushion between him and George.

"Please tell me there's a happy ending," Tinsley said, and Josh opened his mouth. Then she waved her hands. "No, wait. Don't spoil it."

Oh, I spoiled it all right.

Suddenly he had everyone's attention, and while he'd originally planned to beg off or make an excuse to leave, this was his marina family. Besides, he was so sick of not-talking to anyone.

Out it came, a sentence at a time. Until he reached the part of the trip where everything fell apart. His throat constricted as he forced himself to power through. "It was fun while it lasted, but we don't want the same things. In the end, we were just too different."

Silence coated the room, so thick and heavy that he thought maybe they'd all managed to fall asleep with their eyes open. Then Nancy and Tinsley looked at each other. They had an entire conversation without words, glances and raised eyebrows apparently enough for them to communicate.

George scooted to the edge of the couch, and Josh almost asked how he could just leave after all the gut-spilling. But then George put a hand on his shoulder, his grip firm. "Ladies, should I tell him? Or do you want to?"

"Depends on how good a job you do, dear," Nancy replied, and trepidation crept down Josh's spine, leaving him sitting stick-straight.

George nodded at his wife, and then twisted toward Josh. "Son, that's the most pathetic story I've ever heard."

"Because it didn't have a happy ending," Tinsley helpfully provided. "Don't worry, though. We'll work on that."

Work on it? It wasn't some story he could edit, or yeah, he would've made it end happier. This was real life.

"What you're saying is that you met an amazing woman, one you care a lot about"—the wrinkles in George's forehead grew more pronounced—"and you're scared to try again?"

Offense twisted Josh's gut. "Not *scared.* I never said I was scared."

Nancy peered down her nose at him. "We read between the lines."

"Didn't you hear the part about how Danae and I want different things? She wants me to settle down."

"But you're scared." Tinsley swept her long locks over her shoulder, the beaded bracelets lining her arm rattling with the motion. "I get it. After my last relationship, I was afraid, too. But I've opened my heart to love again."

"Right. Sergio."

"Oh, no. He's not the one, so we broke up. I haven't found the right man—yet. But I will. Because I've opened my heart." Tinsley formed a heart with her thumbs and forefingers, her neon pink nails emphasizing the motion as she then mimed that "heart" opening.

Was Josh seriously going to take advice from someone who decorated with fairy lights, made jewelry, and was...happy? Tinsley always had a giant smile and used her boundless enthusiasm to cheer up others. She hosted parties so that everyone in the marina could get acquainted. She also came over and painted Nancy's toenails, since it was hard for her to bend that way anymore.

During the past several days, he'd

missed happiness, his own smile, and the people he'd met—Danae in particular. He'd missed her kindness and sunshiny attitude, how much she cared about her team, and how she got all squeaky over cute animals.

"And like this woman you met," Tinsley continued, "I don't see the point in wasting my time if a guy doesn't see how fabulous I am."

"I think Danae's amazing, and smart and beautiful and fabulous—not that I usually use that term. I just..." How to put it into words?

"Didn't want to get hurt again, so you got scared and messed it up," Nancy said. "Yeah, we know."

If they mentioned the word "scared" one more time! But as he slumped back and truly let himself consider the possibility...

The truth was, he'd dragged his feet from the beginning. Told himself not to let himself get sucked in by Danae's charms or her smile or her absurd planner. He'd declared that he was never settling down. He could only imagine how that sounded to Danae. And instead of trying to find a solution, he'd basically given her an ultimatum and shoved her toward her ex-boyfriend.

He dropped his head in his hands and plowed his fingers through his hair. "I'm an idiot."

While the pat on his back felt a bit condescending, he realized Tinsley didn't mean it that way. Especially since she added, "The good thing about having friends like us at the marina is that we can help you figure out how to fix it."

His phone chimed, and he frowned. That wasn't the usual sound it made when he received a text or a call. As he pulled it out of his pocket, he saw a reminder alert. One he hadn't set.

Just like that, a lightbulb over his head clicked on, glinting with an idea that probably edged a smidge too close to crazy.

Chapter Twenty-Six

JUST AS SHE HAD THE day she'd received the email with the Evite, Danae stared at it until the image swam in two.

You're invited!

Please join us for the official boat-christening ceremony.

Josh Wheeler, Bayside Marina, Slip 7

Danae was fairly certain this was the longest she'd gone without blinking, and despite her watering eyes, she kept her lids plastered open. As illogical as it was, she worried if she blinked, the Evite with Josh's name on it would disappear.

While also hoping that it would magically morph into a different message, because seeing his name picked at a wound that hadn't begun to heal.

She'd ended up opening and gawking at the invitation every day since Monday, when it had first hit her inbox. She had told herself that on Friday afternoon, she was going to find her own sense of closure by deleting it.

Which meant she got to torture herself with it for one more hour.

Seriously, though, how ironic was it that before their trip, she'd been so annoyed that Josh wouldn't email her. Now she was insanely exasperated that he had.

Why did he decide to go ahead with the ceremony? Did I get in his head like he embedded himself in mine?

Or is he proving a point—that he plans on living on his boat forever and ever?

"Hey," Mark said, and she jumped. She clicked to minimize the window but made it bigger instead—on par with her crummy day, really—and guilt curdled in her gut.

There was no way Mark could miss the giant invitation onscreen. Not with the bright blue and yellow and red. Colors that represented stability and cheeriness and passion. It also had a cartoon anchor and the word "ahoy" across the top, and she couldn't imagine Josh picking it out.

Then again, she was probably overthinking, the way she tended to do.

Finally, Danae managed to exit her email, her pulse racing as quickly as her fingers had. With the Evite out of view, she inhaled a fortifying breath and swiveled in her chair to face her ex. "What's up?"

Even though she'd closed the image, Mark's eyes remained fixed on her computer screen. He pressed his mouth into a tight line, and the stack of papers in his hand rustled as he extended them her way. "I brought you some of last year's financials so that we can complete the comparison report."

Phew. It's not about him and me. With every passing day that she couldn't stop thinking about Josh, she grew more certain that she couldn't simply resume dating Mark.

"I also wanted to talk to you," he said. "About us."

Ah, hope. So fleeting. How hadn't she learned that lesson by now?

Mark tugged on his ear, the corner of his mouth lifting in a bittersweet half-smile. "I've been trying to be patient while we finalized the new campaign with Mr. Barton. It's taken up a lot of extra brainpower and time, and I know how you get when your focus is on a project. But we wrapped up that part of the process yesterday, and still, nothing."

"I'm so sorry, Mark. I've been so mixed

up with work and everything else on my brain. I've been meaning to talk to you but not wanting to cross boundaries at work, so I kept putting it off."

"Looks like we've switched places. I'm trying to figure out what's going on in our relationship and you're talking boundaries." His huffed laugh was a smidgeon on the mirthless side. "The longer it took for you to give me an answer, the more I assumed it wasn't going to be what I wanted to hear."

Danae opened her mouth to defend herself, but he perched on the edge of her desk and sighed.

"I should've known."

Thanks to her jittery nerves, her face heated, and she pushed her glasses back up the bridge of her nose. "Should've known...?"

"That you're hung up on Josh. I could see there was some interest there, and it's my fault for acting too late. That sailor swooped in before I could get my act together and ask you out."

"I..." No use in denying it, she supposed. Not when her heart beat faster and harder, and if it could speak, she knew it would be shouting Josh's name. Foolish, silly heart. "Yeah, I'm afraid I fell for him, regardless of telling myself it wasn't a good idea."

"No reason for you to be afraid. I saw it written across his face—he's definitely into you."

"Maybe he *was*. Interested, anyway. But

it doesn't matter. It's...complicated." An annoying phrase, but one that came in handy for times like now, when she didn't want to get into it. "I'm so glad that you and I have been able to move past our breakup, and I don't want to undo all our goodwill. But I also don't want to lead you on or date you when I can't stop thinking about someone else."

A couple of seconds passed before Mark slowly nodded, a resigned expression settling over his features. "I think seeing you with him made me remember the beginning stage of our relationship, when things were so fun and simple. It made me think we should try again. But since we've returned, you haven't been yourself. I figured you were stressed about the campaign, but after seeing the longing on your face when you had that Evite up onscreen, I recognize it for what it is—heartbreak."

The sorrow she'd attempted to hold back for almost two weeks rushed forward at once and demanded to be felt. In theory, she'd chosen the safer option—one that would provide her with a secure future—but all she'd felt since stepping off the ship without even saying goodbye to Josh was unsettled and raw.

Her brain had insisted she had to be true to herself, but now she worried that listening to it in favor of her heart had been a huge mistake. Yes, they were different in a lot of ways. Surely there was some way to make things work with Josh, though.

Rehashing this again and again is only going to hurt. Why do you keep doing this to yourself?

"I'm going to head back to my desk, but if you need anything, I'm here." Mark straightened from his perch on the edge of her desk, and they shared a smile.

Right then and there, they seemed to both realize that while they had loved one another in the past, and they were still fond of each other, they weren't *in love*. And while Mark's dumping her had stung her ego, it hadn't hurt down to her very soul like this.

Maybe a relationship with someone like Mark would be safer, but after experiencing the roller coaster of emotions with Josh—and the way her entire being crackled and hummed around him—mild attraction and affection would never cut it again.

With each passing day, she had hoped that missing Josh would ease up.

Then she'd go through her planner and see her stickers. Recall his joke about gold stars. In a lot of ways, her planner moonlighted as a bullet journal. As if she were no longer in charge of her fingers, they flipped back to the day they'd done alpaca yoga. To the cartoon llama sticker with its legs crossed, hooves smashed together in prayer pose. Across the top, it read *llamaste*.

Josh had looked so out of place as he'd

attempted the poses in his jeans. Then Chewpacca had sniffed him and nudged him. If Danae closed her eyes, she could smell the animals and the grass and the grain that had been sprinkled around their mats. Then she relived tipping too far as she'd laughed, and Josh trying to catch her before they tumbled to the ground together.

Ugh. Every subject somehow led her back to Josh, and how was that even possible when she'd only been around him at sea?

Since she'd stared off into space, she shook herself awake, shoved her planner aside and flipped through the reports Mark had brought her. Nothing sank in, but she'd take them home and study them later. Not like she had anything better to do this weekend.

Nope, she'd be pounding a pint of ice cream by herself tomorrow evening while the rest of her team were at Josh's boat-christening ceremony.

Chapter Twenty-Seven

"OKAY, WHAT NEXT?" JOSH MUTTERED, half to himself and half to Jane, Nathan, Tinsley, and Nancy.

George was in the vicinity, but he'd appointed himself official taste tester of the appetizers. Judging from the stack of toothpicks, he'd eaten several of the barbecue meatballs Nancy had made—at least she'd prepared enough for a small army. Meanwhile Mom and Dad were supposed to be arriving any minute. Another alert he hadn't set in his phone went off, marking thirty minutes till go time. Danae had definitely gone overboard on the alerts, but on top of being sort of useful, they'd served as a reminder of what he was doing all this for.

As Josh scanned the various items he'd bought and tried to recall everything that needed to be done before the party started, he wished he had someone like Danae to help him be more organized, every detail well-planned.

No, not *like* Danae. He wanted the one and only. No substitutions or exceptions, and what if he threw this entire party and she didn't come?

"Josh, don't freak out." Tinsley looped a white string of lights along the bow of his boat, which was facing dockside for the ceremony. She'd assisted with the Evites and arranged things with the marina, so he'd given her free rein to decorate, twinkling fairy lights and all. "This is going to work. I can feel it."

Josh's heart nearly leapt out of his chest when he spotted Vanessa, and he rushed in her direction, his footsteps echoing across the wooden walkway. "Oh, thank goodness, you're here."

Vanessa pushed her large sunglasses up on her head, using them as a headband to secure her dark curls as he led her to his slip. "Wow, the ship is beautiful."

"Compared to Barton's luxury sailboat, it hardly compares, but—"

"Old doesn't equate to broken." Vanessa glided her fingers along the wooden trim of the bow. "I'm at least a decade wiser than you, Josh, so I get it."

His nerves went from tumultuous to a sloshing sway. "*Thank you* is what I should've said. Both for the compliment and for being here."

Already the woman was raising her phone to take pictures, most likely about to post them on tons of apps he'd never heard of.

"Everyone, this is Vanessa," he said as he tugged her toward his mishmash family. "She's the social media director of Barton Boats, and will be shooting videos and taking pictures as we perform the ceremony."

After rattling off introductions, Josh drew Vanessa aside, next to the tarp that covered the gold letters he'd applied yesterday. "Danae's coming, right?"

Vanessa opened her mouth. A squeaky noise that didn't satisfy any part of him came out, and she shrugged. "I truly believe she'll show up."

"*Believe?*" All morning Josh's blood pressure had been sky-high, but that sent it screeching into the danger zone. "Didn't you talk to her? You said you were going to find a way to get her here."

"We all talked to her yesterday before leaving work. We told her that she *had* to come along, or how else could we possibly relive our fun trip? She nodded a bunch, so I thought we were getting through to her." Vanessa grimaced. "But then she said she wasn't sure she could make it and asked me to take lots of pictures, just in case. I know she wants to be here, but she's scared."

Scared. There was that word again. It had been frustrating enough when George and Nancy had used it to describe him, but the idea of Danae being afraid...? Oxygen hissed out of his lungs, leaving his head throbbing from the lack of air. "The entire reason I'm throwing this party is because of her. *For her.* I made Evites. I went food shopping." He swung his arm toward the bow of the ship. "There are blinking lights strung across my ship."

Vanessa gave him a sympathetic look. "I'll call her. Paige, Franco, and Justin were already planning on swinging by her place to pick her up—I'm sure they'll get her here. No promises on how happy she'll be if they end up having to physically drag her from the house and throw her in the car."

In any other circumstance, that image would make him laugh.

Too much was on the line, though. His friends and family had been filled in on how much he liked Danae and wanted to fix things, and with their encouragement, he had allowed hope to filter in. He'd funneled that hope into the stamina needed to clean up the ship, paint the new name, and do everything it took to throw a party.

Honestly, he'd had no idea how intense planning an event was, which gave him even more appreciation for Danae's ability to make it seem so seamless. Even when she had a grumpy, stubborn captain working against her.

"Josh, where should I put the appetizers?" His mother's voice broke through his erratic thoughts, and he turned to greet her and his father. He took the plate of grilled shrimp and pineapple skewers and frowned at the overflowing table piled with fruit platters and veggie trays. Plus the colorful macaroons that Tinsley referred to as "amazing little cookies filled with extra happiness."

"Here." Nancy moved each platter about half an inch, making use of every spare centimeter, and it allowed a perfect gap for the skewers.

Josh glanced at his watch again. Ten minutes to go.

Frantic energy suffused his frame until he practically vibrated with it.

With every guest who arrived, he worked that much harder to hold his smile. To be polite as he greeted them, instead of constantly looking past them to see if the person he *needed* to arrive *had* yet.

A clashing mix of lingering jealousy and relief mingled in his gut when he spotted Mark. Danae wasn't by his side. That she might have been was a possibility he'd done his best to steel himself for.

Mark gave him a sharp nod. "Josh, hello. I wasn't going to come at first, and if you want me to leave, say the word. But I felt like

I should see this thing through. Also, that I'd better be here in case you didn't do the right thing, so at least Danae would have a solid support system."

"I can respect that," Josh said, while praying he wouldn't accidentally send her into the guy's arms again.

Then he was back to scanning the walkway. Most of the people who lived in the marina had shown, and if Josh glanced at his watch one more time, he was going to rip it off and toss it in the water. He found Vanessa in the crowd and raised his eyebrows at her.

She pressed her lips together and shrugged.

Great.

Each step took way more effort than usual, but Josh managed to make it to the front of his ship. He gripped the metal railing and boosted himself onto the bow so he could address the crowd. "First of all, I'd like to thank everyone for coming."

The pang in his throat reverberated all the way down to his toes. This wasn't how he'd wanted this evening to turn out, but his friends and family had shown up, and while it hurt that Danae hadn't, he'd try again. And he'd continue to do so until he could at least apologize and tell her how much he'd missed her. Then he'd add that he was ready to compromise and do whatever else it took to give a relationship with her a shot.

Movement in the crowd caught his eye, and then every face but one faded away. The same face in the picture he'd taken on a beach in Cape Cod, seconds after Danae had spotted a baby seal. He'd pulled it up countless times during the past two weeks, wondering why he was torturing himself, yet unable to stop.

"Uh, so there are appetizers, so feel free to grab a plate and mingle for a few minutes," Josh said. "Then we'll fill our glasses and toast to this sailboat's future journeys, wherever they may lead."

Whereas his feet had been leaden moments ago, they were so light now that he virtually flew off his boat. Although the loud *thud* of his landing on the wooden walkway earned him a few concerned glances.

The crowd parted for him as he headed toward Danae, who was flanked by Paige, Franco, and presumably Franco's husband. Her blond hair hung around her shoulders in loose curls, and she'd worn her glasses. The navy-blue dress she wore flared right below her knees, and due to the beige heels on her feet, she was taller than usual.

She clenched a gift bag in her hands, and as he approached, she lifted it higher, like the wimpiest shield ever. When it came to the woman in front of him, his memory was a sad imitation knockoff that didn't do her justice. She was even prettier than he remembered. The last rays of the day played across the planes of her face, highlighting her freckles and her hair and those endless hazel eyes.

Beauty aside, it was the heart beating within her that he'd truly fallen for. He adored how kind and caring she was. How she'd ignited something within him that he'd thought no longer existed.

"Hi," he said, the simple word coming out strangled with the countless emotions rioting within him.

"Hello. I'm so glad you've decided to christen your boat." Danae's words came out oddly formal, and he wasn't sure how to respond to this robotic version of her. Then she reached up and rubbed the side of her neck, and *there* was the woman he'd been missing so strongly that he ached from it. "I've been worried about you out on the water, unprotected by the gods."

He smiled, a dozen fireworks igniting in his chest at once, and he went ahead and let his hope run free. She'd shown up. She didn't want him hurt.

As her friends tactfully left them alone and boarded the boat, Danae leaned in, close enough that Josh's heart forgot how to beat, and whispered, "Um, who is that woman waving super huge at us? I'd say she was waving at you, because I don't recognize her, but I assume she understands you can't see her when your back is turned."

Josh pivoted around, and sure enough,

a woman was waving at them. He lifted his hand, and Tinsley bounced on the balls of her feet. She snagged Nancy by the arm and whispered in her ear, and then Nancy grabbed George and did the same.

Before long, Tinsley was spreading the news to his parents and Jane and Nathan as well.

Not real subtle, his family and friends. But man, did they care, and more than he'd realized, at that.

"Anyway"—Danae twisted the twine handle of the bag in her hand, leaving it spinning at her side—"I didn't want to interrupt, and I hope it's okay that I'm here, but—"

"It's more than okay," Josh said. "I want you here. That's why I invited you."

"I thought maybe you were just being nice."

"Haven't you and I met before? When have I ever just been nice?"

Everything inside him froze—and then immediately melted—as her signature warm smile spread across her face. He was almost afraid to say more in case he somehow ruined it. "You don't give yourself enough credit, Josh Wheeler. You can be nice." Her grin widened. "When you want to be."

"Thank you. But I wish I had been a lot nicer at the end of our trip. I'm sorry I was a jerk."

"I could've handled things better, too.

I've regretted not saying goodbye, and I've thought a lot about you. About us." Danae tucked her hair behind her ear, each one of her familiar gestures buoying him up and adding another block of courage. "When I lost my dad, trying to control everything became my coping mechanism. I thought the only way to be true to myself was to stick to my goals and usual protocols, no matter what. If you'll give me another chance, though, I'll try not to plan everything. I'm totally up for just seeing where this goes—as long as you still are."

Before he could fully process her words, Danae thrust the gift bag into his hands. "But no pressure, and I'm not expecting an answer now. I just wanted to wish you luck and show my support, and I'm sure it's about time to start the ceremony."

Josh pressed his lips together so a laugh wouldn't burst out of him. "Are you in charge of the itinerary for my own boat christening?"

Her eyes widened. "No. I didn't mean to..." She shrugged, her mouth pulling to the side in a ridiculously adorable way. "Force of habit. But I'll work on it."

Concern hung so heavy on her features that his heart couldn't handle it anymore. He stretched out his fingers until they brushed hers, and then he tentatively folded her hand in his. Everything inside him shouted for joy when she returned his grip full force.

"I've regretted the way things ended, too," Josh said. "I haven't been able to stop thinking about it, and our trip, and you." His throat tightened, the rest of his words requiring extra effort as he prepared to lay it all on the line. "I've also decided that I'm not willing to let you go without a fight. There has to be a way for both of us to compromise enough to make it work, because the other option is...not working for me."

"Really?" Her voice cracked, enough vulnerability packed in that one word that he went ahead and dropped every one of his walls, too. That way they could be susceptible together. Even if it was—as his marina family put it—scary.

"You're the reason I threw this party. Not just because you suggested it, but because I wanted to tell you that I'm crazy about you. I'm ready for a new phase in my life, one where I focus on being happy, and you make me happy, Danae."

She brought up her free hand, covering that gorgeous smile for a moment.

He swallowed hard and took that one last, big leap. "I'm ready to go all in and do the whole relationship thing, as long as it's with you."

Her eyes glistened with unshed tears, and his heart hammered against his ribs, as if it were high-fiving him from the inside. Even as his friends and family had assured him that he could win her back, he'd had his doubts she would give him another chance.

All around them, the rest of the guests were beginning to grow noisier. "Guess I should start the ceremony." Josh slipped his fingers through Danae's. "Will you come with me and help me rename my boat? I could use you by my side for this."

"Who else is going to remind you how it's *supposed* to go?" she teased, sinking her teeth into her bottom lip.

Hand in hand, they strode to the decked-out bow of his ship. "Sorry about the delay," Josh said to his guests. "I needed to take care of something—of someone—first. Everybody, this is Danae. She's the one who suggested this ceremony. According to her, she's not superstitious, but she said she also worried about me being out on a boat without the approval of the sea gods."

"Okay, fine. I might be a pinch superstitious," she said, holding up her fingers, the last glimmer of sunshine glowing through the space between them.

Snickers went around the crowd.

Since it was his party, he took a moment to introduce everyone. Danae said a quick hello to his parents, his sister, George and Nancy, and finally, Tinsley, who was talking so fast that Josh only caught half the words. Enough for him to put together that she was telling Danae how absolutely devastated "poor Josh has been since messing things up with you."

Tinsley wasn't wrong, so he didn't bother protesting. The woman at his side might as well hear what a mess he'd been without her, especially after what he'd put her through.

The bag she'd given him gaped open, and he let go of her hand so he could check out his present. He lifted the tissue and box out of the bag and then peeled away the flimsy white paper.

Affection washed over him, suffusing his entire being with warmth. "You got me a star," he said, and Danae looked over with a shy smile.

"It's one of those lanterns, like the ones we saw on Martha's Vineyard at the gingerbread houses. You don't have to hang it up, but I saw it, and I couldn't stop thinking about that night, and—"

He pulled her into a hug, one tight enough to lift her feet off the ground. "I love it. Thank you so much."

"Well, it'll match the white fairy lights that I'd bet a million dollars you had nothing to do with."

Josh grinned at her, and she grinned back, and when it came to foolish things, this ceremony definitely wasn't one of them. Almost letting Danae go was the most foolish thing he'd ever done, and he was never doing it again.

Forget taking it slow. He'd already fallen for her, and it was the kind of free-fall there was no coming back from. Who would even want to, considering the landing was so soft and kind and beautiful and smart?

Destiny wasn't something he'd ever believed in. But the fact that Danae was here with him suggested it believed in him anyway.

"Just wait until you see how the boat's name looks," he said to her, and then he raised his voice. "Thanks again, everybody, for joining me for the christening of my boat. When I bought her, she was pretty beat up, but after a lot of hard work, she's one of the best boats out there."

"Hear, hear!" George raised his glass of wine, and Nancy told him it wasn't time yet, which made Josh, Danae, and most everyone around them giggle.

"Without further ado, I call upon the sea gods and thank them for keeping this boat safe under her previous names, *Reel Therapy* and *Solitude*. Today, we come together to give the boat a new name..."

He glanced at Danae and, in an attempt to soothe the creases in her forehead, ran his thumb over her knuckles. Why did she look so worried?

"Um, not to tell you what to do," she whispered, "but you don't have to list *Solitude* as the old name."

"It is the old name, though. I never put

it on the boat, but I'd rather be safe than sorry. Especially since I plan on taking you out with me, many, many times."

"Oh-kay," she said, obviously still a bit confused. "Just pretend I never said anything." She mimicked zipping her lips, even though they both knew that zipper would never hold.

"I request all the records of those old names be erased, and ask the gods to bless this ship under her new name and grant her safe passage on all future voyages." Josh lifted the uncorked bottle of wine and then inclined his head to Danae. "Which way do I pour it again? I did my research. I just can't remember it right now."

"I got you," Danae said. "It's east to west. Like the rising and setting of the sun."

Josh poured the small wine sacrifice to the sea gods. Then Tinsley handed him the netted, pre-scored bottle of champagne, and he held it out to Danae. "Will you do the honors?"

"Are you sure?"

"Believe it or not, today I have a plan, and you're a huge part of it. The best part of it, really."

She squeezed his hand, sending a jolt all the way up his arm to settle in the center of his chest, and then took the bottle from him.

Josh cleared his throat. "I christen thee..." He yanked off the tarp, revealing the gold lettering he'd spent hours getting just right. But instead of looking at the boat's new name, he watched for Danae's reaction, much like he'd done throughout their journey together.

Tears welled in Danae's eyes as she studied the gold lettering. As opposed to the staring she'd done at Josh's Evite, instead of not blinking, she blinked, blinked, blinked.

But the gold lettering spelled out the same word she'd originally seen, leading her to believe it wasn't a mirage.

Josh stood and flashed her a smile, and the jagged pieces of her heart smoothed and mended until every part of her shimmered as brightly as the letters that made up the boat's name.

"You're supposed to say the name aloud," Josh whispered. "Then we break the bottle and finish the ceremony."

Sure, if she could manage to speak without bursting into tears. Happiness tingled through her entire body, and she felt her dad, up in the heavens, looking down on her. She swore she even felt a nudge that seemed to say *You're on the right path, NaeNae.*

"We christen thee *Polaris*, after the everlasting North Star," she said past the lump in her throat. "May you guide this ship the way you have guided sailors since the dawn of time."

Expelling a shallow breath, Danae brought the bottle down on the bow of the ship, next to the leafy branch that symbolized a safe return. The bottle cracked and wine sparkled out in a spray, splatters coating her fancy pumps and leaving the tops of her feet slightly sticky.

"Now, George," Josh said, snagging two glasses of champagne from the table and handing one to her.

"Hear, hear!" George raised his glass, and everyone in attendance toasted to Polaris.

The entire evening felt like a dream, one Danae had almost missed because she'd been afraid. She'd worried that if she showed up and things went poorly, she'd have to say goodbye to the possibility of herself and Josh forever. Thank goodness for her team, who'd shown up and insisted she go along. She raised a glass to them, too, and they all seemed to be cheering just for her.

Vanessa was filming, of course, so they'd undoubtedly be social media stars in a few minutes.

Stars.

"I can't believe you changed the name from *Solitude* to *Polaris*."

"Well, someone made me realize that solitude might not be what I'm after. Plus, *Polaris* is the ultimate gold star." Josh grinned, and a euphoric haze settled over

Danae. From now on, happiness was going to factor into more of her decisions. More of her planning.

Josh took her glass and set it and his aside. Then he slipped an arm around her lower back and turned them to face the bay. Pink, purple, and orange streaked the sky, the colors melting into the reflection of the water, the breathtaking setting an excellent match for an amazing night.

Danae turned her head and locked on to eyes as blue as the morning sky. Her breath caught at the amount of affection reflected there, barely able to fathom it was aimed at her.

"You're my Polaris," Josh said, and time screeched to a halt as he curled her closer.

Anticipation shivered through her, tethering her to this moment and this man. At long last, his lips met hers, the mix of prickly scruff and tenderness igniting countless sparks that built and built, until every inch of her burned with the intoxicating blaze.

Suddenly she felt weightless. Thanks to the firm arm banded around her lower back she was unconcerned, delighted to give in to the thrill of Josh dipping her. As if it couldn't help itself, her heeled foot popped up, and then they presented the ideal image of a passionate kiss against the backdrop of a gorgeous sunset.

Later, once the party wound down, she knew they'd sail off toward the horizon and start their own perfectly imperfect version of happily ever after.

Epilogue

DANAE WALKED THE NOW-FAMILIAR TRAIL in the Little Bay Conservation Area with Josh at her side. For their six-month anniversary, she'd taken off Thursday and Friday so they could revisit places from their first sailing trip, where they'd begun their journey of falling in love.

Most weekends they alternated between hanging out at her beloved cottage and his cherished ship, the Polaris. Like the North Star, it had never steered them wrong.

One thing she loved about their relationship was that they made each other better. With Josh, she could relax and be more spontaneous. She trusted him wholly, with her well-being, with her evenings and weekends, and most of all, with her heart.

Josh had learned to send her texts letting her know when to expect him—within a twenty-to thirty-minute window, since the ocean didn't always comply. He checked in when he arrived at ports with WiFi, because he understood she worried about him, and he always, *always* answered her emails.

Eventually.

"By the way, did you buy a present for Jane's baby shower yet?" Josh asked, and she dodged a branch that breached the trail. "The alert went off in our calendar, and I couldn't remember if you were going to choose something, or if we needed to go shopping tomorrow first thing."

"Not only did I pick up several adorable baby girl outfits, they're wrapped and ready to go. That way, when we get home late tonight, we won't have to worry about it. We can sleep in and still be on time."

Using his grip on her hand, Josh drew her close and wrapped his arms around her. "Have I mentioned how much I love and appreciate you lately?"

"It's been at least a couple of hours," she said with a laugh.

He rested his forehead against hers, much like the first time he'd brought her on this very trail. Only unlike that first time, he followed up the move with a kiss.

She lingered a moment, enjoying the

embrace and soaking in his profile and his scent and everything about being with Josh Wheeler. "Have I mentioned how much I love going on adventures with you lately? Both planned and unplanned."

"Although you prefer the planned," Josh said, brushing his nose against hers and kissing her cheek.

"Well, of course. But I'm typically okay with the unplanned now, so that's progress, right?"

"Right," he said. Then they hiked the last few yards to the bench that overlooked the bay.

Even though she'd been here a handful of times, her breath still caught at the amazing view. She heard Josh behind her, lowering his backpack to the bench and rustling around in it for something.

Probably a snack. The guy was always hungry, and she'd learned the one thing he was great at being prepared for was snack time.

"We can eat our granola bars in a minute," she said. "Now's for enjoying the view. If you want to, I mean—you get what I'm saying. No pressure or anything. It's just an incredible view."

"Oh, I'm enjoying the incredible view. It's just that I made a firm plan, so..."

She glanced back to see what he was talking about, figuring he'd packed a heartier snack than the granola bars she'd slipped inside.

Josh was down on one knee, a black velvet box in his upraised palm. "Danae Danvers, from the first email you sent me, I knew my life would never be the same. I didn't know all the ways you'd change me—I'm a go-with-the-flow guy, in case you were wondering." He punctuated his statement with a grin she returned.

Inside, her heart went pitter patter, and she told herself not to fast-forward the here and now and begin making plans. This moment was one she wanted to live in for a while. "I'll put a reminder in my planner. Maybe add a sticker."

His low laugh drifted over to her and reverberated deep in her soul. "The past six months have been the best months of my life. I've learned to embrace other journeys beside sailing. Learned that I'm capable of so much love that I sometimes fear I'll implode from it."

"Like a star?" She bent at the waist and cupped his cheek. "Don't worry, I'll hold you together. No matter what."

"Yet another thing I love about you. The first time I brought you here, I told you about how I'd made one of the biggest decisions of my life as I sat on this bench, one where I was going to focus on living my best, happiest life. And you, Danae Danvers, make me so happy.

"As I said the night of our boat christening..." The lid of the box opened with a *snap*, revealing a diamond ring that winked in the sun.

Danae loved how he referred to the boat as theirs, and she'd begun referring to her cottage as theirs, too. They'd fully merged their lives, and while she believed that meant Josh would be willing to fully settle down one day, she hadn't pushed.

Truth be told, neither of them felt like they'd settled. They'd elevated and enhanced both of their lives by building each other up and weathering the storm of life together. She'd told herself if that was all that ever came from their relationship, she'd consider herself very fortunate.

But this...? The sweetest, most exquisite joy washed away every worry she'd ever had about her future. *Their* future.

Josh cleared his throat, and with his emotions cracking, hers crumbled altogether. "You're my Polaris. My North Star. My everything. I'm completely and utterly in love with you. Will you marry me?"

Danae fell to her knees—they were going to give out on her anyway. Plus, this way she could throw her arms around Josh's neck. "Yes," she said as happy tears spilled down her cheeks. "Yes, I'll marry you, Josh Wheeler."

He pulled back enough to slip the ring on her finger, and she whispered *I love you* onto his lips as they sealed the proposal with a kiss.

The End

Acknowledgments

Thanks to the entire staff at Hallmark Publishing. To my editor, Stacey Donovan, for her boundless optimism and amazing edits. You're an absolute joy to work with, not to mention you've made some of my biggest dreams come true. The members of my awesome small town think I'm famous after being on Home & Family, and everyone there made me feel like I was a star, even if not the best cook. LOL. Thanks to Eunice Shin, and all the other people at Hallmark who help get my book into readers' hands.

The people who always sacrifice and support me the most as I write a book are my amazing family. To my husband and kids, thank you for being so supportive, even when I talk about my characters like they're real people (because they are). Thanks for trying to keep up with the plotlines of several books at once. Thanks even more for all the help around the house and for making dinners and encouraging me to keep going, even on the hard days.

Shout out to my agent of awesomeness, Nicole Resciniti. You're a rock star, and I can't thank you enough for all you've done for my career. Thank you for your guidance and perseverance and for comforting me when my world's on fire. Xoxo.

To my two amazing besties, who also have to keep up with multiple plotlines. Gina L. Maxwell and Rebecca Yarros, thanks for the chats and the writing sprints, and for being my rocks when it comes to writing and lifeing.

Last, but certainly not least, thank you to my readers for supporting my books and sending me lovely messages that keep me going. Find me on Facebook, where you can tag along on my adventures, including burning my dinners, experiencing lots of mom fails, and managing to generate a whole lot of awkwardness.

And thank YOU, dear reader, for picking up this book. You also help make dreams come true.

Crunchy Salmon Cakes

A Hallmark Original Recipe

In *Sailing at Sunset*, Josh, Danae, and Danae's coworkers enjoy a lot of delicious seafood on their chartered sailboat tour of New England. When Josh takes them all to his favorite restaurant and Danae tries the salmon cakes, she declares, "This might be the best thing I've ever eaten. *Ever.*" If you make our Crunchy Salmon Cakes for friends or family, they might just say the same thing.

Prep Time: 15 minutes
Cook Time: 10 minutes
Serves: 8

Ingredients

- 2 cups flaked, cooked red salmon (2 15.5 oz. cans), skin and bones removed, drained
- 1/2 cup fine cracker crumbs
- 1 large egg, lightly beaten
- 1/2 cup celery, chopped
- 1/4 cup red onion, chopped
- 1/4 cup red pepper
- 1/4 cup yellow pepper
- 2 tablespoons parsley, minced
- 1 1/2 teaspoon capers, drained
- Dash hot sauce
- 1/2 teaspoon Worcestershire sauce
- 3/4 teaspoon crab seasoning
- 1/4 teaspoon salt
- 1/4 teaspoon black pepper
- 1/2 cup mayonnaise
- 1 teaspoon Dijon mustard
- 2 tablespoons butter
- 2 tablespoons oil

Preparation

1. Combine all ingredients except for butter and oil.
2. Divide into 8 equal portions and form into patties
3. Heat 1 tablespoon butter and 1 tablespoon oil in a non-stick frying pan.
4. In batches of four, cook salmon cakes for 4-5 minutes on each side over medium heat, or until browned. Repeat with the rest of the butter and oil and cook the other four cakes.
5. When cooked, set onto a paper towel lined plate to catch any extra oil.
6. Serve hot with Remoulade Sauce.

Thanks so much for reading *Sailing at Sunset*. We hope you enjoyed it!

You might like these other books from Hallmark Publishing:

Country Hearts
In Other Words, Love
A Simple Wedding
A Cottage Wedding

For information about our new releases and exclusive offers, sign up for our free newsletter at hallmarkchannel.com/hallmark-publishing-newsletter

You can also connect with us here:

Facebook.com/HallmarkPublishing

Twitter.com/HallmarkPublish

About the Author

Cindi Madsen is a *USA Today* bestselling author of contemporary romance and young adult novels. She sits at her computer every chance she gets, plotting, revising, and falling in love with her characters. She has way too many shoes but can always find a reason to buy a pretty new pair, especially if they're sparkly, colorful, or super tall. She loves music and dancing and wishes summer lasted all year long. She lives in Colorado (where summer is most definitely NOT all year long) with her husband, three children, an overly dramatic tomcat, and an adorable one-eyed kitty named Agent Fury.

You might also enjoy

Beach Wedding *Weekend*

RACHEL MAGEE

Chapter One

Paige Westmoreland was on the verge of pulling off the impossible. Most of the wedding planners who came before her swore it couldn't be done, and there had been a few times (two particular flaming disasters came to mind) when she'd also doubted its possibility. But here she was, about to manage the perfect wedding.

Pride swirled inside her as she stood in front of the two-story wall of windows and looked out over the manicured gardens the way a painter stood in front of her masterpiece. Sure, it might be a little premature to claim it yet. The bride hadn't even walked down the aisle, for goodness' sake. But she had a good feeling about this one. After forty-seven attempts, this was the first time she'd ever gotten this far without so much as a hiccup. Every single box on her pre-wedding checklist was marked off, the kitchen was fully staffed and running right on schedule, and the bride and groom, along with everyone they considered important to their wedding, were in excellent health and fantastic moods. From where Paige stood, she could almost see the glittering pot of gold at the end of the proverbial rainbow. And since the bride of this particular wedding was her best friend's cousin, it made the victory that much sweeter.

She drew in a deep breath, letting the joy of the perfect day sparkle through her. In her opinion, especially on days like today, she had the best job in the world. Every weekend, and the occasional weekday, she got to see love win. And, as an added bonus, she had the privilege of doing it in Hilltop, the charming resort town nestled in the heart of the Texas Hill Country.

Paige ran through the timeline for this particular wedding in her mind. Ten minutes until the groom and his men took their spots and the wedding processional started. Twelve and a half minutes until the bride walked down the aisle at exactly five o'clock. Which meant...

"I made it." The jovial voice echoed through the otherwise empty room, but even this didn't surprise her. She typed 8:30 into the timer on her tablet and pressed start before she looked up at the latecomer.

Aiden Pierce strolled across the marble

floor of Hilltop Resort's famed wedding pavilion, The Chateau. He had the laidback gait and easy smile of someone for whom life always seemed to work out, and the sight of him brightened Paige's already sunny day.

"Cutting it a little close, aren't you?" She gave Aiden a hard time because that's the kind of friendship they had, but inside her pride beamed with such force she wondered if it made her glow. She'd planned this wedding so perfectly that she'd even anticipated his late arrival. Earlier, she'd caught wind that Aiden's golf game on the resort's course was going to be a close finish, and since he was the bride's cousin, she'd prepared a way to sneak him to the front row where his family was seated with minimal disruption.

Aiden tied his sapphire tie as he walked, not bothering to speed up his lazy pace. "The bride hasn't walked down the aisle yet. Therefore, I'm not late."

There was a twinkle in his eye. The same friendly one that won over almost everyone he spoke with. From what Paige had gathered in the eight years she'd known her best friend Ciera's older brother, it was impossible for anyone to be upset with him. Plus he had the kind of charismatic personality that made him instant friends with everyone in the room.

Paige glanced out the window again at her perfect wedding. Almost all of the two hundred white wooden folding chairs were occupied, but she could see the empty one on the end of the second row she'd saved for him. It just so happened that Aiden's very punctual mama, who was also aware of his tardiness, had chosen the seat right next to it. What could she say? While she could plan for most things, she wasn't a miracle worker.

"I'm afraid I'm not the one you have to convince." Paige pulled a face to show her mock concern.

With his tie in a loose knot, he buttoned the top button of his shirt and ran his hand through his wavy, sandy blond hair in a vain attempt to style it. "Mama talks a big game, but she'll be glad her baby boy's sitting next to her."

Paige tightened his tie for him, smoothing it out against the front of his shirt. This was something she did often because he claimed he liked the way she made it perfectly straight. Perhaps, if he wasn't her best friend's brother, she might've appreciated the way his strong chest felt. But he was, and their relationship, since the day she first visited the Pierce household, was nothing more than friendly.

"Or she'll be wondering why her baby boy couldn't pull himself off the golf course early enough to be here on time."

"Is it that obvious?"

She put her hands on her hips and pretended to examine him with a stern eye. Other than his wind-blown hair and his sun-kissed face, there was no sign he'd been swinging a golf club until less than five minutes ago. In fact, she found it a little unfair that he could look so great with such little effort. "I suppose you'll pass."

Half of his mouth pulled up into a guilty grin and he motioned outside. "With a day like this, can you blame me? Plus, it was more business than pleasure. I had to be there." He adjusted the sleeves under his jacket.

"You know what they say about excuses."

He gave her an apologetic shrug highlighted by his charming grin. Yep, it was true. It was impossible to stay mad at him. She pointed to the door on the far side of the room.

"If you slip out that door you can walk down the side and slide into your seat without anyone but your mom noticing."

"Thanks for having my back, Westmoreland." He buttoned the top button of his jacket. "On the bright side, at least I'm not as late as that guy." He nodded his head toward the main entrance above them.

For the first time during this wedding, Paige felt the slight flutter of surprise. Now that Aiden was here, she thought everyone had arrived. She followed Aiden's gaze up the grand stone staircase to the mezzanine level lobby until she saw him.

At that very moment everything stood

still. It was entirely possible even the world stopped turning. Out of all the things she considered that could've gone wrong today, all the contingencies she prepared for, this one never entered her mind. She stood there, stunned.

"Hey, isn't that..." Aiden broke her trance.

"Brody Paxton," Paige finished. Her voice had a sort of breathless quality to it that she hated, but she couldn't help it.

Brody stepped up to the railing and paused. Perhaps he had a valid reason for stopping in that particular spot, but as far as Paige could tell, it was only to smolder. Which, by the way, he did so well it made her weak in the knees.

His dark hair was perfectly styled in his signature Ivy League haircut, and his well-tailored suit accentuated his lean, athletic frame. The light flooding through the door cast a halo-type glow around him, making him look like a vision out of a dream. The string quartet behind them picked that moment to reach their crescendo, and she couldn't be sure, but she thought she even heard angels singing. After all this time, her ex-boyfriend was still the most beautiful man she'd ever laid her eyes on.

He slipped off his sunglasses and gazed out the massive windows. Even from a short distance, she could see the hypnotic sparkle in his cobalt blue eyes, and something inside her fluttered. Was it her or was there a sudden lack of oxygen in the room?

"Didn't he move to Europe?" Aiden asked.

Paige nodded, trying in vain to get her scattered thoughts under control. "His company transferred him to Luxembourg." At least that's what he'd told her thirteen months and eight days ago, when he'd ended their blissful eleven-month relationship with the news that he was moving overseas. Alone.

The familiar ache pinged in her chest.

"Why is he here?" Aiden whispered.

"I don't know." The same question had been swirling around her mind as well. It had been a while since she'd talked to him, but as far as she knew, he was still living in Europe.

Visions of the dismal day she drove him to the airport trickled to the front of her memory. Watching him walk away was one of the hardest things she'd ever done. She knew the move would be good for his career, but it didn't make the ache in her chest hurt any less.

The one thing that had made it easier was hope and a promise. A faint spark of excitement tingled in the tips of her fingers as the pieces of this puzzle started to come together.

On that dreary day in the busy airport, tears had stung her eyes. Brody had told her it wasn't a breakup, just a pause. They weren't saying goodbye, just see you later. His final goodbye kiss still burned on her lips as his airport promise rung in her ears. *Someday, I'll be back.*

She would adamantly deny it if ever asked, but she'd often daydreamed about what their reunion could be like. Maybe she would meet him at the airport with a welcome home sign and a teary-eyed smile. Or perhaps he would surprise her and show up on her doorstep with a bouquet of flowers and, during some of her more hopeful moments, a ring. The setting might have changed, but the ending was always the same; he'd come back, and they'd be together again.

And here he was.

The fingertip-tingles started to work their way up her arms. She hadn't known if it would really happen. Time had a way of changing things, but what they'd shared was special. She'd been certain then he was *the one*, and seeing him now, all of those feelings came rushing back.

She started to call his name, and the excitement flooding into her threatened to launch her up the stairs and into his waiting arms. But as she took the first step, she caught sight of something else. Or rather, someone else.

Brody turned and offered his elbow to the woman stepping through the door. A smitten smile spread across his face. A smile not made for Paige. She froze in her tracks.

"Whoa. Who's that?" Aiden's words didn't help the sucker punch to the gut reality had just dealt her.

An elegant woman stepped up next to Brody. With one hand she tucked a strand of her long, auburn hair behind her ear, highlighting her delicate features, as she slid the other into the crook of Brody's arm. Suddenly the world started to spin again, a little faster than Paige was anticipating, and she swayed on her feet.

The power couple walked the few steps to the grand staircase and paused, as if displaying their beauty and poise for the whole world to see. All the excitement drained out of Paige's body, leaving her limbs feeling limp and heavy. She considered running away. Not to hide, per se, because that would've been juvenile. She liked to think of it as postponing a conversation until she was fully prepared, which seemed rather responsible. And by fully prepared, she meant the ability to speak without sounding like a blubbering idiot.

But it didn't matter if running was responsible or not: her legs wouldn't cooperate. And even if they had, there was nowhere to escape in this otherwise empty, massive room. So she stood there, with no choice but to face him, scattered thoughts and all.

Brody's gaze landed on her. His polite

smile turned up the corners of his mouth, accentuating his strong jaw, before he whispered something to the girl next to him. Her gaze drifted to Paige, then refocused on him. Paige's stomach dropped when his intimate look confirmed their relationship was more than friendly.

The girl smoothed the emerald dress that elegantly hugged her curves and then draped her hand over the railing. Then they started down the wide stone steps in perfect unison.

Brody stepped with his usual steady confidence. The girl moved with the grace of a dancer, each of her footsteps skimming the surface of the stairs. The four-inch stilettos at the end of her toned legs seemed to be an extension of her foot, as if she were made to wear them. Everything about her radiated beauty and poise.

Paige glanced down at her own look in comparison. About the only similarity between them was they'd both chosen to wear almost the exact shade of green. Other than their shared penchant for emerald-colored garments, Paige was the complete opposite of the beauty on Brody's arm.

OXFORD WORLD'S CLASSICS

WILKIE CO[illegible] n of a successful painter, William C[illegible] and after an unhappy spell as a clerk in a tea broker's office, during which he wrote his first, unpublished novel, he entered Lincoln's Inn as a law student in 1846. He considered a career as a painter, but after the publication, in 1848, of his life of his father, and a novel, *Antonina*, in 1850, his future as a writer was assured. His meeting with Dickens in 1851 was perhaps the turning-point of his career. The two became collaborators, and lifelong friends. Collins contributed to Dickens's magazines *Household Words* and *All the Year Round*, and his two best-known novels, *The Woman in White* and *The Moonstone*, were first published in *All the Year Round*. Collins's private life was as complex and turbulent as his novels. He never married, but lived with a widow, Mrs Caroline Graves, from 1858 until his death. He also had three children by a younger woman, Martha Rudd, whom he kept in a separate establishment. Collins suffered from 'rheumatic gout', a form of arthritis which made him an invalid in his later years, and he became addicted to the laudanum he took to ease the pain of the illness. He died in 1889.

JOHN SUTHERLAND is Lord Northcliffe Professor of Modern English Literature at University College London, and is the author of a number of books, including *Thackeray at Work*, *Victorian Novelists and Publishers*, and *Mrs Humphry Ward*. He has also edited *Vanity Fair*, *Pendennis*, and *The Way We Live Now* for Oxford World's Classics.

OXFORD WORLD'S CLASSICS

For almost 100 years Oxford World's Classics have brought readers closer to the world's great literature. Now with over 700 titles—from the 4,000-year-old myths of Mesopotamia to the twentieth century's greatest novels—the series makes available lesser-known as well as celebrated writing.

The pocket-sized hardbacks of the early years contained introductions by Virginia Woolf, T. S. Eliot, Graham Greene, and other literary figures which enriched the experience of reading. Today the series is recognized for its fine scholarship and reliability in texts that span world literature, drama and poetry, religion, philosophy and politics. Each edition includes perceptive commentary and essential background information to meet the changing needs of readers.